"This is a matter of the future, yours and the baby's."

Nancy stared out over the corral. "But marriage? I just buried my husband."

His gut bunched at the memory. "I know. But I also know you're going to be too busy soon to run a ranch. And that baby will need a father."

Tears were gathering in her eyes again. "That's true," she murmured. "But I'm not ready to be a wife."

"And I'm none too ready to be a husband," Hank assured her. "But I made you a promise, and I intend to keep it."

The tears were falling now. "Oh, Hank, that's so kind of you. I don't know what to say."

Kindness wasn't his reason, but he didn't correct her.

"Just think on it," he urged, fisting his hands to keep from wiping the tears from her cheeks. "And I'll understand if you'd rather find a better fellow than me."

She turned then and stood on tiptoe to press a kiss against his cheek. "I'm beginning to think there is no finer fellow than you," she murmured.

* * *

LONE STAR COWBOY LEAGUE:
THE FOUNDING YEARS—
Bighearted ranchers in small-town Texas

Stand-In Rancher Daddy—
Rene~~e Ryan, July 2016~~
A Fam~~ily~~
Louise M~~...~~
A Ranc~~...~~
Regina S~~...~~

Regina Scott has always wanted to be a writer. Since her first book was published in 1998, her stories have traveled the globe, with translations in many languages. Fascinated by history, she learned to fence and sail a tall ship. She and her husband reside in Washington state with their overactive Irish terrier. You can find her online blogging at nineteenteen.com. Learn more about her at reginascott.com or connect with her on Facebook at Facebook.com/authorreginascott.

Books by Regina Scott

Love Inspired Historical

Lone Star Cowboy League: The Founding Years

A Rancher of Convenience

Frontier Bachelors

The Bride Ship
Would-Be Wilderness Wife
Frontier Engagement
Instant Frontier Family

The Master Matchmakers

The Courting Campaign
The Wife Campaign
The Husband Campaign

The Everard Legacy

The Rogue's Reform
The Captain's Courtship
The Rake's Redemption
The Heiress's Homecoming

Visit the Author Profile page at Harlequin.com.

REGINA SCOTT

A Rancher of Convenience

⟨H⟩ HARLEQUIN® LOVE INSPIRED® HISTORICAL

Special thanks and acknowledgment are given to Regina Scott for her contribution to the Lone Star Cowboy League: The Founding Years miniseries.

Recycling programs
for this product may
not exist in your area.

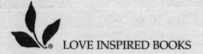

LOVE INSPIRED BOOKS

ISBN-13: 978-0-373-28374-3

A Rancher of Convenience

Copyright © 2016 by Harlequin Books S.A.

www.Harlequin.com

Printed in U.S.A.

For I was hungry and you gave Me something to eat,
I was thirsty and you gave Me something to drink,
I was a stranger and you invited Me in.
—*Matthew* 25:35

To my sister authors Renee Ryan and Louise M. Gouge
for humoring and encouraging me
through the writing of this book; and to the Lord,
for opportunities, leadings and most of all love.

Chapter One

Windy Diamond Ranch,
Little Horn, Texas, July 1895

She was a widow.

Nancy Bennett shook her head as she stood on the wide front porch, looking out at the ranch her husband had built. Across the dusty ground in front of the house, a horse corral clung to a weathered, single-story barn. Beyond them, scrub oak and cottonwood dotted windblown grass where longhorns roamed, content.

She could not find such contentment. One hand clutched the letter that could spell the end of her dream. The other hand rested on her belly where it was just beginning to swell inside her black skirts.

She and Lucas had been married only ten months. She was still learning how to be a wife, hadn't yet accustomed herself to the idea that she would one day be a mother. Now Lucas was dead, killed because he had rustled from their friends and neighbors. And her whole world had been upended like a tumbleweed turning in the wind.

Sheriff Fuller had tried to be kind when he'd brought her the news two weeks ago. She'd been pressing the pedal of the wrought iron sewing machine Lucas had ordered for her, finishing the seam on a new shirt for him, when she'd heard the sound of a horse coming in fast.

Such antics would have been so like Lucas, particularly since he'd bought that paint from her friend Lula May Barlow. Having been raised on a prosperous horse ranch in Alabama, Lucas liked fast horses, fine clothes. She'd never understood why he'd advertised for a mail-order bride, or why he'd chosen her. Perhaps he hadn't been satisfied with his options here in Little Horn. Lucas, she'd learned, wasn't satisfied with much.

Still, she'd risen to go greet him, like the dutiful wife she had tried so hard to be. She'd known everything was exactly the way he liked it—stew simmering on the stove with just the right amount of rosemary to spice it, parlor swept clean of the dust he perpetually brought in on his expensive tooled-leather boots and horsehair-covered chairs at precise angles facing each other in front of the limestone fireplace. She'd taken a peek at herself in the brass-framed mirror near the front door to make sure her long brown hair was carefully bound up at the top of her head with tendrils framing her oval face. She'd even pinched color into her cheeks, which had recently been far too pale, according to him. Surely there was nothing to set him on edge this time.

Smile pasted firmly on her face, she'd opened the

door and stepped out on the porch. But instead of her husband, Jeb Fuller was climbing the steps.

The sheriff immediately removed his broad-brimmed hat and ducked his head in respect. The damp dark blond hair across his brow told as much of the warm summer air as his hard ride.

"Mrs. Bennett, ma'am," he said, voice low. "I'm sorry to bring you bad news. Your husband was shot."

Nancy felt as if the solid planks of the porch were bucking like one of Lucas's feisty horses. She must have swayed on her feet, because the sheriff's arm reached out to steady her as he drew level with her.

"Where?" she asked, panic and fear tangling inside her. "When? How bad is it? Please would you take me to him?"

"I'm afraid it's not so simple, ma'am," he drawled, brown eyes sad. "Your husband was caught with other men's cattle in his possession, and when he was confronted, he drew down on his neighbors. He was stopped before he could harm anyone."

Nancy stared at him, mouth drier than the Texas plains. "Stopped? You mean he's dead?"

The sheriff nodded. "I'm afraid so. I took the liberty of having the body sent to Mr. Agen, the undertaker."

She choked, the breakfast she'd shared with Lucas threatening to claw its way back up her throat. "It must be some kind of mistake. Lucas would never steal. He already has a ranch full of cattle."

"And we'll need to have your hands round them up," the sheriff said. "Just to make sure there aren't others that should be sent back to their rightful owners."

"No," Nancy said. As his brows jerked up, she took a shuddering step back from him. "No. Lucas can't be dead. He can't be a thief. He's my husband!"

Sheriff Fuller ducked his head again. "Yes, ma'am. And I expect I'll need to ask you some questions about where he was on certain occasions, so we'll know if he had any accomplices."

Accomplices? She'd swallowed hard. Surely none of their hands had helped Lucas steal. Did the sheriff think she'd helped? She hadn't even known!

But she should have.

The look on Sheriff Fuller's face and the voice crying in her heart both said the same thing. She was Lucas Bennett's wife. She woke with him in the morning, fed him, kept his house and garden and went to church services and civic functions on his arm. She'd thought him overly exacting, yes, moody certainly, especially in the last few months. But how could she have missed downright evil? Was she no judge of character? Had she lost the sense God had given her?

What kind of wife knew so little about the man she'd married?

Ever since, she hadn't been able to face the towns-folk of Little Horn, staying in the shelter of the house and relying on her husband's foreman, Hank Snowden, to return Lucas's body and arrange the burial on a hill behind the house. Her friend Lula May had spent the first night with her, but Nancy had only felt guilty taking the widowed rancher away from her family. Nancy hadn't bothered to alert any-one to the ceremony, certain that few would want to attend after what Lucas had done. As it was, only her boys had stood by her side while Preacher Stillwater had read over Lucas's grave.

How Lucas had laughed when she called his hands her boys.

"They're grown men more used to steers than civilized society," he'd told her. "I wouldn't get attached."

At first, she'd believed him. When she'd moved to the dry Texas Hill Country from the lush Ozark woods, everything had seemed so big, so vast. The massive cattle and the laconic men who tended them gave her a shiver. She'd stayed safely in the house, to Lucas's encouragement and approval.

But as his warmth cooled, his approval had become impossible to earn, and she'd gradually realized something about the three men who lived in the bunkroom at the back of the barn. They might be rough, but they treated her better than her husband did.

Isaiah Upkins was the veteran, his short-cropped hair iron gray, his blue eyes pale, as if the color had leached after years of watching cattle in the sun. Billy Jenks was the youngest, with hair as red as the nose he habitually burned despite her admonition to wear the broad-brimmed hat she'd urged Lucas to buy for him. She wasn't sure Billy was even eighteen yet. He seemed to be trying to shave, if the plaster sticking to his chin on occasion was any indication.

Then there was Hank Snowden. Raven haired and blue eyed, he had all of Billy's boyish energy and little of Mr. Upkins's pessimism. She knew by the times she'd seen Mr. Snowden with her husband that Lucas had come to rely on him. Lucas had even appointed the cowboy their representative in the Lone

Star Cowboy League, a cattle association that had started in the area.

But the three hands seemed all alone in the world. She knew that feeling. So, she baked them cakes on their birthdays and special occasions. They brought her wildflowers for the table, eggs from prairie chickens. She nursed them with honey and mustard plasters when they were ailing. They sang songs outside her window when she was worn out from weeping.

Now none of them knew what to do with her, and she didn't know how to direct them. Lucas had never explained his business. She had no idea how to run a ranch. But she was trying.

Then the letter had come, and once again her world threatened to upend. This time she refused to sway, refused to hide, refused to give up. She could not lose this ranch. And she needed Hank Snowden to help her keep it.

She could see him now, examining a horse by the barn. Like all her husband's hands, he was tall and rangy, but he moved with a languid grace that reminded her of a mountain lion she'd seen leaping a hill once. His attention at the moment was all for the horse. Perhaps the sandy-haired creature had been ailing. Mr. Snowden seemed to know when things were hurting. He'd certainly kept close to the house the last two weeks, as if he realized she might need him.

Likely he was planning to leave after the roundup. What reason could he have for staying? A boss who didn't know anything about cattle except they were big and had impossibly long pointy horns? Any of their neighbors would be glad to hire someone of his experience.

But Mr. Upkins hadn't the temperament to teach her. And Billy was too young to know everything she needed to learn. As poorly as she'd understood her husband, she didn't trust herself to hire someone new. It had to be Hank Snowden.

Taking a deep breath to steady herself, she raised her hand. "Mr. Snowden! I must speak with you. It's about your future at the Windy Diamond."

At her call, Hank looked up from examining the mare's hoof. Mrs. Bennett was standing on the porch, one hand pressed against her middle. He could hear the tension in her voice. Had the gossip reached her despite all his efforts? Did she know the truth?

You know it was an accident, Lord. I only meant to disarm Lucas Bennett, not kill him. Why won't my conscience let it go?

He lowered the mare's hoof and gave the tied horse a pat before moving toward the house. Dread made his boot heels drag as if the dust of the ground pulled at his spurs. But he could see as he approached that she looked more concerned than angry, teeth worrying her lower lip.

He'd always thought Lucas Bennett had everything a man could want—nice spread over sparsely wooded hills with good, reliable water. Big ranch house just waiting to be filled with a family. Lovely young wife who doted on him. Even now, after two weeks of mourning and in those heavy black skirts and fitted bodice, she was still one of the prettiest gals in Little Horn. How could he not admire the warm brown hair that looked softer than silk? Those eyes that could seem the color of loam or oak leaves in turn?

But it wasn't just her looks he admired. Nancy Bennett had a kind heart. That had been evident within weeks of her coming to the Windy Diamond to marry. Hank still remembered the day she'd come running to help him.

He'd been out mending a fence, the sky overcast and heavy with the threat of a storm. The cattle seemed to prefer his company, for a number were milling around the area. When that first clap of thunder broke, they moved, fast. He was down before he could think to mount his horse. As it was, he'd barely made it back to the barn and slid to the ground, arm hanging uselessly at his side. Mr. Bennett had immediately ridden for the doctor, while Upkins and Jenks surrounded Hank.

And then, all at once, Nancy Bennett had appeared beside him, brows furrowed and mouth turned down in compassion. She'd gathered her skirts and knelt. "What happened?"

No need to worry the lady. Hank managed a game smile. "I thought to myself when I woke up this morning, 'Seems like a good day to break your arm, Hank.' Guess I was right. But don't you worry. Mr. Bennett's gone for the doctor."

She glanced up toward the drive, then back at Hank. They both knew it might take her husband an hour to get to town, locate the doctor and bring him back. Hank tried to ignore the throbbing ache in his arm.

"I know a little about doctoring," she assured him, voice as soft as the notes of a favorite hymn. "Will you let me look at it?"

Upkins and Jenks shifted around him, and Hank

could feel their doubts. She was the newcomer, the outsider. And ladies generally did not concern themselves with cowhands.

"I wouldn't want to put you out, ma'am," Hank said.

Still she refused to move, watching him. He sighed in resignation and lowered his hand. The elbow hung at an odd angle. His stomach bucked at the sight of it.

"It's not bad," she said. "But we need to hold your arm still until the doctor gets here so we don't do more damage." She glanced up at his friends. In short order, and with the sweetest of phrasing, she had Jenks heading for the house for material to use as a splint and helped Upkins lift Hank to his feet. But as she reached for Hank's arm, he couldn't help flinching.

"How did you come to know doctoring, ma'am?" he asked as she accepted the things Jenks had returned with and began to wind a length of cotton material around two of her wooden mixing spoons to hold the bone immobile.

"My mother was a midwife," she explained. "She taught me."

Upkins barked a laugh. "Midwife, eh? Well, it's right good to know Hank's arm might be expecting. We could sure use another cowpoke of his skills."

They'd all laughed, and Hank had thanked her profusely for her efforts. The doctor had been even more complimentary when he'd arrived with Mr. Bennett, claiming her quick thinking had likely saved Hank's gun hand.

And look how he'd repaid her. That gun hand had robbed her of a husband.

He stopped at the foot of the steps now and removed his hat. He could feel his hair tumbling onto his forehead, but he knew pushing the coal-black mop back in place would only make him feel more foolish standing here like the penitent he was. "Something wrong, ma'am?"

She clasped both hands before her, prim and proper. He could see her chest rise and fall as she drew in a breath.

"First, I want to thank you, Mr. Snowden, for everything you've done since Mr. Bennett passed on."

She was trying to be businesslike, but that gentle voice and those wide hazel eyes made it nearly impossible for her to seem so serious. Still, he nodded. Even if he hadn't felt so guilty over her loss, he would have stepped in. The Good Book said that a husband and wife were partners in life, but it had become clear that Lucas Bennett hadn't shared a bit about ranching with his mail-order bride. Hank had had to help her make decisions as if he were the boss. Still, if it hadn't been for Nancy Bennett, he would likely have been making plans to ride away after the roundup.

Since he'd shaken the dust of Waco off his boots five years ago, he'd never worked on any ranch long. Moving on was the best way not to get attached to folks who would only end up expecting more from him than he was able to give. He'd never found a way to please his family, had lost the one woman he'd thought to marry. What made him think others would be any more willing to take him as he was?

"From what you told me," she continued, "this ranch has every chance of succeeding. Unfortunately, the bank thinks otherwise."

He frowned. "Bank, ma'am? I was under the impression Mr. Bennett owned this spread outright. You shouldn't have to worry about a mortgage."

Were those tears brimming in her eyes? Something inside him twisted even as his hands tightened on the brim of his hat.

"I didn't think I had anything to worry about," she said, peach-colored lips turning down. "Lucas told me he originally came here to build this ranch on property his family owned. His father gave it to him after Lucas married me. But apparently Lucas thought we needed money." She opened her fingers to show Hank a crumpled piece of paper there. "Billy brought back the mail from town. We had a letter from the Empire Bank in Burnet. Lucas took out a loan from there a month ago."

A month ago? But that made no sense. Sometimes ranchers had to take loans right before roundup if a well went dry or a tornado tore down a barn. They knew they'd soon have money from the sale of their cattle to pay what they owed. There'd been no such disaster on the Windy Diamond. And Lucas Bennett had been thieving. Surely he'd had money enough. Why take out a loan?

"What are their terms?" he asked. "Might be enough in the ranch account to pay it off."

She shook her head. "I sent word to the clerk in Little Horn after Mr. Bennett left us. There's little money in the ranch account, barely enough to pay wages this quarter. Small wonder Lucas took out a loan."

She was giving the fellow credit Hank refused to allow. If her husband had drawn money from the bank, it hadn't been for anyone's benefit but his own.

"Best we ask for time to pay it off," he advised.

"We had time," she said. "Lucas had six months to repay the loan, but the bank is calling it in now. It seems they have no faith in my ability to run a ranch. See?"

Hank stepped up to her side then and took the note from her, fighting the urge to take her in his arms, as well. If ever a woman needed comforting, it was her. Come all this way to marry, try to make a life with a stranger, and then discover the fellow was a no-account rustler. What had Lucas Bennett been thinking to jeopardize not only his spread but his marriage?

He glanced at the note. It was politely worded, expressing condolences on her loss, explaining the bank's policy, the bankers' need to be fiscally responsible. What about responsibility for neighbors, kindness to widows and orphans? With this sort of threat hanging over her head, what choice did she have?

He handed her back the letter, careful not to touch her fingers in the process. "Maybe it's for the best, ma'am," he said, throat unaccountably tight. "You weren't always happy here."

"I was becoming happy," she said, gaze going off toward the hills. "I was trying. And then everything changed."

She bit her lip again, to hold back harsh words or tears for the husband who had left her in such a bad way, he wasn't sure. He couldn't help reaching out and touching her hand. It felt so small, so fragile. Yet when he'd been hurting, her hands had cradled his broken arm even as she'd taken away his pain.

"You could do what cowboys generally do," he suggested. "Move on, start fresh. If you sell the place, you could pay the bank and still have money to live elsewhere."

Her hand returned to her belly. "No, I need to stay here, keep the ranch, for...for the future."

He stiffened, staring at her hand, at the gentle swell beneath it. The other cowpokes might tease him about his ability to read a heifer—when one was content, when one was yearning, when one was ailing. A feeling would come over him, and he'd know. Call it intuition, experience or the Lord's leading. He'd only been wrong once.

And right now, a feeling was coming over him about Nancy Bennett. Unless his senses didn't work as well when applied to females—and he had cause to know they'd failed spectacularly with a certain lady back in Waco—Nancy Bennett had a reason for wanting to keep the ranch.

She was pregnant. He'd not only cost her a husband, but he'd cost her unborn child a father.

She turned her gaze on him. "I thought if I could convince the bank I can care for this ranch, they might give me more time to pay. I need your help, Mr. Snowden. I want you to stay on as foreman. I won't be able to pay you what you're worth, not at first, but if we can get our cattle to market, that will change. And I need you to do something even more challenging, I need you to teach me everything you know."

If he was any kind of smart he'd refuse. He could feel her expectations, her hope, hemming him in more surely than a barbed wire fence. And he wasn't sure teaching her to run a ranch was such a good idea. Ranching was tough, hard work, work he'd just as soon spare this kind, gentle lady.

Yep, if Hank was smart, he'd thank her kindly for her faith in him, refuse her proposal, fetch his gear and his horse Belle and ride on out of here.

But he'd never claimed to be smart. And how could he turn away from an innocent woman and her babe who needed his help?

"Glad to be of assistance, ma'am," he said. "I'll stay as long as you need me, do whatever you want."

And hope his efforts would finally put his conscience to rest.

Chapter Two

He'd agreed to stay. Nancy felt as if she could draw a deep breath for the first time in weeks. She was ready to learn more about this ranch, about the gigantic cattle that roamed it and would provide a living for her and her baby. And she intended to start as soon as possible.

So, she rose even earlier than usual the next morning and dressed in her sturdiest outfit. The heavy brown twill was beginning to feel tight, though the cinnamon-colored jacket over the white cotton bodice was as comfortable as always. Sombrero covering her hair, she met her boys coming out of the barn just as the sun was breaking over the hills behind the house to the staccato serenade of a flock of warblers.

Mr. Snowden was the first to catch her gaze as she approached. Handing the reins of his horse to Mr. Upkins, he hurried to meet her. Those blue eyes looked darker in the golden light, and his face was tight. "Is everything all right, ma'am?"

His gaze roamed over her as if searching for injuries. Was it her imagination, or did it linger on her belly? Did he know? Lucas had decided not to tell anyone until she was further along.

"You can never be sure about babies out here," he'd warned.

The thought of losing a child frightened most women, she knew. But her mother had taught her well. Since shortly after her father had died when Nancy was twelve, her mother had involved her in midwife duties. Nancy had helped dozens of mothers through pregnancy, had brought dozens of babies into the world. She could tell her baby was growing and healthy and strong. If she'd had any doubts, the nightly kicks would have been enough to prove it! But Lucas had insisted, and so she had remained silent.

"Everything's fine, Mr. Snowden," she said, forcing herself to smile. "I thought I might come with you this morning. See how the herd is doing."

Mr. Upkins was frowning at her, and Billy froze in the act of mounting.

"Don't see how that's a good idea, ma'am," Mr. Snowden said, pulling off his hat. His thick black hair was already beginning to curl with the heat, for the air was warm even overnight during the summers here. Her hand positively twitched with the urge to reach up and smooth down the waves.

Instead, she looked from one of her boys to the other, putting on her sweetest smile.

"But why not?" she asked. "Surely, I need to understand how the ranch works. You agreed to teach me, Mr. Snowden."

Mr. Upkins shoved back his hat at that, and Billy shook his head. Mr. Snowden took her elbow and turned her toward the house.

"We're riding the line today, Mrs. Bennett," he explained. "That means we'll leave now and won't be back until sundown. No telling what we might run into—rattlers, mountain lions, coyotes. It's no place for a lady."

No place for a lady. She'd heard that claim often enough, first from the townsfolk in Missouri who had decided to entrust future babies to the new doctor rather than rely on an unmarried woman, then from Lucas when she'd asked questions about the ranch. She'd never appreciated such coddling, and she certainly couldn't afford the indulgence now.

"Lula May Barlow tends to her ranch," she reminded him, digging in her heels to keep from moving farther back.

To his credit, he released her arm. "Mrs. Barlow has two nearly grown stepsons to help. And you have us." He lowered his voice and his head to meet her gaze straight on. "Besides, riding line wouldn't be good for the baby."

She felt as if he'd thrown a bucket of spring water over her head. "How did you know? Did Lucas…?"

He shook his head, straightening. "Mr. Bennett didn't share much with the hired help. It was the glow about you, the way you move. About five months along, I reckon."

He'd guessed something she'd had to explain to Lucas. "You should be a midwife, Mr. Snowden," she told him.

He chuckled, a warm sound that beat back the chill she'd felt. "And here I thought I was one, for a whole herd of heifers." He sobered suddenly, dropping his gaze. "Not that I meant to compare you to a heifer, ma'am."

It was her turn to laugh. She couldn't remember the last time she'd done so. "Certainly not, Mr. Snowden. I don't have horns."

He glanced down at her. "And your eyes are much prettier, and you don't weigh nearly as much."

"Why such compliments, Mr. Snowden," she teased. "You'll quite turn my head."

Was that a tinge of red working its way into his firm cheeks? "Only speaking the truth, ma'am," he murmured. "Now, if you'll excuse me, I should start out so I can be back by nightfall."

She caught his arm. His muscles tensed under her hand, and she realized she was being too bold. Immediately she dropped her hold and stepped back.

"I'm willing to stay behind for the good of the baby," she told him. "But you promised to teach me to run this ranch. How can I learn if you're out on the range?"

He eyed her a moment, then blew out a breath. "You're right. I'll send Upkins and Jenks along and stay with you. If they spot any trouble, they can always ride back, and we can tackle it tomorrow."

She couldn't believe how buoyant she felt as she watched him send her other boys off. He returned to her side and walked her to the porch, insisting that she sit on one of the wicker chairs there and even handing her the padded cushion from another of the chairs to put behind her.

"You're fussing," she accused him.

Now she had no doubt his cheeks were reddening. As if to keep her from noticing it, he paced around the chairs and finally took one not too far from hers, setting his hat on the table between them. Even then, his knee bobbed up and down, as if he'd rather be out riding.

"Perhaps," she said, hoping to put him at his ease, "we should agree on a few things. First, if you are going to be my teacher, I think it would be appropriate for you to call me Nancy. Shall I call you Henry?"

His knee froze. "No, ma'—Nancy. That's my father's name too, and I never cottoned to it. He had a way of saying it, all drawn out like it was three or four syllables, and I'd know I'd disappointed him again. Call me Hank."

Hank. Though she'd known that was what Lucas called him, she hadn't considered the name until now. It was strong, steady, not unlike the man sitting next to her. "Very well, Hank. I want you to know I'll be a very attentive and eager learner."

He shifted on the chair as if he wasn't so sure about his own role as teacher. "What exactly did you want to know about ranching?"

What didn't she want to know? She felt as if she'd lived in a cocoon of her husband's making and hadn't yet emerged as a butterfly. "Everything?" she suggested.

He took a deep breath. "That's a tall order. Maybe we could start with what you know and work from there."

Nancy waved toward the hills. "We have land. It supports cattle. And apparently rattlesnakes, mountain lions and coyotes. We sell those cattle and turn a profit." She faced him fully. "What I want to know is how."

He ran a hand back through his hair, spiking curls in its wake. "And I thought riding the line made for a long day."

"I told you I knew nothing," she reminded him.

He nodded. "All right, then. To start off with, cattle don't just spring up like tumbleweeds. We generally bring in a bull or two around this time of year."

Nancy frowned. "Don't we have any bulls?"

"Not enough to service a herd this size."

She made a face. "I don't understand."

He was turning red again, and his gaze refused to meet hers. "Maybe we should start with the other end of the story. This isn't a conversation I'm prepared to have with a lady."

She thought for a moment, going back over what he'd said, then brightened. "No need. I think I know what you're talking about. Bulls plus cows equals babies."

He sagged back against the chair as if he'd run a race. "Bulls plus cows equals calves. But yes, that's what I mean. And calves are born in the spring, get branded and grow into steers we sell at a profit a year later come fall. Make sense?"

"Yes," she said. "You don't have to hesitate to talk about birthing with me. I'm not afraid to talk about babies, mine or anything else's. I understand them. Cattle are what scare me."

He chuckled. "Cattle are big babies, if you ask me. Won't listen to what you tell them. Want their own way. Then they look at you all sweet like, and you know they have you right where they want you."

"Well, if cattle are babies, I'll be running this ranch in no time," she told him, offering him a smile.

He stared at her mouth as if she'd done something amazing. Was a smile so important? Or was hers that special to him?

Even as her cheeks heated under his regard, he

turned and gazed down the long drive toward the wrought iron gates that marked the edge of the Windy Diamond.

"Someone's coming," he said, standing. "I'll be right back."

"Where are you going?" Nancy asked as he stepped down from the porch and headed for the barn.

"To get my shooting iron."

A flutter started in her stomach, and she pressed a hand against her waist to still it. Did he think it was outlaws? Some other kind of trouble?

It couldn't be Sheriff Fuller again. She'd been grateful he had been considerate when he'd returned to question her further about Lucas. She only regretted she hadn't been any help to the lawman. She truly hadn't known a thing about her husband's shady business dealings. It seemed to her she hadn't even known her husband.

She was just glad to recognize the occupants of the wagon that rattled onto the flat before the house. Edmund McKay, a tall, serious-looking rancher who had a spread to the southwest of town, was at the reins, and her friend Lula May sat beside him. Lula May gave her an airy wave, then gathered her blue cotton skirts. Though the young widow was perfectly capable of climbing down, Mr. McKay came around and lifted her from the bench. His gaze seemed to linger on hers before he released her.

Now, there was a sight. Only a month or so ago Nancy and Molly Thorn had teased Lula May about refusing to let Edmund help her down. Now there was a tenderness between her friend and the rancher that tugged at Nancy's bruised heart. It seemed she'd missed a romance in the last couple weeks she'd been staying close to the ranch. The thought made her smile, but the frown on Mr. McKay's face as he walked toward her set her stomach to fluttering again.

She scolded herself for the reaction. Edmund McKay had never struck her as a harsh man. He might even be accounted handsome with his chiseled features, hair the color of the sandy soil, and dark coat emphasizing his muscular build. He walked with the confidence of a man at rest with his conscience. Lula May, who was tall for a woman, looked positively petite at his side, her strawberry blonde hair confined behind her head, blue eyes crinkling around the corners with her smile.

"Nancy," she said, climbing the porch to enfold her in a hug. "I was hoping you might feel up to company today." She cast a glance at Edmund as if to encourage him to speak. He yanked the brown Stetson from his head.

"Mrs. Bennett," he said with a nod that seemed respectful enough. "How are you faring?" The way he shifted on his feet told her she wasn't the only one concerned about this meeting. She resolved to welcome him all the same.

"We're faring well, thank you, Mr. McKay," she told him. "Mr. Snowden sees to the ranch for me, along with Billy Jenks and Mr. Upkins. I don't know what I'd do without them."

Edmund nodded. "They're a good bunch. Sheriff Fuller said they were real helpful making sure there were no more stolen cattle on the range."

All her good intentions vanished, and Nancy cringed despite herself. "I'm so sorry, Mr. McKay. I had no idea Lucas was stealing."

"There, now," Lula May said, reaching out a hand. "I told the other members of the Lone Star Cowboy League that you had nothing to do with any of it."

That only made her feel worse. She'd appreciated her neighbors' efforts in banding together to help each other in times of need. But Lucas had shrugged off the idea.

"Any fool knows it's every man for himself out here," he'd scoffed. Still, he'd agreed to let Hank represent their interests in the league. She'd thought Lucas was merely trying to do his civic duty. Now she was fairly sure he'd used the information the cowboy brought him to help plan his thieving.

"She convinced us," Edmund was saying, with a glance to Lula May that was all pride. "There isn't a man—"

"Or a woman," Lula May put in.

"Who holds you accountable," Edmund finished.

Nancy drew in a breath. How easy it was to latch on to their forgiveness. A shame she could not forgive herself.

"Thank you," she said. "But I should have realized what was happening. I should have warned the league, told the sheriff. Because I was blind, you all suffered. I'm so sorry."

The clink of spurs told her Hank had returned.

"No call to be sorry," he said, stepping onto the porch behind Edmund. "If there's anyone to blame for this mess, it's me."

Edmund McKay shook his head, and Lula May, as she'd asked the league members to call her, had that lightning sparking in her eyes again, but Hank knew he spoke the truth. McKay knew it too. He'd been there the day they'd caught Lucas Bennett with a whole herd of cattle not his own.

The members of the Lone Star Cowboy League had been trying to discover who had been stealing cattle from the area. The rustler had hit nearly every spread for miles around, caused a fire that had leveled the Carson barn. But it had taken Lula May to put the pieces together. And the picture she painted had made Hank sick.

His boss was the rustler, and Hank had unknowingly fed him the information to plot the thefts.

When Sheriff Fuller offered to deputize Hank, McKay and another local rancher named Abe Sawyer to go with the lawman after Lucas Bennett, Hank hadn't hesitated. He'd ridden with the other men to confront his boss. Hank had been pretty sure where the man was hiding, in a box canyon on the spread. But when they found him with more than three dozen head of cattle, Bennett and McKay had squared off, with Bennett drawing fast. The sheriff and Hank had both fired at the same time. Hank knew which shot had hit home.

Nancy Bennett was a widow, and it was all his fault. He was about ready to admit it, take his licks as his due.

But she turned on him, hands going to the curve of her hips. "Nonsense, Mr. Snowden," she said, hazel eyes wide. "You're the best hand my husband ever had. He told me so himself."

He felt as if she'd twisted a knife in his gut. He'd always prided himself on doing a good job, but the fact that Lucas Bennett had bragged on him only made Hank's betrayal worse.

He tugged the hat off his hair. "Just doing my duty, ma'am. I'm glad to see other folks come out to help, as well." He nodded to Lula May and the rancher.

"Anything you need," Lula May assured her friend.

He waited for Mrs. Bennett to brighten. That was one of the many things he appreciated about her. She was mostly quiet—shy, he was coming to realize—but when she smiled, it was like the sun rising, warming the whole earth with its glow. She hadn't been smiling much since even before her husband had been killed. When she'd beamed at him earlier on the porch, he'd about slid from his chair in thanksgiving.

But now she merely lowered her hands and her gaze as she turned to her visitors. "Where are my manners? Please come in. I don't have anything baked, but there's cool water from the spring."

"And I brought a lemon cake," Lula May announced. She put her hand on the rancher's arm. "Would you fetch it from the wagon for me?"

She didn't fool Hank. Lula May was one tough lady, who'd managed her husband's horse ranch after he'd fallen ill. Now a widow, she was the only woman in the Lone Star Cowboy League, and the member most respected by the others. If she was asking McKay to do her fetching and carrying, she was up to something.

He was just as glad for it, for it gave him a moment to talk to his friend alone. As the two women passed him to enter the house, he hurried to pace the rancher.

McKay cast him a quick look, green eyes thoughtful. "Mrs. Bennett says you're doing right by the ranch. I wouldn't have expected less."

Hank put a hand on the man's shoulder to stop him before he reached the wagon. "I promised her I'd stay as long as need be. But there's something you should know. Lucas Bennett took out a loan from a bank in Burnet before he died."

The rancher frowned, turning to face him. "From Burnet? Why didn't he come into Little Horn or approach one of us? We'd have loaned him money or found a way to fix whatever he needed."

"I don't think he wanted the money to fix anything," Hank told him. "He may have convinced the bank he wanted to improve the ranch, but he sure didn't use the money on anything worthwhile."

McKay nodded. "Lula May tells me he may have been gambling with her uncle while he was in town."

Hank felt as if he'd eaten something that had sat in the sun too long. "It wouldn't surprise me. Not after what else he did."

McKay shook his head. "I can only feel for his widow."

Hank too. "It gets worse," he said. "The bank is threatening to call in the loan. Seems they don't think Mrs. Bennett is skilled enough to turn a profit ranching. I thought maybe the league could help her out."

"I'll ask Lula May to call an emergency meeting for tomorrow night," McKay promised, starting for the wagon once more. "You can make the case then."

Hank joined him at the wagon. "I might not be the best advocate. I've already done enough damage, carrying everything we discussed about keeping the ranches safe to the very thief we were trying to protect ourselves from."

"You didn't know you were telling tales to the wrong person," the rancher insisted. "No one holds you accountable either. Lucas Bennett fooled us all."

Hank dusted his hands on his Levi's, wishing he could wipe away the last two weeks as easily. "At least we know it's over. We stopped the rustler. Everyone can go about their lives."

Everyone but him and Nancy.

"I wouldn't be so sure." McKay reached into the wagon and carefully drew out a basket covered with a gingham cloth.

Hank frowned. "What are you talking about? Lucas Bennett is dead. I buried him myself."

The rancher eyed him. "He may be dead, but even alive he wouldn't have been able to take all those cattle to market by himself."

"Upkins and Jenks had nothing to do with it," Hank said, widening his stance. He recognized the gesture and forced his body to relax. What, was he going to draw on Edmund McKay now?

"I believe you," his friend assured him. "I thought maybe Bennett was stealing those cattle to build his herd. But if he was so desperate for money he'd mortgage his spread, he had to have been planning to sell them."

"Nobody in these parts would buy stolen cattle," Hank protested.

"Nobody we know," McKay agreed. "But someone must have made him an offer. He would have known he couldn't hide the cattle long before one of you spotted them. And he'd need help to drive that many to a buyer, one who wasn't concerned about the brands."

His friend was right. Hank's only solace for shooting Lucas Bennett had been that he'd stopped the man from shooting anyone else and he'd ended the rash of thefts that had plagued the Little Horn community. But if someone had been aiding Lucas Bennett, they still had a common enemy.

"If I were you," the rancher said, green gaze boring into Hank's, "I'd keep a close eye on the spread. Where one rustler steps out, another may think to step in. There may be more than rattlers hiding in those hills, and Nancy Bennett is going to need protection from them."

That kind of protection was normally the job for a lawman or a husband. He was no lawman. And Jeb Fuller had the whole county to watch over. He couldn't focus all his efforts on the Windy Diamond.

So did Hank dare think of himself as a husband?

He'd tried before. His father, in his usual proud way, had picked out the girl. For once, Hank hadn't been willing to argue. Mary Ellen Wannacre had been downright beautiful, with hair brighter than sunshine and eyes the color of bluebonnets. With her on his arm, he'd felt like the man his father was always goading him to be—powerful, confident. Every fellow in Waco had been green with envy. He'd allowed himself to fall in love.

But in the end, he'd come in second best. She'd chosen to marry his friend Adam Turner, who at least had had the decency to stammer out an apology. Hank couldn't blame either of them. He'd never managed to measure up to his father's expectations. It didn't come as a surprise he didn't measure up to hers.

It had taken him five years to begin to meet his own.

Was he willing to set those aside for someone else's, to keep Nancy Bennett and her baby safe?

Chapter Three

"It can be overwhelming, can't it?" Lula May said as she took a seat in Nancy's parlor. The two brown horsehair-covered chairs still sat at precise angles in front of the stone fireplace, as if waiting for Lucas to come through the door. Nancy sank onto the one opposite her friend and focused on the red-and-blue diamond shapes woven into the rug on the plank floor.

"Yes," she admitted. "And I can't help thinking I might have spared everyone this pain if I'd just recognized what Lucas was doing."

Lula May raised her chin. "That's enough of such talk. Why, I'd known Lucas longer than you had, and I had no idea what he was doing. I didn't even know he was from Alabama, raised near where I grew up, until recently. And Edmund had no idea either, for all the two worked side by side during roundups."

Nancy managed a smile for her friend's sake. "Edmund, is it?"

The prettiest pink blossomed in Lula May's cheeks. "He asked me to marry him."

Nancy reached out and took her hands. "Oh, Lula

May, I'm so happy for you! You deserve a fine fellow like Edmund McKay."

They talked of weddings and babies and other things that lifted her spirits as they waited for the men to rejoin them. When he heard the news, Hank went out of his way to tease Lula May and Edmund about their upcoming nuptials, but his smile seemed strained, as if he expected trouble. Surely her friends were no danger. What was wrong?

He stood on the porch as she waved goodbye to them, and she could feel the tension in his lean body.

"What is it, Hank?" she asked. "Did Mr. McKay tell you something I should know?"

He flinched as if she'd poked a sore spot. "Not exactly. I should get back to work. We can talk more later." Shoving his hat on his head, he strode off toward the barn.

She didn't call for him to stay this time. Much as she needed to learn, she'd hardly help the ranch succeed by keeping him continually from his job.

What she could do, she realized, was deal with the bank. Returning to the house, she wrote a letter requesting more time and stating the steps she was taking to ensure the ranch earned enough profit to pay back every penny Lucas had borrowed, with interest. She could only hope that would be sufficient, for now.

The next week, she spent as much time as she could out on the range, taking the team to keep up with her boys. She'd driven her mother's small buggy back in Missouri, but the clattering wagon took a little getting used to. And she didn't stay out past noon, when the sun was beating down hot enough to fry her lunch on the limestone reaches that ringed the ranch.

But the six hours away from the house opened her eyes. Sitting on the porch, even tending the garden behind the house, she'd never realized the terrain surrounding the ranch was so rough. The house, barn and corral were on flat ground near Hop Toad Springs, but even a half mile away the land began crumbling like a paper crushed in a fist. Limestone reaches thrust up; streams cut draws and canyons. And everything was covered in tall grass and dotted with clumps of short oak trees and cottonwoods.

She also learned that while the cattle roamed free over the wild and windswept acres, there was always something that needed tending. If Kettle Creek was running low, the whole herd had to be driven closer to the house to Hop Toad Springs, which drew from groundwater and never failed. Fences encircling their land had be to constantly patrolled and mended, or the cattle would wander too far afield. And Hank and her other boys kept a close eye on the herd to protect the cattle from predators, four-footed and two-footed.

The last gave her pause.

"You mean there are others out stealing cattle?" she asked Hank as he sat astride his horse next to the wagon. They were about a mile away from the house, resting under the shade of a copse of trees, the oak leaves chattering in a rising breeze that brought the scent of dry dust and clean water.

"Always those who want more than their share, ma'am," he answered, gaze roaming the area as if he expected an outlaw to leap out from behind a bush.

She could believe that Lucas had turned to rustling from greed. He'd always seemed to want more than what he had. From what she could see, he'd certainly owned more than most people. Hadn't that been sufficient?

Hadn't she and their baby been sufficient?

"Look there," Hank said, pointing to where a longhorn was ambling out of the shade. "See that white circle high on her shoulder? That's our Rosebud, fairest of them all."

Nancy raised her brows. "You name the cattle?"

He winked at her. "Only the special ones. Miss Rosebud, they tell me, has never failed to calve since she was old enough to bear."

Sure enough, a calf, nearly grown now, trotted after its mother. A dozen more cows plodded in her wake.

"You get Miss Rosebud on your side," Hank said, "and the rest of them will follow you anywhere. Upkins says it's on account of the way she swings her tail all sassy like."

Nancy smothered a laugh, and he had the good sense to color. "I didn't mean anything by that, ma'am," he hastened to assure her.

"I didn't think you did," Nancy replied. But she couldn't help smiling at the idea that her brash and bold boys gave their favorite cattle pet names.

She tried not to interfere with their activities, but she could tell by their terse answers to her questions, their sidelong glances, that she made them nervous. Like Lucas, they seemed to prefer her safely inside the house. But how was she to learn if she didn't come out?

Evenings were better. She'd take some fruit or a piece of pie to the porch to wait for her boys to come riding in. Mr. Upkins and Billy always tipped their hats as they passed before dismounting to lead their horses into the barn. One or the other would embolden himself to come closer, ask her about her day, make some comment about the ranch. But they always scurried back to the barn as if concerned they were being too forward.

She made sure Hank didn't escape so easily. She'd call to him before he could take his horse into the barn, and he'd usually hand the reins to one of the others before joining her on the porch. His boots would be covered with dust, his shirt telling of hard work, yet he always managed a smile.

She'd hand him an apple or a sweet, and he'd lounge against the uprights and tell her about what had happened on the ranch after she'd left him. It took a lot of questions to get the answers she wanted, but she eventually learned that her husband had amassed a herd of about one hundred cows, plus eighty steers getting ready to go to market.

"Is that good?" she asked, before taking a sip of the lemonade she'd brought with her. A fly buzzed close, and she swatted it away.

"Fair to middling," he said. "If we can get a good price, you'll have enough to keep things going another year and pay the bank what you owe."

That's what she wanted to hear. She had to believe she could make a go of things, for her child.

But the bank must not have had faith even in Hank, for they sent someone to confirm her claims.

Mr. Cramore arrived one afternoon in a black-topped buggy she was surprised had made it the thirty miles from Burnet over rough country roads. A portly fellow, dressed in black with a silk tie at his throat, he hitched his horses to the rail surrounding the corral as if not planning to stay overlong, plucked a satchel off the seat and moved with solemn strides to the porch.

When she met him, he removed his top hat and bowed his head as if to give thanks.

"Mrs. Bennett," he said in a deep, slow voice, double chins quivering. "My most heartfelt condolences. I'm Winston Cramore of the Empire Bank in Burnet. I had the privilege of knowing your husband well. He will be missed."

She was only glad the story of Lucas's illegal activities must not have reached Burnet, or Mr. Cramore might not have been so quick to claim acquaintance. And she sincerely doubted anyone had known her husband well, or someone would have realized his intentions.

"It was very kind of you to come all this way to talk," she said, leading him to one of the wicker chairs on the porch. "May I offer you something to eat, lemonade?"

"Both would be welcome," he assured her, taking a seat and perching his hat on the knee of his black trousers. He smiled as if dismissing her. With a shake of her head, Nancy went inside and fetched him the food.

When she returned, she found him pulling papers from his satchel.

"You will of course want to see the agreement your husband signed," he said, waiting until she'd set down the plate of ginger cookies and a glass of lemonade on the table at his elbow before handing the sheath to her.

Nancy took a seat on the chair near his and glanced

over the papers. The tiny lettering and legal terms were difficult to decipher, but there was Lucas's arrogant scrawl agreeing to them all.

Mr. Cramore was frowning out toward the barn. "It appears Mr. Bennett did not have time for the improvements he'd planned before his untimely demise."

The planks on the barn were turning a dull gray as they bleached in the sun. But she could see where someone had patched them.

"Mr. Snowden and the other hands have been working hard," she told him.

"In my experience, cowboys seldom work hard without proper leadership," he replied.

"I'm pleased to say my boys—er, hands—are very industrious," she told him. Holding the papers in her lap, she made sure to sit up properly, hoping she looked like the leader of the spread.

Mr. Cramore picked up a cookie with dainty fingers and took a bite, then smiled at her. "I believe your husband had other plans, as well. Did those come to fruition?"

She could hardly tell him she had no idea what her husband had planned. He'd only think her even less competent to run the place. She glanced out over the spread, looking for inspiration. A cloud of dust appeared to be coming closer, fast.

"That's likely Mr. Snowden now," she said, rising and setting the papers on her seat. "I'm sure he can answer any questions you might have." As Hank and his horse appeared out of the dust, she fled down the steps and hurried for the corral.

He reined in beside her. "Who's your company?" he asked with a nod toward the house, eyes narrowed.

"Mr. Cramore from the bank," she explained as Hank dismounted. Just having him here made her ridiculously glad. "He's asking questions about the ranch."

"Well, let's answer them then." He let his horse into the corral, then turned for the house. His spurs chimed as he started for the porch, Nancy beside him. As they climbed the steps, the banker rose.

"Mr. Cramore," Hank said, extending his hand. "I'm Hank Snowden, Mrs. Bennett's foreman. How can I help you?"

Mr. Cramore tutted as he glanced at Nancy. "A foreman, Mrs. Bennett? He's clearly no more than a hired hand. It seems we were right in our assessment that you have no interest in running the ranch yourself."

She couldn't leave him with that impression. She returned to her chair, resettled the loan agreement on her lap and nodded for the men to be seated, as well. Then she leaned forward to meet the banker's gaze.

"It isn't my interest that's lacking, sir," she told him. "I know I must learn before I take on the leadership of this ranch. Mr. Snowden is teaching me."

She smiled at Hank, who nodded. But the banker shook his head.

"Surely you see the problem, dear lady," he said, face sagging with obvious concern. "You are relying on a man who has no interest in the future of this establishment."

Hank stiffened in his seat. "I've promised Mrs. Bennett I'll stay as long as she needs me."

Just hearing him repeat the words made it easier to draw breath. Mr. Cramore was not nearly so assured.

"Forgive me for saying so," he replied, "but such promises are difficult to keep when circumstances change. You would not be the first man to find it too much of a challenge to live out here."

He was talking to the wrong man, Nancy thought. She couldn't see Hank turning tail because times got tough. She waited for the cowboy to refute the assertion, but Hank looked out over the ranch as if taking stock of it for the first time. Had she misjudged a man's character again?

Mr. Cramore continued, each statement like a nail in her confidence.

"And if you are as skilled as Mrs. Bennett claims," he said to Hank, "you will certainly receive offers to improve your situation. Ranches are always looking for good hands. No, sir, I stand by my assessment. With nothing to tie you here, you are at best a weak reed on which to lean."

Three weeks ago, she would have had a ready answer. She knew her boys. None of them would abandon the ranch willingly. But then, she'd thought herself married to a fine, upstanding man too. What did she really know about the hands her husband had hired?

What did she know about the man she'd asked to teach her?

Hank frowned at the banker, but his face was turning pale. Was he about to leave her?

"You're wrong," he grit out. "I'll have a solid tie to this ranch. I aim to ask Mrs. Bennett to marry me."

There, he'd said aloud the conviction that had been building in his heart. But it was a question who looked

the more shocked by the statement. Both Mr. Cramore's and Nancy's mouths were hanging open. He'd
sure picked a poor time to propose.

But what else could he do? The banker was obviously working up to demanding payment, or the ranch
in lieu of payment. And the members of the Lone Star
Cowboy League had regretfully acknowledged there
was little they could do to help.

"I understand Lucas Bennett left his wife in a bad
way," Abe Sawyer had said when Hank had made the
case last week at the meeting Lula May had called.
"But I doubt we could raise the money needed to pay
the loan fast enough to satisfy the bank, and until
roundup, there isn't a lot of extra money to be had."

"There must be something we can do," Lula May
had argued. "Nancy Bennett is carrying her first
child. We can't let her lose the ranch that should be
that child's inheritance."

McKay had rested a heavy hand on Hank's shoulder. "Do what you can, Hank. This might be a case
where hard work will win through."

Hank wasn't so sure. He'd worked pretty hard back
in Waco on his family's ranch, and it had never won
him a place in his father's affections. He'd thought
he'd been the perfect suitor—attentive, complimentary, encouraging—but his sweetheart had chosen
another man. Truth be told, he'd been surprised and
honored when Lucas Bennett had asked him to represent the Windy Diamond's interests in the Lone
Star Cowboy League, and even more honored when
the other members accepted him among them and
listened to his input.

He'd thought maybe helping Nancy learn about

ranching would be enough to salve his conscience. It seemed now that the bank would never be satisfied with her skills. Like his father, they had a narrow view of life, and only a man running a ranch gave them any confidence. He had a feeling that even if he introduced them to Lula May Barlow, they'd point to her stepsons as the brains behind the ranch's success. They'd be wrong, but no amount of talking was going to change their minds.

Only action would do that.

The banker recovered first now. "A poor jest, sir," he said with a heavy shake of his head. "It is never politic to make light of a lady's loss. And I'm certain Mrs. Bennett is too soon a widow to wish to take up with another gentleman."

The way he said the word gentleman told Hank the banker thought no cowboy could live up to the name. He couldn't argue in his case. He wasn't Lucas Bennett with a shiny reputation and a fancy spread. But that shiny reputation had become tarnished, and the spread was crying out for someone who actually cared. He could be that person.

"That's for Mrs. Bennett to say," Hank replied, hooking his thumbs in his belt loops and casting a glance at the lady in question. What he saw wasn't encouraging. She had managed to close her mouth, but now her lips were shut so tight honey wouldn't have squeezed past.

Cramore waved a hand. "Can't you see you've put her in an impossible position? It's clear the bank must step in. I will appoint someone to run the ranch for her, until such time as the loan is paid in full."

Nancy stood to move between them, face pale but

head high. When she spoke, her usually soft voice had a firm edge to it. "That will not be necessary, sir. I can make my own decisions, in matters of this ranch and in matters of my heart. Will you excuse us for a moment?" Setting aside some papers, she nodded to Hank and practically ran down the steps.

"This isn't a matter of the heart, Nancy," Hank hastened to tell her as he followed her toward the corral. "This is a matter of the future, yours and the baby's."

She stopped next to the buggy, back toward the porch and gaze holding his. "I know that, Hank. But I will not have you sacrifice yourself for us."

Hank shook his head. "Not much of a sacrifice, if you ask me. I was working here anyway."

She cringed, and he realized how that had sounded.

"Sorry, ma'am," he muttered. "I didn't mean that marrying you would be a chore. And I surely see that you'll get a number of offers once you've put off your widow's black. But you need help now, and it sounds like the bank won't accept a hired hand in that role."

She stared out over the corral. "But marriage? I just buried my husband."

His gut bunched at the memory. "I know. But I also know you're going to be too busy soon to run a ranch. And that baby will need a father."

Tears were gathering in her eyes again, turning the hazel green as spring. "That's true," she murmured. "But I'm not ready to be a wife."

"And I'm none too ready to be a husband," he assured her. "But I made you a promise, and I intend to keep it."

When she didn't answer, he leaned closer, determined to make her understand. "The way I figure it, we just have to show the bank we're both serious about the success of this ranch. We don't have to act like husband and wife otherwise. I can sleep in the barn like I usually do, take my meals with Upkins and Jenks. Nothing has to change. You and the baby will just get the protection of my name."

The tears were falling now; he could see them tracking down her pearly skin. "Oh, Hank, that's so kind of you. I don't know what to say."

Kindness wasn't his reason, but he didn't correct her.

"Just think on it," he urged, fisting his hands to keep from wiping the tears from her cheeks. "And I'll understand if you'd rather find a better fellow than me."

She turned then and stood on tiptoe to press a kiss against his cheek. "I'm beginning to think there is no finer fellow than you," she murmured. Then she ducked her head and hurried for the house.

He touched his cheek, feeling as if his skin had warmed. He knew there were plenty of fellows willing to marry a pretty widow in possession of a ranch, baby and all. But none of them had his need to make amends.

Still, he had little doubt what her answer would be if she knew he was the one who had killed her husband.

Chapter Four

Nancy's mind was still reeling as she returned to the porch, where Mr. Cramore stood waiting. The portly banker looked as nervous as she felt, shifting back and forth on his dusty patent leather shoes.

"Well, Mrs. Bennett?" he asked. "What would you have me make of all this? Do you intend to marry this cowboy?"

Nancy glanced at Hank, who had followed her up the steps. His gaze was hooded, his face still pale, as if he expected her to denounce him in front of the banker despite her appreciation for his kindness.

"I will do the same as any other rancher given a proposal," she told the banker. "I will give the matter due consideration before answering."

Cramore blinked, looking a bit like an owl she'd surprised near the spring once. "But surely you see he is merely attempting to profit at your expense."

Hank widened his stance. "That's a mighty judgmental thing to say about a fellow you met a quarter hour ago."

Mr. Cramore's pudgy nose lifted, as if he'd smelled something unpleasant. "I know your kind, sir."

"And I've known a few bankers in my time who were a little too quick to get their hands on a spread in trouble," Hank countered. "But I didn't assume you were one the moment we met."

Neither had Nancy, but perhaps she should have. Oh, was this more proof of her inability to see the truth about people? Could Mr. Cramore be unscrupulous? Was greed rather than caution the reason he'd come to see how the ranch was faring?

And what of Hank? Was he hoping to take over ownership of the ranch, shut her up in the house as Lucas had?

As if he could see the thoughts churning feverishly in her mind, the banker looked from Hank to Nancy. "You must realize the bank's position," he insisted. "We have invested good money, and it is our duty to see it returned."

"I understand the bank's position," Nancy told him. "Please understand mine. I hope to keep this ranch, with or without Mr. Snowden's help. Nothing I've seen says you have any right to appoint managers or otherwise interfere with our operations."

He puffed out his chest, swelling the paisley-patterned waistcoat until the silver buttons winked. "Now, see here, madam. The word of the Empire Bank is sacrosanct."

"So you say," Nancy replied. "And I'm willing to believe we owe you the money based on the information you've provided. But you will have to believe that I will pay that money back according to the agreement."

"And if you're not willing to believe," Hank put in, "you better bring the law with you the next time you come."

"Fine." Mr. Cramore reached for his hat and patted it onto his balding pate, then snatched up the papers from the table and stuffed them back into his satchel. "I will expect to hear your decision on this ridiculous proposal, Mrs. Bennett, within the month. Or I will speak to your sheriff about foreclosing on the ranch."

A shiver went through her as the banker clumped down the steps and headed for his buggy.

"He's bluffing," Hank said, watching the man untie his horses.

Nancy wasn't so sure. Had she been in his position, she too might have questioned whether someone with less than one year's experience living on a ranch would know how to manage it properly. And he was right that she had no ties on Hank to keep him here. The Windy Diamond was surely a risk to the bank.

But in the end, none of that mattered. She had no intention of losing the ranch.

Or her heart.

She confessed as much to Lula May when they attended their quilting bee the next day. The ladies of Little Horn had taken to meeting weekly at the Carson Rolling Hills Ranch to complete important sewing projects and encourage one another. Nancy hadn't been able to attend for some weeks, first because of a rocky beginning to her pregnancy that had kept her housebound, and then because of her shame over Lucas's thefts.

But she badly needed her friend's advice now, so

she'd gathered her sewing box and taken the wagon west to her nearest neighbors.

Sixteen-year-old Daisy Carson, the oldest sibling still in the Carson home, led her to the room off the kitchen that her mother Helen had set aside for their meetings. Like her mother and older sister, she was a pretty blonde with a winning smile. She and the other members of the quilting bee had been stitching quilts to sell and raise money for the new church, but the frame stretched out in the middle of the warm, wood-paneled room seemed a little small to Nancy as she moved toward the chair between Lula May and her soon-to-be-sister-in-law Betsy McKay. Betsy smiled in welcome before bending to check on her toddler, who was napping under the quilt frame.

Helen Carson sat at the head of the frame, with her friend Beatrice Rampart at the foot. Daisy and Mercy Green, owner of the café in town, sat across from Nancy, but another woman was in the chair usually reserved for Molly Thorn, Helen's oldest daughter. Nancy recognized the sturdy blonde as Stella Donovan Fuller, the mail-order bride who had recently married the sheriff. She nodded a greeting as Nancy took her seat.

"Molly wasn't feeling well," Helen announced as she threaded her needle. "But you all might have seen that we've framed a new quilt." She glanced around the room with a smile to each lady. "That's because our Nancy is going to have a baby."

It was for her? Nancy stared at the delicate blue-and-pink flowers on the material until tears blurred her vision as congratulations echoed around her. She managed a smile. "Thank you so much. I don't know what to say."

"No need to say anything," Stella Fuller declared. "Just stitch."

The others laughed and set to work.

Betsy paused to put a hand to her back. "I hope your pregnancy is better than this one," she told Nancy. "I've never had a baby move around so much."

"I remember those days," Helen put in. "I thought Donny was going to kick his own way out."

"My ma said boys are like that," Stella commiserated.

"Not in my family," Lula May insisted. "Pauline was just as vigorous in the womb, and she's not much quieter outside it!"

Nancy smiled as the women laughed. As Beatrice asked Mercy for the recipe of the apple bread she'd brought to the last Sunday social at church, Nancy leaned closer to Lula May.

"We had a problem at the ranch," she confided, voice low. "Lucas took out a loan from the Empire Bank in Burnet, and the bank has such little faith in me that they sent a man to see how I was running the Windy Diamond."

Lula May bit off a thread as if she would have liked to sink her teeth into a few recalcitrant bankers. "Let me guess. They want a man to run the ranch."

Nancy nodded. "And Mr. Cramore, the banker who came out to quiz me, says Hank doesn't count as he will only leave me."

Lula May tsked as she pulled out another color of floss and threaded it through her needle. "Sounds like he never met Hank. That man is devoted, Nancy."

"Apparently so." Nancy swallowed. "He asked me to marry him."

Lula May's brows, a shade darker than her strawberry blonde hair, shot up. "Well, well," she mused, starting to stitch on the baby's quilt. "And what did you say?"

"I told him I'd consider the matter. I see the benefits, Lula May, I surely do. But…"

Lula May regarded her out of the corners of her eyes. "But you're not ready."

Nancy blew out a breath. "I'm not sure I ever was. I came out here with this wide-eyed notion that two strangers could make a good marriage. Now I understand I never even knew my husband. How much do I know about Hank?"

Lula May lay down her needle and looked Nancy in the eyes. "You know he's loyal—he stayed at the ranch when he could have moved on."

Her words were loud enough that Nancy could see other gazes turning their way.

"My husband, Josiah, says he's a hard worker," Betsy put in as if she'd heard every word of their hushed conversation. "I know he's seen him on several roundups now. He says Hank Snowden is a man you can rely on to keep his word."

"Always nice to us when I see him in town," Stella Fuller added. "Tips his hat like a gentleman. And he's kind on the eyes."

Nancy's cheeks were heating.

"Everyone in the Lone Star Cowboy League thinks the world of him," Lula May told her.

Nancy nodded. "We all thought the world of Lucas too, and he proved us fools."

The others quickly returned to their sewing, but Lula May's mouth tightened.

"Hank Snowden is no Lucas Bennett," she insisted. "I'd stake my ranch on that."

And that, Nancy realized, was exactly what Hank had asked her to do—trust her future and the baby's future to him. How could she when she couldn't even trust her own judgment?

She barely saw the dusty road as she drove the wagon home through the clumps of oak and cottonwood. She had to figure out what to do about Hank's proposal. If only she felt comfortable trusting her own reasoning.

All her life she'd tried to make the best of circumstances. When her father had died, leaving her and her mother without support, she'd helped her mother develop a trade as a midwife. When her mother had left too soon and the townsfolk didn't want Nancy to continue that trade, she'd answered Lucas Bennett's ad for a mail-order bride. When Lucas's initial interest in her had faded into disdain, she'd still tried to be the best wife she could.

Now she had a baby on the way, and the home and livelihood she had thought would sustain her and her child were being threatened. Hank's offer could solve those problems. But would accepting his offer create other difficulties? What if he was demanding, forcing her to change things to suit his whim as Lucas had done? Could she work hard enough to satisfy him? What if his kindness turned cold? Could she make herself go through that again?

What if he was abusive? She had confided in no one the night Lucas had come home late, smelling of alcohol, and demanding dinner when she'd already banked the stove for the night. As she'd tried to explain, he'd cuffed her. Immediately he'd apologized, but he'd made sure she knew it was her fault for provoking him. How could she let someone like that back into her life, into her child's life?

Hank Snowden is a good man.

The thought came unbidden, but firm in its conviction.

If only she could believe it.

Nancy was absent from the porch the next two nights when Hank and the others rode in. Hank might have worried she was sick, except he could see her from his post, going about her chores of washing and working in the vegetable patch. She didn't ask him to stay behind in the mornings and teach her either.

She was hiding in the house the same way she'd done when her husband had first brought her home as a bride. He didn't think that boded well for her acceptance of his proposal, but he wasn't about to badger her over the matter. That surely wouldn't make her any more amenable to the idea.

Given her retreat, he was surprised to find a note waiting for him in the barn when he, Upkins and Jenks returned from working the next day. The Windy Diamond had bunks for a small contingent of hands. More workers were generally hired during branding in the spring and roundup in the fall. The barn had a stall for a milk cow and a coop for chickens plus a wide room at the back with bunks, a long table and a cook stove, counter and storage.

Over the past year, Hank had grown accustomed

to the room, which always smelled like beans, leather and saddle soap. Jenks never made his bunk, and the narrow bed was crowded with a wad of colorful blankets and bits of leather, horse hair and string the youth intended to make use of. Upkins was always complaining about how the sixteen-year-old made room for every barn cat that wanted a place to hunker down for the night.

The veteran was more fastidious—blankets tucked in at right angles and smoothed down flat, hat hung on a peg above his head and belongings stowed in a trunk that slid under the bed. Hank slept on the top bunk above him and tried to keep things neat, if only to prevent them from falling on Upkins below.

He didn't much care about his belongings, except for the quilt. He'd won it in a raffle to raise money for the new church that was being built in Little Horn. In truth, he wasn't even sure why he'd bought all the tickets to win the thing. It was pretty and warm and sweet. All the local ladies had stitched at it, and he knew some of the carefully placed threads had been put there by Nancy. She'd been so determined to help raise the money. What man could resist those big hazel eyes?

Still, the folded pink paper sitting on the table was at odds with the mostly masculine setting. Hank could only hope it wasn't a note dismissing him from his post for his bold suggestion.

"What's that you got there?" Upkins demanded as he came into the room.

"Looks like a love letter," Jenks teased, flopping down on his bunk and setting the lariat he was braiding to sliding off the blankets.

Hank ignored them, reading the politely worded note before tucking it in his shirt pocket. "Mrs. Bennett wants to see me."

Upkins scrunched up his lined face. "She wants a report, most like. You can tell her the herd is hale and hearty."

Jenks nodded. "Good water, good grazing, no sign of trouble."

Hank nodded too, though he thought trouble was likely waiting for him, at the ranch house.

He cleaned himself up before answering her summons, and if he tarried over the task neither Upkins nor Jenks berated him for it. It wasn't often a respectable lady requested a cowboy's company. His friends no doubt thought he was slicking down his hair, shaving off a day's worth of stubble and changing into his best blue-and-gray plaid shirt and clean Levi's to make himself more presentable. He knew he was just delaying the inevitable.

His steps sounded heavy without the chink of spurs as he climbed the steps to the porch. Shaking a drop of water off his hair, he rapped at the front door and heard her call for him to come in. With a swallow, he opened the door and stepped inside.

It was the second time he'd been invited into the ranch house, and he still thought it didn't look like Nancy Bennett lived there. Oh, it was neat as a pin, the wood walls painted a prim white and the dark wood floor scrubbed clean. But the entryway had only a mirror and a brass hat hook to brighten it, and the parlor leading off it, with its dual chairs flanking a limestone fireplace, looked as if no one stayed long enough to muss it up. Surely a house that Nancy lived in would have more charm and warmth.

"Back here," she called, and he followed the sound of her gentle voice down a hallway that led toward the rear door. Three closed doors lined the left wall, and, near the back of the house, a doorway opened onto a wide kitchen.

And Nancy Bennett glowed in her kingdom. He could see her reflection in the silver doors on the massive black cast-iron stove on the back wall, smell the savory results of her efforts from one of the two ovens. How she must take pride in her own hand pump so she didn't have to go outside to fetch water, and the big pantry lined with shelves where preserves glittered in the lamplight.

But nowhere was her touch more evident than on the long oval table that stood in the center of the room. The expanse was covered with a lacy white tablecloth dotted with shiny brass trivets, a pair of rose porcelain candlesticks dripping crystal and a china vase full of daisies. The entire affair was surrounded by a dozen high, carved-back black walnut chairs. Lucas Bennett must have been expecting company or hoping for a passel of children, because he'd never invited his hands to sit at that table.

Nancy was standing at the head now, wearing a blue dress with green trim, reminding Hank of a clear summer sky and good grass.

"I thought you might join me for dinner," she said, "so we could discuss your proposal."

He had a feeling his nerves would make the delicious-smelling food taste like straw, but he nodded. "I'd be honored."

She smiled, making his legs feel all the more unsteady. "Go on," she urged, nodding to the foot of the table, where a place had been set with silver cutlery and a crystal glass of lemonade. "I'll just set out the food."

His mother had taught him never to sit in the presence of a lady unless the lady sat first. So he stood awkwardly while she carried a tureen of stew smelling of garlic, a basket of biscuits piping hot from the oven and a pot of apple-and-plum preserves to the table and laid them all out on the trivets. Then she gathered her skirts and sat, and Hank sank onto the chair and gazed at her through the steam.

"Shall I say the blessing or would you like to?" she asked.

He could barely swallow much less recite a prayer. "You go ahead."

She closed her eyes and clasped her hands. "Be present at our table, Lord, be here and everywhere adored. These mercies bless and grant that we may live in fellowship with Thee. Amen."

"Amen," Hank managed.

She served him, filling a plate and then rising as if to bring it to him. He leaped to his feet and rushed around the table to take it from her. Her brows went up, but she didn't speak again until he'd returned to his seat and taken a few bites.

All the while thinking it was a crying shame he couldn't enjoy the food more, because it was *good*.

"I've been considering your proposal," she finally said, fork mixing the stew about on her plate. "And I have one question."

"Only one?" he asked, smile hitching up. "I must

have been more persuasive than I thought. Not that I was trying to pressure you," he hastened to add. Why was it he could never say the right thing with her?

"You have been very kind," she assured him. "What I want to know is why."

His mouth suddenly felt as if he'd eaten sand for the last week, and he reached for the glass of lemonade and gulped it down. He knew why his nerves were dancing. Here was his opportunity to tell her the truth. Yet if he told her, would she allow him to make amends? The need to right the wrong he'd done was like a burning mass in his gut.

"I suppose I feel guilty," he allowed, setting down his glass. "By reporting on the business of the league, I aided Mr. Bennett with his thieving. Seems only right to help his widow and child."

Her gaze dropped to her still-full plate. "Not everyone would think that way. Lucas always said you and Mr. Upkins and Billy would ride on when you tired of the place. You marry me, Hank, and you stay here. This would be our home."

He realized his knee was bouncing and forced it to stop. Staying put might not be so bad. He'd been a tumbleweed for too long. He couldn't have faced a future in Waco, not with all the bad memories of his father and Mary Ellen, but maybe Little Horn could be home.

"I can settle," he told her.

She didn't look as if she believed him, fork once more rearranging the food on her plate.

"I must ask one more thing of you," she murmured, gaze following the movement of the silver. "If we marry, we would put this ranch in trust for the baby.

You and I would have to agree to any changes in that trust."

He nodded. "That's as it should be. A man wants his children to inherit what he built." If that man could believe in his children. His father never had.

She drew in a deep breath. "Very well, then, Hank. We can talk to the lawyer in town, set up the papers to be signed the day of our marriage."

Hank stared at her, feeling as if the stew had multiplied in his stomach. "Our marriage?"

She nodded, laying down her fork at last. "Yes, Hank. I am agreeing to your proposal. I will marry you."

Chapter Five

Hank wandered back to the barn after dinner, steps still decidedly wobbly. Nancy had agreed to marry him. He was going to be a husband and a father. He wasn't sure what to do, what to think.

Upkins caught his shoulder as Hank stepped into the bunk room.

"Whoa there, son," he said, frowning into Hank's face. "What happened?"

Jenks shifted away from his belongings. "Did Widder Bennett toss you out?"

Hank shook his head, more to clear it than to answer their questions. "She's going to marry me."

Upkins released him so fast, Hank nearly fell.

"What!" the veteran demanded, stepping back.

Jenks scrambled off his bunk, sending a cat dashing out the door beside Hank. "Why'd you go and do something so low-down?"

"Low-down?" Hank frowned at him. "I offered her my name, my protection. You know she can't run this place by herself."

"We can." Upkins widened his stance, though his

six-guns were safely in their holsters by his bunk. "And I thought we were doing a good job of it too. No reason for you to push yourself forward."

"Taking advantage of a lady in her time of need," Jenks agreed, coming to join the older cowhand.

"It's not like that," Hank told them. "I'll be her husband in name only."

Jenks looked from him to Upkins. "What's that mean?"

Upkins shrugged, clearly as puzzled.

"It means I'm bunking with you and riding out like always," Hank explained. "But as far as the Empire Bank is concerned, Mrs. Bennett has a man running the ranch."

Jenks scratched his ear as if he couldn't have heard right. "So what's she calling you? Mr. Bennett number two?"

Not while he lived. "She'll be Mrs. Snowden now."

Upkins shook his grizzled head. "Makes no sense. Wives rely on husbands for more than the change of name, as far as I can see."

Jenks nodded. "Spiritual leadership and genteel companionship as the years go by."

Hank started laughing. "Well, guess I won't make much of a husband, then. Seriously, boys, nothing's going to change."

Upkins still didn't look convinced. "You really going to settle for my cooking when you have the right to sit at her table?"

Dinner hadn't been all that comfortable tonight, but the food had been far tastier than the cowboy's. Hank could imagine sitting next to Nancy after a long day, sharing stories, planning for the future. She'd smile, and he'd know that all was right with the world. He wouldn't have been surprised if he wasn't smiling just thinking about it. He put on a somber face.

"We didn't agree on specifics," he admitted.

"Then I reckon you ought to," Upkins told him. "Are you obliged to drive her to services every Sunday? Is she going to expect you to take on chores around the house? Who's giving the orders to ride, you or her?"

Hank shook his head. "Maybe you should have offered to marry her. Seems you have it all figured out."

"I've got the questions, son," Upkins retorted. "That don't mean I got the answers."

"Neither do I," Hank said. "But there's something you should know. She's carrying Bennett's child."

Jenks's brows rose so high they disappeared under his thatch of red hair. Upkins let out a low whistle, then narrowed his eyes at Hank.

"You aim to be its pa?"

"Yes," Hank said. "You have a problem with that, best you ride on now."

For a moment, Upkins held his gaze, and Jenks seemed to be holding his breath. Then Upkins nodded.

"We'll all help," he declared with a look to Jenks, who nodded so fast Hank thought the boy's head might rattle.

"You'll make the babe a good pa," Jenks agreed.

Hank didn't know how Jenks could be so sure. He wasn't. He didn't even have a good example to follow, unless it was to do what his father hadn't.

"I intend to try," he told them both.

Once more Jenks glanced between Hank and Up-kins. "So, we're going to have a wedding."

Hank laughed. "I reckon we are, and as soon as possible. I guess I better talk to Pastor Stillwater."

As it turned out, the local minister wasn't the only one Hank had to talk to about his and Nancy's wedding. Hoping for a word with the pastor, Hank took Nancy into Little Horn that Sunday for services in the old revival tent the town used while the first church building and parsonage were being constructed nearby.

He hadn't had a chance to attend services very often in the past. Cattle didn't know much about keeping the Lord's day, so Hank had generally been working. Besides, back in Waco only the fine folk went to services, and he was no longer part of that company.

Now, as he escorted Nancy into the shelter of the tent, he couldn't deny the peace that flowed over him. He'd grown up worshipping among polished wood pews to the bellow of a massive pipe organ. The little tent with its packed dirt floor, rough wood benches and rickety piano felt more like home. After all, it hadn't been in the fancy church he'd come to know his God but in the simple cathedral of a cowboy's saddle.

Still, sitting with Nancy, holding the hymnal for her, his spirits rose. How could he not feel proud to have her beside him, pretty and sweet as she was?

Easy now, cowboy. Pride goeth before a fall. He'd felt same way about Mary Ellen, and his feelings had been built on nothing more substantial than air. Nancy wasn't here vowing undying devotion. She stood with him because she needed his help to save the Windy Diamond. And he was here to atone.

As the others listened to Pastor Stillwater's message, Hank bowed his head.

I know You forgive easily, Lord. The Bible talks about a lost son being welcomed home and You eating with sinners. I know You won't hold Lucas Bennett's death against me. Help me help Nancy so I won't hold it against myself.

Nancy shifted beside him, hand going to her back, and he stepped closer, offering his arm to lean on. Her smile was his reward.

After services, he left her with some of the other ladies and went to seek the pastor, who assured him of his support and willingness to perform the marriage ceremony. But Hank had no sooner stepped away from the minister than McKay and an older rancher in the area, Clyde Parker, closed in on him.

"We have everything under control," Parker assured him, hitching up his gray trousers with self-importance. "The Lone Star Cowboy League is at your service."

If the league came through with the money to save the ranch, Hank wouldn't have to marry Nancy. For some reason, that made his spirits sink. "Then you found a way to pay the loan after all."

"No," McKay told him. "That's not what he means."

The dark clouds lifted. What was wrong with him? He ought to be disappointed they hadn't been able to help Nancy.

Parker laughed, sounding a bit like the wheezy piano. "The story's all over town, boy. You made the sacrifice to marry Nancy Bennett. Lula May says we should throw you a reception after the wedding. Think of it as a service to the community. We all need a reason to celebrate after the troubles this summer."

Hank held up his hand. "Hold on. Marrying Mrs. Bennett is no sacrifice. I'm the one honored by her trust. And I'm not sure she'll want a fuss."

"Mrs. Bennett?" Parker teased with an elbow to Hank's gut. "You should be calling her by her first name now."

She'd given him leave to do so in private, but he found it difficult to use her first name in public. Funny how just being with Nancy made him remember the manners his mother had tried to instill in him. Ladies were to be treated with respect, helped into and out of any building or conveyance as if they were delicate flowers that might wither at a harsh word. Even with her quiet voice and shy smiles, he knew Nancy was made of stronger stuff. Look at the way she was trying to learn to run the ranch her husband had left her.

Excusing himself from the ranchers, he walked toward the piano, where Nancy was surrounded by the local ladies, looking a bit like spring wildflowers with their pretty dresses and bright-ribboned hats. Several of the group giggled behind their gloved hands as he approached. The only one who wasn't watching him closely was John Carson's girl, and Daisy had her head turned as if she was studying someone behind him.

"Ladies," Hank said with a nod. "May I steal Mrs. Bennett away from you for a moment?"

"Only if you promise to bring her back as Mrs. Snowden," the sheriff's wife teased.

Nancy blushed and excused herself. Hank drew her toward a corner of the tent where the velvet bags that were passed for offering were stored. He could see Mrs. Hickey, the town gossip, craning her scrawny neck to get a view of the two of them, but he put his back to her to shelter Nancy.

"Seems like everyone knew before I ever told them," he said, rubbing his chin.

"I know." Nancy sighed. "I mentioned to Lula May at the quilting bee that you had proposed, and of course the other women encouraged me to accept."

Of course? Who knew the ladies of the town thought that much of him? He couldn't help grinning.

"They must have assumed I'd taken their advice," Nancy continued. "I'm sorry, Hank."

"No need to be sorry," he assured her. "I didn't call you away because of the rumors. Seems the league wants to throw a big reception for us after the wedding."

She paled. "I can't accept their kindness. We both know we wouldn't be in this position if Lucas hadn't broken the law."

"True," Hank said. "He caused heartache for a number of folks. But this reception may be a way to put all that behind us."

She was chewing her lower lip again, a sure sign, he was coming to understand, of her concern. "Well, I suppose we could take them up on their offer. For Little Horn. Maybe Lula May can help me bake."

Hank took her hand and gave it a squeeze. "Don't fret. I'll take care of everything."

She raised her brows. "Everything?"

"Everything," he insisted. After all, it was the least he could do.

Two weeks later, Nancy stood up with Hank and said her vows in front of a goodly portion of Little Horn's finest. She couldn't help contrasting her weddings. She and Lucas had been married in the big church in Burnet, because Lucas refused to be wed in a tent. He'd even had a blue satin dress made for her so she looked the part of an affluent rancher's wife, and she'd felt a little awed to be standing up beside such a prosperous fellow, bouquet of white roses in her hands from the wife of the town mayor.

This time, she carried a bunch of yellow daisies Billy had picked from the ranch and handed her, red-faced, as he stammered his best wishes. Mr. Upkins, dressed in a black suit and bow tie she hadn't known he possessed, had insisted on giving her away. Her green dress with the ruby roses embroidered down the front had been sewn by the ladies of the quilting bee and designed to be let out as the baby inside her grew. It was all quite lovely, and she felt like a complete fraud accepting the attentions.

But somehow, she managed the words, and when Preacher Stillwater held her and Hank's hands together and declared them husband and wife, she even found a smile.

As they turned to face the applauding crowd, Hank tucked her hand in his elbow.

"Phew," he murmured in her ear. "I thought he'd never stop talking. Let's eat."

That made her laugh, but then she was fairly sure that had been his intention.

The ladies of Little Horn had done themselves proud, Nancy saw as Hank led her to the two long tables in the field to the south of the tent. Besides the spice cake Lula May had baked for the wedding, its sides dripping icing, there were peach pies with golden crusts and cobblers plump with sweet biscuit topping, crisp ginger cookies and cinnamon rolls dotted with currants. The café owner Mercy Green had even provided gallons of vanilla ice cream. Hank filled Nancy's plate with the delicacies and mounded one for himself before escorting her to the head table, where a spot waited for them.

"This isn't so bad," he mused after they'd eaten their fill. He leaned back so the narrow wooden chair tilted on two legs. "Fine vittles, pretty lady at my side, friends and family celebrating. What's so hard about marriage?"

"We've been married all of a quarter hour," Nancy reminded him. "You just wait and see how hard it can be."

Immediately he sobered, the legs of his chair thudding down onto the dry ground. "Sorry, Nancy. I reckon you had it harder than many. I know Mr. Bennett had a temper at times. And I know he rode off when he should have stayed home."

She didn't want to remember how her first marriage had failed. "No more mention of Mr. Bennett. Not today."

As if he agreed, he hopped to his feet. "Let's not talk at all. Let's dance."

From the middle of the field, Nancy heard the

scrape of a bow on strings. Glancing that way, she saw that Bo Stillwater was tightening the clamp on his guitar while several of the other local men tuned up fiddles and pipes. Around them, couples were forming, men leading ladies and ladies grabbing their sweetheart's hand and tugging the fellow toward the music. Daisy Carson was twitching her skirts and glancing to where Calvin Barlow and his family and Edmund McKay were waiting.

But to stand up in front of them all with Hank? She wasn't sure she was ready for that.

"Oh, I don't think dancing is necessary," she demurred.

Hank cocked his head, sapphire eyes catching the sunlight. "It may not be necessary, but it will likely be fun. You remember fun, don't you, Nancy?"

Did she? She seemed to recall playing with other children in the schoolyard, but after her father's death she'd spent most of her time with her mother. That had been rewarding, and she'd never regret growing so close, but she could not call it fun.

"I don't believe we've been introduced," she said, keeping her tone light.

He raised his dark brows. "Well, then, it would be my pleasure to acquaint the two of you." He held out his hand.

She hesitated. She'd been surprised no one had seen fit to berate her for marrying again so soon, barely a month after Lucas's death. Surely she shouldn't be out there kicking up her heels. However badly Lucas had behaved, he'd still been her husband.

So was Hank.

The thought sent a tremor through her. For all

they'd agreed on a marriage in name only, surely she owed him some duty.

She must have hesitated too long, for he lowered his hand. "Are you morally opposed to dancing, ma'am?" he asked with a frown.

A moment ago, he'd called her Nancy. She was building a wall between them when none was necessary. She raised her head to meet his gaze. "No, certainly not."

"Then is it bad for the baby?" he pressed.

"No, it's not that." She bit her lip, trying to think of a way to explain to him when she'd been the one to ask him not to talk about Lucas.

He nodded, plopping himself down on the chair again. "Don't fret. I understand. I probably wouldn't want to dance with a cowboy if I was a fine lady either."

Nancy surged to her feet. "Nonsense. Any lady would be pleased to dance with you, Hank."

He stood, but she could see him eying her warily. "What are you saying?"

Nancy held out her hand. "I believe you asked your wife to dance, Mr. Snowden."

His grin spread. "I believe I did, Mrs. Snowden."

It seemed as if the pigeons that favored Hop Toad Springs had taken flight inside her as Hank cupped her hand and led her out onto the grass.

Harold Hickey, husband to the chatty Constance Hickey, was standing by the makeshift band, ready to call the dance, as Nancy took her spot across from Hank. The ladies stood in one long line, the men opposite, with lots of looks flashing from one side to the other—amusement, delight, excitement. At the last minute, Calvin Barlow dragged Daisy into the group, and they took their place at the bottom of the set.

"Let's start with something fast," Harold said with a nod to the band, who launched into a lilting horn-pipe. The wiry fellow began tapping his toe in time, gray head bobbing.

"Greet your partner," he called, and the couples took two mincing steps forward. Hank bowed, and Nancy curtsied, her skirts belling out around her. She thought the ladies of the quilting bee hadn't gathered up all that material to watch it flow in the dance, but then again, maybe they had!

"Swing your partner," Harold called, and they linked elbows. Hank spun her around in a circle, first one way, and then the other. A smile broadened her lips.

"And a do-si-do," Harold called. Nancy lifted her skirts and skipped around Hank.

"Mighty graceful, Mrs. Snowden," he said as she passed.

And she felt graceful: light, buoyant, free. Why had she protested?

"First couple, take a jaunt," the caller demanded.

Next to them, Edmund McKay took Lula May's hands and danced her down the center. Nancy clapped in time with the other couples as their friends came back up to their spot.

"Reel her on down, Edmund," Harold ordered, and the pair linked elbows, first with each other and then with the opposite dancer. Edmund nearly lifted Nancy off her feet as he turned her. Then Nancy was clapping again as Edmund and Lula May progressed down and skipped back up.

"And let's peel away," Harold said over the music, and Nancy followed Lula May around the line. She couldn't help noticing the spring in her friend's step. Nancy was fairly sure hers matched it.

"Make a bridge," he called, and Edmund and Lula May took hands and held them high, Lula May on her tiptoes to more closely match Edmund's reach.

Hank took Nancy's hands and led her up to the top. And then it was their turn to swing around the couples. As she steepled her arms with Hank at the foot, she felt laughter bubbling up.

"See," Hank said as they lowered their hands after the last couple had danced through. "I knew you were acquainted with fun. You just forgot. I think we should have him around more often."

She couldn't argue with that.

They finished the dance to applause for the band and caller. Harold nodded his thanks. "Now, how about something a little slower for us old-timers? Let's have a waltz."

Unmarried couples exited the square, and married couples gathered closer. Hank smiled at Nancy and turned to leave.

"And let's have our newlyweds lead the pack," Harold called out.

Hank stopped, glanced back at Nancy. For a moment, she thought she saw panic in his bright eyes. Didn't he know how to waltz? Her mother had taught her, though Nancy had never partnered a gentleman. Lucas hadn't liked dancing, at least with her.

She stepped up to Hank and took his hand. "It's not hard," she murmured. "I could lead if you like."

"It's not that," he murmured back, gaze searching hers. "My mother always said waltzes were for married couples."

Nancy smiled at him. "You're married, cowboy. Or have you forgotten your vows already?"

His grin lit up the field. "No, ma'am. Let's waltz." He swept Nancy into his arm and turned her around the circle.

She was flying, soaring, safe in his embrace. The joy welled up from inside her, until she thought she might burst. How had she forgotten how much she loved to dance?

The other couples seemed to fade, the music to quiet, until it was only she and Hank, moving together, skimming the grass. That blue gaze drew her closer, like cool water in the summer heat. She couldn't look away.

Until he stopped and bowed, and she realized everyone was clapping again, for them. His smile was all for her, his hand cradling hers gently.

And for the first time, she wondered exactly what she'd done when she'd agreed to be Hank Snowden's wife.

Chapter Six

She was a wonder. Hank left Nancy at their table to go procure some punch for the two of them. He couldn't figure out why she'd been so hesitant to dance. Twirling her around the grass, he'd felt as if they were flying. Now she positively glowed from their efforts, even though she was a little out of breath. A fellow could learn to love that sweet smile.

He stumbled on the grass and had to rein in his thoughts. He'd promised her a marriage in name only. And just because he admired her didn't mean the feeling was mutual.

He'd learned that lesson well. He wasn't about to go building castles in the air again. He'd do as he'd promised, save the ranch for her and her baby. He'd treat her with the respect due the real owner of the ranch. He didn't have to hand her his heart with a pretty blue bow on it.

CJ Thorn was standing by the refreshment tables, head bowed as if he couldn't make up his mind about which of the many offerings to sample.

"I'd advise the peach pie," Hank told him, reaching for the tin punch ladle. "Unless you're partial to cinnamon, and then there's nothing finer than Mrs. Carson's rolls."

CJ managed a smile. The same height and build as Hank, his friend had dark brown hair and eyes that could look downright broody at times. Of course, he'd had a lot to deal with the last year, with his brother disappearing and leaving him custody of his twin four-year-old nieces. CJ had been smart to latch on to Molly Langley's help. The two had wed earlier this summer, and Hank thought the marriage had lifted many a burden from the rancher's shoulders.

"I was looking for something easy on the stomach," he told Hank now. "Molly hasn't been feeling well for the last couple weeks."

Hank frowned as he poured the rosy punch into a glass for Nancy. "Sorry to hear that. Maybe you should talk to Mrs. Bennett—er, Nancy. She knows something about doctoring."

"Molly's a little embarrassed about the whole thing," CJ confessed. "She's used to being the helper, not the one who needs help. I'm just glad I can stay close to the ranch right now."

Hank took his time pouring a glass for himself. "Haven't had any more trouble with rustling, then?"

Now it was CJ's turn to frown. "No. And I didn't think I would. We ended that problem."

"I thought we had," Hank admitted. "But McKay brought up the fact that we don't know what Lucas Bennett intended to do with the cattle. Likely he hoped to sell them to someone, and that person is still riding free."

CJ's breath hissed through his teeth.

"I think," Jeb Fuller said, elbowing his way between them to reach for a cookie, "that you all ought to let the law do its work on the matter."

Hank felt himself bristling and forced his hand to relax before he spilled the punch.

"No one's trying to take the law into his own hands," CJ assured Jeb with a look to Hank. "Even when you rode out to confront Bennett, you deputized Snowden and McKay."

"And we left you out," Jeb remembered, rubbing the cookie between his thumb and forefinger so that drops of ginger flitted to the ground like falling stars. "I wanted to keep the number of people small so we wouldn't risk any vigilantes. You know how Clyde Parker can be."

Hank and CJ nodded, both having been around the peppery rancher when he got riled up.

"But McKay is right," Jeb continued. "Lucas Bennett couldn't have driven all those steers to a buyer alone. And while we seem to have stopped the thefts locally, at least for the moment, there's been trouble from Oakalla in the north down to Burnet in the south. Lucas Bennett couldn't have covered all that ground."

Hank felt as if the fine food had soured in his mouth. "Then there's more than one rustler, and someone is buying stolen cattle."

"Very likely," Jeb replied. He popped the cookie in his mouth and chewed as he eyed Hank. "I advise you all to keep up the patrols, just in case. But I don't want anyone out looking for trouble."

Something poked at Hank's heart. "I'm not a vigilante."

"Never said you were," Jeb replied. "Just know that I'm looking into the matter, and the folks in Burnet hired a former Texas Ranger to help. Between the two of us, we'll bring the culprits to justice."

Hank wished he could believe that. But cattle had been disappearing for months, and it had been the Lone Star Cowboy League, not Sheriff Fuller, who had realized that Lucas Bennett was the thief in their area. Besides, the sheriff had a lot of ground to cover. He couldn't be everywhere. What if more cattle were stolen? What if Nancy's cattle were taken? The Windy Diamond couldn't survive the loss.

As Jeb and CJ discussed plans for roundup now that the air was finally cooling toward fall, Hank looked out of the tent across the field. Harold Hickey had called up a polka, and ladies and gents were bobbing about the grass, hands clasped. Some of the boys had set up an alley for ninepins and were crowing as Donny Carson mowed down the wooden pins in a single roll. Daisy Carson was walking around the edges of the field on the arm of the oldest Barlow boy, under the watchful gazes of their mothers. Music, laughter and conversation flowed, bright as the summer day.

Was he the only one to see a dark shadow looming over them all?

Nancy folded her hands against the pretty bodice of her green wedding dress as Hank drove the wagon back to the Windy Diamond. The calls of their well-wishers still echoed in her ears. Lula May had insisted that Nancy throw her bouquet, and everyone had been surprised when Daisy Carson caught it. Mrs. Carson had snatched the bouquet from her daughter's grip and taken her aside. Nancy could hear Helen insisting that there was no need for a sixteen-year-old to be thinking about marriage yet in this enlightened day and age.

Nancy could only agree. She wasn't sure she was ready for marriage a second time at twenty-six. She certainly wasn't sure of the man beside her. He'd been quiet since their dance, as if it had set him to thinking and those thoughts weren't particularly pleasant. Were all men moody after they married?

"Penny for your thoughts," she said.

"Probably not worth a penny," he answered as he guided the horses toward the iron gates where the shape of a diamond canted to the right, as if blown by the wind.

"It was a nice party," Nancy ventured.

The thud of the horses' hooves against the dusty road was as loud as the blow of a hammer. "Real nice," he allowed.

"Thank you for asking me to dance," she said.

"My pleasure," he returned. "That is, I didn't do it for my pleasure. I mean, it was pleasurable, but I was thinking more about you having fun than me. Not that I didn't have fun."

Nancy put a hand on his arm. "It's all right, Hank. I know what you mean. And I did have fun. I probably would have enjoyed myself even more if I hadn't been thinking they shouldn't have been so kind to us."

She felt his muscles tense under her hand. "How so?"

Would he make her point out the obvious? "Lucas stole from them, lied to them."

"Started the Carson fire," he added.

Her stomach cramped. "That too? I don't know how Helen can bear to so much as look at me!"

"You?" He pulled on the reins to turn the horses through the gate. "This is no fault of yours. I heard you apologize to McKay and Lula May when they came to visit. But you have no reason to feel sorry. You didn't help him, didn't know what he was doing."

Maybe she would have if she'd been a more attentive wife. But after he'd raised his hand to her that night, she'd stayed away from him as much as possible, and he'd seemed to prefer it that way. But if she'd tried harder, leaned closer instead of pulling back, things might have been different.

She tucked those thoughts away. God had given her a second chance to be a wife, and she was going to do her best this time.

Unfortunately, Hank didn't make it easy for her.

"Would you like some dinner?" she asked as he stopped the wagon in front of the house.

He patted his flat stomach. "No, ma'am. I am fuller than a pig the day before slaughter."

Not a pretty picture, but she got the point. "Then will you come in for some lemonade?"

He hopped down and came around for her. "Best I go help Jenks."

Billy had stayed behind to watch the herd. "Of course," she said.

He lifted her down, and she couldn't help remembering the tender way Edmund McKay had looked at Lula May in the same circumstances. Hank let go of her so fast she thought her dress might be on fire. He tipped his hat.

"Good night, Nancy. Sweet dreams."

She supposed she would have to be satisfied with that.

He was up and out of the barn even earlier than usual the next morning, for she saw his horse was gone from the corral when she rose. She thought surely he'd join her for dinner that evening, so she spent the day cooking a roast with tomatoes and beans fresh from the garden, cornbread, mashed potatoes with a hint of garlic and a peach pie. She tidied up the house, made sure the table was set just right, combed her hair until it shone.

Then she sat in the parlor and waited.

And waited.

As the sun sank toward the horizon, fear tingled like a splinter under her skin. What if he'd run into a mountain lion? What if he'd stepped on a rattler? What if one of the cattle had turned on him and trampled him?

What if he was a rustler?

She stood up, paced the room. Oh, this was no good! She went to the kitchen, sliced the roast and left it warming in the oven. Maybe she'd see him coming in if she went out to the porch.

Maybe Mr. Upkins would be bringing Hank's body.

She burst through the door and made herself stop and take a deep breath. Everything looked calm, certainly calmer than she felt. A few of her cattle had wandered closer to the house. She could see their coffee-colored hides moving among the oaks. An owl called from the bushes while its mate swept over the grass, seeking prey.

And a light glowed from the barn.

It seemed her "husband" was going about his life. That's what he'd said he'd do. She shouldn't have expected otherwise. Yet somehow she felt empty, abandoned. Her father and mother had left her through no fault of theirs. Through his own actions, Lucas had ended up leaving. In the matter of Hank Snowden, she was the one who must act.

She picked up her blue skirts and swept to the barn.

She'd never actually been in the barn before. Lucas had felt a lady shouldn't sully her hands. Billy milked the cow and gathered eggs. The warm smells wrapped around her the moment she pushed through the wide doors—cow and rabbit stew and hay. In the dim light, the tall, long building seemed entirely masculine, with pitchforks stuck in piles of hay, ropes looped on hooks and axes and saws hanging from nails. The milk cow stood resting in its stall, dark eyes gleaming at Nancy as she passed. The chickens clucked a scold. A cat darted away into the darkness.

Voices called from the doorway near the rear. That must be the bunk room. Surely it was improper for her to invade their space.

The prim voice in her head sounded suspiciously like some of the Missouri town women who had insisted it wasn't proper for an unmarried woman to be a midwife. There was nothing improper about her checking on her boys. She owned this spread.

Raising her head, she moved to the door and rapped.

Voices cut out. Spurs chimed as boots strode to the door. The panel whipped open to reveal Billy, eyes wide and hair damp from a dunking. Behind him, Hank and Mr. Upkins held their guns ready.

"Mrs. Ben—Snowden, ma'am," Billy stammered, dropping his arm. "Is something wrong?"

"I had hoped to see Hank when you rode in," Nancy said, keeping her voice steady. "I believe he was going to give me a report."

Hank holstered his gun in the sheath hanging over one of the bunk posts and started forward. Behind him, she saw the quilt she'd helped make, carefully folded on the bunk. The thought of him sleeping under it made her feel warm.

"I believe you're right," he said as he reached the door. "Apologies, ma'am. Allow me to escort you back to the house."

Under her boys' watchful eyes, she stepped aside to let him join her.

"When I didn't see you on the porch as we rode in," he murmured as they crossed the barn, steps quiet in the scattered hay, "I thought you might be tired of my company."

"I am never tired of your company," Nancy told him as he held the door open for her to exit the barn. He regarded her as she passed, and she realized how that must have sounded.

"You were going to teach me how to run this ranch," she pointed out. "To do that, we have to spend time together."

"That's true enough. It's just that things are a little busy now." He walked her across the flat of the front yard and up onto the porch, but there he paused as if refusing to go farther.

Nancy opened the door. "Perhaps you can tell me all about it over dinner. Now come inside and eat,

Hank." Delighted by her boldness, she sashayed back to the kitchen.

He followed.

A little thrill went through her, but she shook it off. She wasn't trying to boss the poor fellow around, but surely they must come to some agreement on their unorthodox partnership. She went to the stove, took down a pad to protect her hands and brought the roast out of the oven.

She heard him inhale. "That smells mighty good."

Nancy smiled to herself. "Please have a seat while I bring everything to the table."

Turning with the roast, she saw he remained standing at the foot of the table, where she'd laid his place. Lucas had always sat at the top and her at the bottom, but she wasn't about to admit that to Hank. There had to be some benefits to running a ranch. She brought the rest of the food to the table, arranged it to her liking, filled a plate for him and herself, then took her seat and bowed her head.

She could hear the drippings simmering in the pan.

Raising her head, she saw that he was watching her. "Will you say the grace?" she asked.

He drew in a breath. "Yes, ma'am. If it pleases you." He cleared his throat, and she lowered her head and closed her eyes, waiting for the familiar words.

"Lord," he said, voice soft and humble, "thank You for bringing us through another day safe and whole. Thank You for the sun to warm us, the breeze to cool us. Thank You for clean water and good food and friends and family to share them with. May they all be the blessing You intended. Amen."

Nancy raised her head to stare at him. He picked

up his fork and dug in, gaze on the plate below him. Her father and mother had recited the same prayer every night, the words running together from frequent use. Lucas had prayed with great purpose, using fancy words, loud and occasionally long enough that the food had cooled and he'd complain as if it had been her fault.

She'd never heard anyone pray like Hank, simple and true and from the heart. And somehow, dinner felt easier because of it.

Then she took a bite of the potatoes and frowned. "Forgive me. Too much garlic."

He shrugged, lifting another forkful of the fluffy mass. "Tastes fine to me. But then, I'm used to the way Upkins cooks. I reckon he didn't learn much from his mama."

She hid a smile. "I fear I didn't learn a great deal from mine either. My mother always preferred to cook alone. She said having an extra person in the kitchen flustered her. So, I suppose I didn't know much about cooking when I came to Little Horn."

"You must have learned fast," Hank said, rising up to help himself to another slice of the roast.

"Well, I had to," she admitted, smile breaking free. "I had a husband to feed, and he liked things done to his satisfaction."

He grunted, slicing into the meat so fast she thought he was concerned it was about to flee. In fact, now that she noticed, he was bolting down the food. Was he trying to finish the ordeal and escape?

Annoyance pricked her. "So how did things go on the ranch today?" she asked.

"Fine," he acknowledged between bites.

"No problems?" she pressed.

He picked up his napkin and wiped the crumbs from his mouth. "Not really."

"You were saying there was a lot to do right now," she tried, temper threatening. "What exactly are we doing?"

He frowned a moment as if thinking. "Best we move the herd farther west."

West? But that was away from the house and the reliable spring. That was where she couldn't see what he was doing.

Suspicion tugged at her sleeve for attention. She focused on Hank. "But shouldn't we keep them closer to the house for safety?"

"We handled the biggest danger," he replied, and she knew he meant Lucas. As if he'd realized his gaff, he flushed and changed the subject. "So you learned to cook from your ma. I hope she won't be disappointed you married a cowpoke."

"My mother's gone," she replied, still finding it hard to say the words. "My father too. That's why I agreed to become a mail-order bride. There was nothing left for me in Missouri."

He swallowed. "Sorry for your loss." He started to reach for the pie, then glanced at her with upraised brows.

"Please," she said, "help yourself."

He grinned, dragging the tin closer and cutting out a good chunk of pie to put on his plate.

"What about your parents?" she asked, suddenly curious. "What will you tell them about our marriage?"

He blinked, peach dropping from his fork to the

plate with a plop. "I wasn't going to tell them anything. I haven't had word from them in nearly five years. I'm not sure they even know where I am."

As close as she'd been to her family, she couldn't imagine not at least writing once in a while. She'd never met Lucas's family in Alabama, but she'd written to let them know about his death and the upcoming birth of his child.

"You must write to them," she insisted, digging into the potatoes. "They'll want to know you married."

"I'm not so sure about that." As if that was all that needed be said, he rose and carried his emptied plate, cup and utensils to the sink. "Anything else, ma'am? Morning comes early."

"I'm well aware of when morning comes, sir." There went her temper. Lucas would have blamed it on her pregnancy making her moodier than usual. She thought it had more to do with feeling as if she was being boxed into a corner.

As Hank turned from the sink, head hanging as if he expected a scold, she fought to keep her tone civil. "It's becoming more difficult for me to go out on the ranch with you," she explained. "So I need you to come to me. I'd like you to eat dinner with me in the evening. Tell me about the ranch. Help me understand not only what must be done but why it must be done. Can you do that?"

"If that's what you want," he said.

"It is," she said with conviction.

He nodded. "I want to move the cattle west because the grass closer to the house is getting thin. We need to give it time to recover. Plus, there's a line shack there where we can begin to stage them for the roundup."

At least that made sense. "And when is roundup?" Nancy asked.

"About a month from now. The league members have already begun talking about it. We'll need to coordinate with them. The bigger the group heading to the railhead, the better."

"Because of mountain lions, rattlers and rustlers," Nancy remembered.

He smiled. "Yes, ma'am."

"You promised to call me Nancy." As soon as she said it she cursed herself for being too forward. Theirs wasn't a true marriage. He didn't have to treat her with any intimacy.

"So I did. Forgive me, Nancy."

That smile warmed her more than her stove.

"I should go," he said, backing toward the kitchen door. "Is there anything else you want?"

"No, thank you," she said, and he escaped before she could tell him the truth. What she'd asked for was only the beginning of what she wanted, but feared she'd never have.

Chapter Seven

Over the next week, life settled into a routine. Nancy spent the days doing her usual chores, with the occasional visit from Lula May or one of the other ladies who were members of the quilting bee. Behind the house, peaches were coming on in the small orchard which also held plum and apple trees, and blackberries were ripening on the brambles near the spring. The fruit must be picked, scalded and canned for use in the cooler months.

Then there was the vegetable garden to tend and washing to be done. There were relatively few dirty clothes with Lucas gone, but when she suggested to Hank that she could wash his things, he'd turned red.

"Cowboys are used to dirt," he'd joked.

At least when evening came, Hank would join her for dinner and report on the ranch. She listened and learned, but she went to bed feeling unsettled. Something more seemed to be waiting, just beyond her fingertips, but she wasn't even sure which way to reach or what she'd find when she did.

The baby was by far the brightest spot in her life.

She could feel the changes in her body and knew that meant changes were taking place inside her too. Her feet and legs cramped from time to time, but she knew how to flex and massage them to ease the discomfort.

In fact, she was flexing under the table at dinner one night and must have grimaced, because Hank rose to go to the pump. She shifted in her seat.

"What are you doing?"

Clean water splashed into a glass he'd taken from the cupboard. He shook the drops off the sides and brought the water to the table.

"You need this," he said, handing the glass to her. "It will help you and the baby."

Her mother had always said plenty of liquid led to a better birth, but she was surprised to hear the advice coming from him. "How did you know?" she asked, accepting the glass.

He flushed. "Well, it works for the heifers."

She knew another woman would take umbrage about being compared to cattle, especially as her figure spread, but knowing how her boys felt about their herd, she counted it a compliment.

Not everyone, however, was so pleased to hear about the baby. She was sitting on the porch, taking a break from her work and sipping at a glass of lemonade, when Billy brought her the mail from town. The young cowboy rode into Little Horn once a week to perform the service.

"Letter for you, ma'am," he said now, ducking his red-haired head as he climbed the steps. He handed her the missive. "Hope it's good news."

It wasn't. Nancy read the letter twice, the second time with trembling fingers. She'd tried to be kind.

How could anyone see it as evil? Was she so different from the world? Is that why she kept misunderstanding people's motives?

She tried to put the matter aside, go about her day, but Hank always seemed to know when something was bothering her.

"Jenks said you got a letter today," he said, dipping his spoon into the beef and barley soup she'd made. "Bank giving us more trouble?"

Nancy could barely look at the soup or the slice of freshly baked oat bread beside it. "No. The letter wasn't from Mr. Cramore. It was from Lucas's father."

Hank went still. "I didn't know you were in contact with Mr. Bennett's relatives."

"I never contacted them when Lucas was alive," Nancy told him. "We'd get a letter from Alabama once in a while. Lucas always said it was family business and nothing to concern me. I thought I should tell his family that he'd died but was leaving a child behind."

Hank stirred his soup, the steam rising past his chiseled jaw. "Did they invite you to come stay with them?"

Nancy choked back a laugh. "No. In fact, Mr. Bennett told me I'd ruined his son's life. It seems Lucas became bitter after our marriage and told his father off for not bringing us home to Alabama once Lucas had made a success of the ranch. His father warned me never to contact him again or he'd seek legal action. He seemed to think I was trying to press him for money."

She couldn't look at Hank. She'd hadn't been asking for money, but she still felt as if she'd stepped in mud.

She heard the chair scrape against the wood floor as Hank pushed back from the table, then the thud of his boots as he came to her end. His arm slipped around her shoulders.

"You did the right thing writing," he murmured. "Most folks would want to know they'd have a grand-baby to look forward to. The shame's on him."

She drew in a breath and nodded. "I know. But it's sad the baby won't have a chance to know Lucas's family."

"That's why we need to give the baby a family," he said, straightening.

As if in agreement, the baby danced inside her.

Nancy pressed a hand to her belly, smile trembling on her lips. "He seems to agree with you."

Hank raised his brows. "Does he?" He bent over. "Well, hey there, little feller. I sure am looking forward to meeting you. Not that I want you to come anytime soon," he hastened to add with a glance up at Nancy. "You just sit nice and warm in there 'til you're ready. Just know you have a mighty pretty mama waiting for you out here."

She felt the baby shift, as if listening to everything Hank said.

"I think he likes your voice," she marveled.

Hank jerked upright. "Can he really hear me?"

Nancy shrugged. "Who knows? Mothers have told me their babies reacted to loud noises or soft music. My baby seems to like you."

He blushed, the red growing in his cheeks like a sunrise. "That's a real honor." He bent low again. "Thanks, little feller."

He turned his head and met her gaze. "Or should I be saying little lady?"

With his face so close to hers, she could see that he

had the longest lashes, thick and black, like his hair. Nancy had to force herself to focus on his question.

"My mother claimed she could tell whether a baby was going to be a girl or a boy," she told him. "She was seldom wrong. I think she'd say this is a boy."

"Well, then," he said, turning to address her belly again, "we're going to have a whole lot of fun together."

He sounded positively eager. She smiled. "And Hank knows about fun," she told her baby. "He even took your mama dancing."

"We'll teach you," Hank promised the baby. "You'll be a fine-looking feller. Stands to reason with the parents you had. You'll be real popular with the ladies."

"Everyone loves babies," she agreed. Then she remembered the note from Lucas's father. "Well, most everyone."

"Anyone with any sense loves babies," Hank maintained. He must have tired of bending, for he pulled out the chair next to hers and sat, gaze still on the baby. "You just wait. Why, the first day we take you to services, those quilting gals will all be reaching out to hold you."

Nancy laughed. "Yes, they will! And I expect you'll smile and coo like the charming baby you'll be."

Hank sobered. "Don't go putting expectations on him, especially not so young. That's a powerful burden on a child."

Hurt washed over her. "I know how to take care of babies, Hank."

"I imagine you do," he allowed. "But I have a few opinions in that area myself. I reckon we need to come to terms."

* * *

It was the wrong thing to say. He could see it in the way her jaw set, her head raised. He couldn't seem to find the right words with her, always brought up sore subjects. But in this case, he knew what needed to be said.

"Let me tell you a story," he started, aiming his look and voice at the baby he could imagine growing inside her. "I was a baby like you once, odd as that may sound to you."

He didn't dare look up at her, but he could see her fingers relax and could imagine her look softening. "No, really?" she teased.

He smiled to himself. "Afraid so. I was the youngest, the last of four, and all the rest girls. Now, I got nothing against girls, and if you turn out to be one despite what your mama says, I'll be proud to teach you to ride and rope and raise cattle so you can help your mama run this ranch."

He dared to glance up at Nancy. She was watching him, head cocked, as if she wasn't sure what he was doing. He licked his lips and launched into the next part of the story.

"My daddy thought different," he explained to the baby. "He'd been waiting a long time for a son. He wanted the best for me—the best teaching, the best food and clothing."

"Lucas wanted the best of everything too," she murmured.

"And we know where that led," he answered.

She nodded, and he pushed on.

"But my pa also expected the best from me. I had to ride better, rope faster, than anyone else on the spread, even the hands who'd been working for years. He told me who I could be friends with, who wasn't good enough for me. He expected me to think just like he did."

"Oh, Hank," she whispered, and he didn't dare look at her again or he knew he'd lose his nerve.

"Now, I tried hard to be a good son, do all the things he wanted, but it seemed I was always a disappointment. So, when he told me he wanted me to marry the daughter of the man who owned the ranch next to ours, I didn't argue. No man would. She was pretty and sweet, and every gent within a hundred miles of Waco was hoping to have her stand beside him. I reckon it was love at first sight."

He saw her hand move to her cheek as if she couldn't imagine anything more romantic. "And then what happened?" she urged.

She should know the story hadn't ended well, or he wouldn't be here in Little Horn, working as a foreman.

"Did I mention she was smart?" Hank asked. "Smart enough to know I wasn't the man she wanted. Seems any feelings between us were all in my head. She up and married my best friend. And I left Waco before Pa could tell me what a disappointment I was again."

His throat was tightening, and he swallowed hard. "That's why I don't like expectations, little feller. They're a noose that chokes you, a rope that binds. The way I see it, the only expectations a man should try to fulfill are the ones he puts on himself, the ones spelled out in the Bible. And even then he might prove a disappointment now and again."

He couldn't look at her face. Her expectations were starting to become important to him, and he knew he couldn't go down that road again. But he could see her hand fall, her fingers knitting together over her belly.

"I know something about expectations too," she said, and he wasn't sure if she was addressing the baby or him. "Lucas had a lot of them. Food had to be cooked just so. The house must be kept pristine. He didn't like a lot of noise at the end of the day, so not much talking and no using the sewing machine while he was in the house."

There were moments he didn't like Lucas Bennett overly much. "Must have been hard," he murmured.

"I thought it was me," she said. "I just tried harder, asked Lula May's help in learning to cook better, scrubbed the floors more often."

No wonder the house looked as if no one had ever lived in it.

"But no matter how hard I tried," she continued, "I never could meet his requirements. I thought if I was just a better wife, more attentive to his needs, maybe he'd come home more often. Maybe he'd be happy."

Now his eyes burned. "Funny thing about happiness. It's different for each person. That's why the only person responsible for your happiness can be you."

"But he was happy, at first," she protested. "We used to tell each other about our lives and laugh. Then he seemed to lose interest and drift away. I never knew why. His father seemed to think he was expecting to move back to Alabama. Maybe he felt like he was in exile here."

"Trying to prove himself to his father," Hank realized. He wasn't sure how he felt to know he and Lucas had had that trait in common.

"But why not enjoy his success?" Nancy asked, soft voice vibrating with hurt feelings. "His father gave him the ranch. Why not settle down?"

He was fairly sure of the reason, but he hadn't wanted to darken her husband's memory any further. Still, he couldn't see her so hurt and confused. Maybe it was time she knew at least part of the truth.

"I can't be sure," he murmured, "but I think he was gambling. He'd leave us with the herd, go riding off toward Burnet. And he'd always come back sullen or angry and missing something he'd left with—his fancy silver belt buckle or his pearl-handled pistol."

"I wondered what happened to that belt buckle," she put in. "When I asked him about it, he said he was tired of it."

Another excuse. Hank sighed. "He even tried to get Upkins and Jenks to play cards with him for their pay."

He saw her bristle. She didn't much like anyone mistreating her cowboys. She was going to make a great ranch manager. There wouldn't be a man in the county who wouldn't want to ride for her brand.

"They refused," he assured her. "But it made us all uneasy. I figure he took out that loan to fund his obsession."

"I wish I'd known," she said. "Maybe I could have talked to him, helped him see that he was hurting himself and everyone else."

"Nothing you could have done," he assured her. "I've seen a few men in that situation. Once gambling fever sets in, it takes more than love and sweet words to cure it."

Her breath sounded shaky. "Oh, Hank, what am I going to tell the baby about his father?"

For once, he knew how to answer. "Good things and bad."

He could hear the doubt in her voice. "And bad?"

"By the time he's old enough to understand, most folks will have forgotten what his father did," he said. "But someone will remember and tell him. He should hear it from us first."

He glanced up. For some reason, his statement had made her smile, and he felt as if the air smelled sweeter, like sage after a rain.

Still, she raised a brow. "And what good can I tell him?"

"Plenty." He nodded toward the baby. "Your pa was a real pistol. Never knew a man who could ride faster, break a horse better."

Nancy chuckled. "That's true enough. Clyde Parker used to ask Lucas over to help break his horses."

"He was a charmer too," Hank continued. "Why, there wasn't a fellow in Little Horn who didn't call him friend."

Her smile faded. "That was true too, before the gambling and stealing."

Hank wasn't willing to allow the darkness in. Not now when he had her smiling. "And he was willing to take a chance on a stranger," he told the baby, "give him a place to live, a job to do."

"Take her into his house, give her a home and a child," she agreed, smile threatening to return.

Hank nodded. "And he had a smile and a twinkle

in his eyes that made you feel like you were someone special."

"I remember." She pressed her lips together as if
to keep from saying more.

He reached out and put his hand against hers.
"That's the fellow we should remember, Nancy. That's
the man we should talk about with his son."

The son Hank hoped to help raise. But the real
question remained—what was he to do about the baby's mother? These conversations whispered to something inside him, gave him hope he wasn't sure was
warranted.

How was he to help Nancy without risking his
heart?

Chapter Eight

Nancy wasn't sure why, but that night marked a change in her relationship with Hank. Where he hesitated to talk to her, he had no trouble talking to the baby. He showed up each evening, face scrubbed and shaved, chaps and spurs removed, and sat at the foot of the table. He told her about the ranch, asked her input on any changes he was considering and told the baby stories.

She had to admit that she enjoyed the stories the most.

"One time," he said, forking up the potato salad she'd made that day, "my closest sister Matilda, she goes by Missy, and I took two of the cow ponies and rode as far as we could out onto the range. We lost sight of the house, we lost sight of the herd. I was starting to get a little worried, only I wouldn't let on to her. Finally, I couldn't take it any longer.

'Missy,' I told her. 'We're lost.'

'No, we're not,' she says. 'I stole a sack of dried pinto beans from the cupboard and put them in my saddle bag. I've been dropping them as we rode. All we have to do is follow them home.'"

"That was smart," Nancy said with a smile.

"I thought so," Hank agreed. "Until we tried to follow them back and discovered that between sparrows and gophers, most of the beans had been eaten. We managed to get home, after dark. Pa was furious. I don't know what made him madder—that we might have had to spend the night alone and undefended on the range or that we'd lost a whole sack of pinto beans."

Nancy laughed, then clapped a hand to her stomach, feeling as if the baby had giggled, as well.

Hank was on his feet and coming around the table. "Are you all right?"

"Fine," Nancy assured him, lowering her hand. "The baby likes your stories almost as much as I do."

He snatched up her emptied plate and turned for the sink as if that had been his intent all along. But he didn't fool her. She'd seen the flush in his cheeks. He liked sharing those stories with her and the baby.

He was just as considerate about sharing other things. He brought her treasures from the range—a rabbit or duck he'd shot and prepared for cooking, fresh-picked thyme or Mexican plums that grew wild. She made sure to use his gifts in the meals she prepared. She was trying not to be sensitive about her efforts—he wasn't critical like Lucas—but she couldn't help noticing his grimace over the rabbit, which she'd served in gravy on toast.

"I can stew it with rosemary instead," she suggested.

He shook his head. "Wouldn't help. I never was partial to rabbit."

Nancy frowned. "Then why did you bring it to me to cook?"

"It's good for the baby," he said. Then he cocked his head. "Isn't it?"

"Very likely," she assured him, touched. "Babies need good food of all kinds to grow."

"There you are, then," he said, lifting his fork. "I'll just have to learn to like rabbit."

He was thoughtful that way about other areas of their lives. One day she heard his steps in the hall earlier than usual as she was finishing edging a gown for the baby on the sewing machine. It was getting harder and harder to reach the pedal, as she had to sit farther and farther away the less she fit against the table.

She sighed, glancing at her sewing machine. It was the latest model from Singer, with gold etching on the rise, a steel faceplate and an actual bobbin winder. She'd been thrilled when Lucas had brought it home in the wagon after ordering it to come by train.

"Do you like sewing?" Hank asked, watching her from the doorway.

She smiled. "Yes. There's something about taking a few bits of fabric and turning them into something useful and pretty. But I can hand sew for now, and I can use the machine again after the baby is born." She passed him in the doorway. "Dinner wasn't supposed to be ready for a bit. I'll see if I can hurry it along."

"Take your time," he said. "I can occupy myself."

Very likely with chores out at the barn. She still found it hard not to think of that as his domain while the house was hers. But as she crossed the hall to the kitchen, she had to own that she liked her domain. Her pots and pans and mixing bowls were all in easy reach. Her stove, the best Little Horn had to offer, cooked fast and predictably. She knew what she was doing, and the results proved she was good at it.

She was returning the chicken and dumplings, a recipe Lula May had given her, to the oven when she heard an odd buzzing coming from across the hall. Had hornets invaded the house?

She hurried to the hall and paused in the doorway to her sewing room. Hank stepped away from her sewing machine, saw in one hand. Four wooden cylinders lay on the floor, surrounded by sawdust. And her chair was a good few inches shorter.

"What did you do?" she asked, starting to laugh.

"Couldn't figure how to raise the machine," he said. "So I lowered the chair."

And it worked brilliantly.

"He's the perfect husband," she confessed to Lula May at one of the quilting bees at the Carson ranch. "Anything I want done, he does, and he often realizes it needs doing before I think to tell him."

"Just as I expected," Lula May assured her.

But after Hank's story of his upbringing, Nancy was careful not to expect too much. She knew the pain of feeling inadequate. She would never knowingly inflict that on another.

Besides, she had more reasons to smile than to worry. They christened the new church building and parsonage the middle of September with the wedding of Lula May and Edmund. The entire community turned out, and Nancy helped bake and decorate beforehand.

"Should you be doing so much?" Hank asked her as he drove the wagon into town for the wedding.

In truth, she had found it hard to sleep lately. She'd let out her gowns, made up the clothes and diapers she'd need for the baby and laid up jars of beans, beets, peaches, plums and blackberries for later, besides doing her usual chores.

"I'm fine," she assured Hank. "I wanted to make Lula May and Edmund's day special, after all they've done for me."

And it was a special day. Stella Fuller had brought a rosebush out West with her little brother and still had some blossoms to contribute to the wedding. With their perfume dancing on the air, the hint of fresh paint was barely noticeable from the whitewashed walls. The benches from the meeting tent had been installed, but Nancy knew that Lula May was already campaigning for proper pews. What was most important was the carved wood cross that hung behind the altar, drawing all eyes to it.

The ceremony was simple; Preacher Stillwater read it from the book, and Lula May and Edmund recited the words as required. But when Lula May looked up into Edmund's eyes and promised to love, honor and obey him all the days of her life, Nancy felt her own eyes turn misty.

Hank was silent as they drove home. Evening was coming sooner every day now, and the sky was rosy with twilight as the horses plodded down the dusty road. The oaks rustled along creeks that were starting to bubble again after summer's heat.

"I spoiled things for you," he said in the quiet.

Nancy frowned. "Spoiled what?"

"The wedding. Marriage." He cast her a glance, face lined by shadows. "I saw how McKay looked at Lula May, how he treated her like she was the finest person ever to come to Little Horn. I never saw my ma and pa look at each other that way. I never knew anyone who did, outside CJ and his wife."

"Lucas didn't look at me that way either," Nancy remembered. "Of course, we'd only known each other a few days when we married, so that's to be expected, I suppose."

"So you think it just takes a while?" he asked.

Was that hope she heard in his voice?

"I suppose it's different with each couple," she said. "My mother birthed babies for couples who'd known each other two weeks before getting married, and they seemed just as happy as the couples who'd grown up together before marrying. And she birthed babies when the mother and father could barely stand to look at each other, whether they took a short while or a long time to wed."

He sighed. "I'm sorry, Nancy. Maybe if I hadn't married you, you might have found a fellow you could look at that way."

A yearning rose up inside her. Maybe it was the tenderness between Lula May and Edmund, maybe it was the lack of tenderness in her own life. Whatever the reason, she was not about to admit the feelings. She wasn't ready to take a chance on falling in love. Her poor heart still felt battered by Lucas's death and all the secrets it had uncovered.

"The same goes for you," she reminded Hank instead. "If I hadn't married you, you might have found a girl you could love."

"I had one once," he said. "That was enough."

She knew he meant the girl in Waco. "It's hard losing someone you love."

His voice came out gruff. "She deserves to be happy with Adam."

"You deserve to be happy too," Nancy said, surprised by the vehemence in her voice.

He clucked to the horses. "I'm happy enough."

Was there such a thing, the perfect limit to happiness? She remembered a verse in the Bible that talked about being content in all things.

"I suppose I'm happy," she said.

"You suppose?" She could hear the tease in his voice. "Do I have to call fun to come around again?"

Nancy laughed. "Oh, no. I couldn't dance right now."

"Must be other ways of having fun," he insisted. "We just need to look for opportunities." He glanced at her, then quickly out to where the gates of the Windy Diamond were rising against the hills beyond.

Opportunities for fun. She'd never thought about life like that. But then, he saw things differently than she did in so many ways—dealing with the cattle, praying.

"What do cowboys do for fun?" she asked.

He wiggled his lips a moment as if chewing on the answer. "Sing songs, tell stories, make up rhymes."

"Rhymes," she said. "Like poetry?"

"Yes, ma'am. I never could get the words to match, but Upkins has a way with it."

"Mr. Upkins?" she asked, unable to picture the tough old cowboy reciting poetry. "Our Mr. Upkins?"

"The very same. Only don't ask him to share it

with you. Some of the language might be a bit…odd to a lady. I can't see him declaring at one of my mother's literary teas."

She couldn't picture that either. She'd assumed Hank's mother was a ranch wife like her too busy to hold literary teas. "But I thought you said your family owned a ranch."

"They do," he assured her. "But Mother came from money in Dallas. She never forgot how to be a lady. I think she'd like you."

Nancy blinked. "Me? Why? I'm no fine lady."

They were nearly at the house. He guided the horses closer to the barn. "Finest lady I know," he insisted. "You remind me every day how it feels to be a proper gentleman."

"I refuse to set expectations on you," she protested as he set the brake.

"I know." He hopped down and came around. In the dim light, she couldn't see his face under the brim of his hat. "But I'd be no kind of man if I didn't have my own expectations of how a lady should be treated." He reached up and lifted her off the bench, setting her on the ground so gently she might have been made of fine crystal. For a moment, she stood in his embrace.

"You deserve to be treated like a lady, Nancy," he murmured. "That's what a husband should do, show his wife every day how much she means to him."

Her heart started beating faster. Was he saying he wanted to be a real husband? Was she ready to be a real wife?

Not yet. Not until she felt more sure of herself.

She stepped out of his arms. "Thank you, Hank. I

appreciate everything you do around the ranch. See you at dinner tomorrow."

"Yes, ma'am," he agreed, but she couldn't help hearing the least bit of disappointment in his tone as he turned to the horses.

Opening the corral and letting the horses inside, Hank shook his head at his own stupidity. What was it about weddings? Women cried when they should be smiling. Men started thinking about their futures. Why had he gone and hinted to Nancy that they might fall in love?

He'd tried with Mary Ellen, and it hadn't turned out well. The only thing the experience had taught him was that love wasn't something achieved by yearning or striving. The seeds either grew or they shriveled, and he'd never been certain how to make them grow. He was a cowman, after all, not a farmer.

Besides, he was pretty sure any warm feelings Nancy might have toward him would only cool, and fast, when she learned how her husband had died.

He'd tried a dozen times to tell her and always the words dried up in his throat. He knew the story was best coming from him, but this wasn't a tale he could tell with a smile and a wink like he did when he was talking to the baby.

The best thing he could do, he reasoned as he headed to the barn for the items to groom the horses, was to stop the man who had been taking the stolen cattle off Lucas Bennett's hands. That fellow was as responsible as Bennett for the losses in the area. Sheriff Fuller had warned Hank to back off, and he'd tried to put the matter behind him, but he felt it like a sore tooth, a constant ache until something ratcheted the pain higher.

He'd questioned Fuller again this afternoon at the wedding. It seemed the law in Oakalla had arrested a group of outlaws they thought might be the rustlers, but the leader had escaped. The sheriff had been reticent to tell Hank anything more. Likely he feared Hank would ride off half-cocked if he heard the suspect's name. Likely he was right. Yet, try as he might, Hank could not figure out who would be so brazen.

"Of course we didn't think Mr. Bennett was involved either," Upkins pointed out when he and Hank were discussing the matter later that night in the bunk room. Jenks had already fallen asleep. With the gang rounded up, Hank was hoping they might do away with night riding for a time.

"We should have realized something was up the way he kept going off by himself," the older cowhand was saying. "And I can think of a half dozen things I should have wondered about."

"Such as?" Hank asked.

Upkins tilted out of his bunk to look up at Hank. "Such as the way he kept directing us away from the canyon where you found him. Gave us some excuse about flash floods when there wasn't a cloud in the sky. And he mentioned how he had his own room at the house, when any man with any sense would have been proud to bunk with a pretty wife."

Hank hadn't realized Lucas Bennett had kept his own room. Had Nancy cleared it out after his death? If not, would the things Lucas Bennett had squirreled away give Hank any clue as to who was helping him?

He knew Nancy was planning on going to one of

her quilting bees the next day, so he made sure to stay close to the barn with the excuse of hitching up the wagon for her. He watched until she was out the main gate, then hurried for the house.

It was quiet as he let himself in, a shell of a place without Nancy to animate it. The chime of his spurs echoed as he started down the hallway.

He knew from experience that the parlor and kitchen lay on the south side of the house, and the last room on the north side was Nancy's sewing room. So, he pushed open the door to the first room and peered inside.

This had to be Nancy's room. The iron bedstead was draped in a soft blue quilt embroidered with daisies, and the curtains on the windows were frilly and white. The clean scent of her colored the air. He couldn't help the smile that formed as he closed the door and headed for the next room.

There was no question this one had belonged to Lucas Bennett. The bedstead was covered in a fine blue-and-gold quilt, Bennett's tan Stetson still resting cocked over one of the end caps. A carved chest sat under the window, and a tall dresser and wardrobe stood along one wall. Nancy must not have been able to force herself to clean out the room, because a tortoiseshell brush and comb and shaving kit stood ready for Bennett when he woke.

Except he never would wake this side of eternity.

Shaking off the guilt, Hank headed for the chest. Kneeling on the bright-patterned rug before it, he lifted the lid and poked through its contents, which appeared to be coats and wool shirts for cooler weather. Feeling a little like a two-penny thief, he checked the pockets and discovered only a penknife, three bits and a clean handkerchief embroidered with the initials *LB*. The thought of Nancy working the stitches set his gut to twisting. He shoved the things back in the chest and rose.

Where would a man keep his secrets?

He picked up the Stetson and looked inside the brim, feeling the blocked wool firm in his hands. Why couldn't Lucas have stood so firm? By all accounts, he'd never known want. Yet he'd wanted more and more until he'd lost it all.

Hank drew in a breath, returned the hat to its spot. Feeling as if a shadow hung heavy over the room, he hurried through his search, checking the bed, the wardrobe. He even bent and peered under the bed but saw nothing except dust, a sure sign Nancy had been avoiding the room.

There was only one place left. He strode to the dresser and looked things over. Again, Nancy's handiwork was evident, for everything was neat and tidy and arranged at precise angles. Or maybe it had been Bennett who wanted things so perfect. The only thing out of place was a brass key, stuck back next to the mirror.

Hank pulled it free, hefted it, balanced it in his hand. It was heavy and ornate, and he was fairly sure it didn't belong to any of the outbuildings on the ranch. He couldn't recall a lock on the front or back door of the house either. Folks didn't bother locking up much around Little Horn. So why had Lucas Bennett needed a key?

"Hank?"

The sound of Nancy's voice had him spinning on

his heel. She was standing in the doorway, her sewing basket in one hand, brows up in surprise.

"You're back," he said, and nearly winced at the obvious statement.

She made a face. "I forgot my sewing basket of all things. My mother said forgetting things during pregnancy was a way for a lady to make room in her head for being a mother. When I came back inside, I saw this door ajar and thought I must have left it open. Why are you in Lucas's room?"

There was no suspicion in the question, only curiosity. She trusted him, had no way of knowing he'd already violated that trust. He refused to damage it further.

"I thought maybe if I looked through his things I might find something that would tell us about why he was stealing," he told her.

She frowned. "But you told me you thought he was stealing because he was gambling."

"That's the only reason I know," he assured her. "Right now, I'm interested in learning who was helping him."

She raised her head. "No one was helping him. Mr. Upkins and Billy and you wouldn't do that."

"I know," he said, keeping his tone soft. "But he was selling those steers to someone."

She blanched. "Doesn't Sheriff Fuller look into such things?"

"He does," Hank acknowledged. "But I'm not sure he has all the information he needs."

Her face was puckering, and the look tightened his gut again.

"Don't get in the middle of this, Hank," she begged. "Please. I don't want you hurt too."

He crossed the room, then put a hand to her elbow. "I won't be hurt. But that thief needs to be brought to justice, Nancy."

"Then let Sheriff Fuller bring him in," she insisted. "I've already been made a widow once. Don't make me one again. I don't know what I'd do without you, Hank."

Chapter Nine

It was a dangerous confession. She didn't want to raise Hank's hopes that they might fall in love. Perhaps he would put the statement down to the fact that she needed him around the ranch. But she knew the sentiment went beyond that. She was so tired of losing people.

As if he realized it, Hank gave her arm a squeeze. "Now, I'm not going anywhere."

"Neither was Lucas," she pointed out.

He dropped his hand. "I'm not Lucas Bennett. I'm no thief."

Yet he probably felt like one, looking through a dead man's belongings. That was one of the reasons she hadn't cleaned out Lucas's things. It made her feel as if she was robbing him.

"I never said you were a thief," Nancy told him. "But accidents happen. People get sick. There are many ways to be parted. All I'm asking is that you don't go looking for trouble."

A smile threatened one corner of his mouth. "And here I thought trouble was my middle name."

Nancy touched his hand. "Don't tease me, Hank. I'm serious. Lucas got involved in rustling and ended up dead. Please, be careful. The baby and I need you."

He lowered his gaze to her belly. "And how is the little feller this afternoon?"

She loved the way his voice softened when he spoke about the baby. "Feeling his oats. He's kicked me three times already."

His gaze jerked up, and he stared at her. "He kicks?"

She couldn't help giggling at his reaction. "Yes. And he twists and wiggles, and sometimes I think he's practicing for those dances you promised him."

He stepped back, pushing his hat up on his forehead. "You're joking."

"Not at all." She reached out and took his hand, then pressed it to her waist. He stood frozen like a rabbit caught outside its den, unsure of the danger.

"Wait a moment," she encouraged him, feeling the twitch starting.

And then the baby moved, a gentle ripple inside her. Hank pulled back, mouth agape.

"I felt that." The words came out awed.

"So did I," she promised.

"Is he supposed to be doing that?"

Nancy smiled. "My mother said a moving baby is a good sign. I just wish he'd watch where he puts his feet. Now, I should leave, or I'll never have time to visit at the quilting bee."

"I'll walk you out." He followed her from the room and paced her down the hallway, the chime of his spurs a counterpoint to the thud of his boots against the plank floor. How nice to have a gentleman beside her, looking out for her, sharing the amazing start of her child's life.

She couldn't lose Hank.

She shoved the panicky thought away. He was here now. That's what she wanted to appreciate.

His hand on her elbow, Hank escorted her down the steps and to the wagon. She'd tied the horses to the corral fence, but they were fretting as they waited.

"Be careful now." The words came out despite her best efforts as she and Hank reached the wagon.

In answer, he put his hands to her waist, his touch gentle and reverent, and lifted her to the bench. Eyes as sharp as sapphires cut across her gaze.

"I'm always careful," he murmured.

She wanted to believe him. If only she could trust the evidence of her own eyes, listen to the advice of her heart. Yet both had proven dangerously untrustworthy.

Would he?

Hank made himself smile up into Nancy's troubled gaze. He'd given her every reason to trust him, but telling her he still hoped to catch Lucas's accomplice had frightened her. Her reaction would be worse if she knew he'd pocketed that key. But how else was he to learn where Lucas Bennett had been selling the cattle?

He went and untied the horses, then handed her the reins. "I'll see you at dinner tonight," she said with a smile. As Hank stepped back, she clucked to the horses, who happily turned the wagon to head off down the road.

He saddled up and rode out to where Upkins and

Jenks were watching the herd. He showed them the key, but both agreed with him that it didn't belong to any building or chest on the ranch.

"Puts me in mind of a key I saw once, when I was coming off a big roundup in Abilene," Upkins said, frowning at the chunk of brass. "Opened the door to a room in a fancy hotel."

"Nearest fancy hotel is in Burnet or Austin, I reckon," Jenks put in.

Hank didn't think Lucas had frequented Austin. He hadn't been gone long enough on any of his disappearances to have ridden to the city, and he'd never taken the train to Hank's knowledge. On the other hand, Lucas had made no secret of the fact that he rode to Burnet on a regular basis, and that town was the location of the Empire Bank, where he had taken the loan that had landed them in this fix.

It looked as if Hank needed to visit Burnet.

Nancy wasn't going to like the idea. She had come to rely on him around the ranch. And very likely him going to Burnet would remind her of how Lucas had left her alone so many times. Hank needed a way to ease into the conversation.

So he decided to make dinner for her.

He hadn't smelled anything cooking when he'd been in the house earlier, which meant she intended to do all the work when she returned from the quilting bee. Leaving Upkins and Jenks with the herd, Hank rode back to the house.

This time, he came in through the back door, to the kitchen that was all Nancy. Though it too was neat and tidy, the pots hanging from hooks on the wall looked ready for use, not decoration. A quick peek in the pantry told him just what to do. He had never cooked back in Waco—his family had a staff in the big ranch kitchen—but he'd learned to throw a few things together over the fire, and he'd tried his hand at finishing up what Upkins had begun. He could do this.

He had everything about ready when he heard the rig coming in. Jenks had already ridden in, so Hank had the cowboy help Nancy with the wagon and team while Hank kept working. A few moments later, and she was in the kitchen with him.

She looked as pretty as a picture, cheeks pink from the wind, eyes nearly brown over her cinnamon-colored jacket. She stopped by the table and frowned at him. "What are you doing?"

"Fixing you dinner," he said, turning the steak in the pan to a satisfying sizzle. "You just put your feet up. Everything will be ready soon."

She removed her jacket and came to the head of the table. Glancing over, he saw she was still frowning.

"Something wrong?" he asked.

"No, I…" She looked up at him. "You moved the place settings."

That he had, and about time too. He was tired of gazing at her clear the length of that table. "It's hard talking to you from so far away," he said. "I figured since I was cooking, it was my choice."

She nodded, then took her seat.

He served her a generous slice of the steak, plus golden fried potatoes.

"Hope you don't mind johnnycake," he said as he added the flattened corn bread to her plate. "I wasn't sure I was up to biscuits."

"It looks delicious," she assured him.

He took a seat beside her. "How about you say grace tonight?"

She bowed her head and clasped her hands. "Be present at our...wait." Hank heard her draw in a breath before she started over. "Dear Lord, thank You for this food. Thank You for helpers to come alongside us when we need them. Most of all, thank You for Your endless provision to Your children. Amen."

"Amen," Hank echoed before picking up his knife and fork and cutting into the steak.

Her cuts were more dainty, refined. She was a lady through and through. She glanced up and caught his gaze on her. "What?"

He smiled and returned to his food. "Nothing. Just glad you seem to like it."

"It's very good," she assured him. "Is this what Mr. Upkins generally cooks?"

"Yes, ma'am. But he can bake biscuits heavy enough to sit with you for two or three days."

She giggled. He loved that sound almost as much as he loved seeing her smile. But with her in such a good mood, maybe now was the time to make his suggestion.

"I've been thinking," he started. "You've been working hard. We should do something fun."

He thought she might protest, but she brightened. "Oh, that would be wonderful. You could take me out to see the herd."

That wasn't exactly his idea of fun. "I was thinking of a trip, say to see the sights in Burnet."

She made a face. "I'd rather go see the cattle. I haven't felt up to staying with you all morning, but

I could manage an hour or two. I'm supposed to be learning, after all."

Much as he was itching to discover the secrets of that key, he couldn't fault her logic. In fact, he was rather proud of her tenacity in trying to understand this enterprise she'd been left. And with her beside him all morning, he'd have other opportunities to convince her to go with him to Burnet or let him go alone.

"All right, then," he agreed. "It would be my pleasure to take you and the little feller out to see the cows."

She put a hand to her belly. "I've been thinking too. We should name him. We can't keep calling him little feller forever."

He chuckled. "I'll leave that to you. Cowboys name critters, not babies. Unless you want him called Wild Eye or Snake-Killer."

She shuddered, but he could see it was all in fun. "No, thank you. I was thinking Ben."

He nodded. "Like Bennett, for his pa."

"For both his fathers," she corrected him. "His last name will be Snowden, after all."

Warmth filled him. "That's right." And the thought still amazed him.

She rose and picked up her plate. "Now, you let me clear the table. Then we'll both have some of Lula May's famous lemon cake. She sent two pieces home with me from the quilting bee."

"Sounds good to me," Hank said. He started to lean back in the chair, tilting it off two legs, then remembered where he was and set it down. Nancy was a good influence. His mother would be delighted to know he still recalled how to be a gentleman. But he thought she'd feel the same way Nancy did if she knew he intended to stop the rustling.

The next morning, as he'd promised, Hank collected Nancy, and they headed out onto the range. She wore a brown dress with strips of green and yellow diamonds running down it, her cinnamon-colored jacket over the top. Her hair was confined behind her head, and she'd tied on a coffee-colored sombrero with fringe on the brim to shade her.

With the rising sun warming their faces, he drove the wagon with Belle tied behind. Upkins and Jenks had gone ahead to round up a few head of cattle and drive them closer to the house so Nancy wouldn't have to travel so far to see them.

"Is that Rosebud?" she asked as she and Hank joined the group. Upkins and Jenks had brought the cattle into a small clearing surrounded by oaks and were riding along each flank to keep the small herd from wandering. A shame Bennett had refused to allow them a dog, claiming all cattle dogs were flea-ridden curs. He'd have to bring up the subject to Nancy, see if they couldn't find a good herder from one of the other ranchers.

Hank nodded now toward the cow that was contently grazing on grass that had sprung up in the September cool. "The lady herself in all her glory."

The roan-colored longhorn raised her head and regarded Nancy as if acknowledging her own worth.

"She's a fine cow," Nancy said.

"The queen of all she surveys," Hank agreed. "But don't let her fool you. She weighs in at more than one thousand pounds of pure muscle. Those horns can rip a man's leg open from ankle to thigh."

"I see."

The words came out so strangled that he turned to look at Nancy. She was as white as a bone bleached in the sun, and both hands were pressed over her belly as if protecting the life within.

What was he thinking? "I'm sorry, Nancy. I didn't mean to scare you. You can trust that Upkins and Jenks and I know what we're doing. We've been riding herd for years."

Her hands relaxed to her sides. "No, I should be the one to apologize. I shouldn't be so afraid of a few head of cattle."

"Now, there we disagree," Hank said, shifting on the bench. "Cattle can be trouble, pure and simple. And you have every reason to be cautious, what with little Ben and all."

She sighed. "I'm finding it hard to be cautious and still learn to run a ranch."

"Once Ben is born, I'll help you learn to ride and rope and do anything else you want on the range," he promised. "It's just right now, you need to be careful. So, let's see what you can learn from here." He glanced about, then nodded toward Rosebud. "I mentioned to you that we brand them in the spring. That tells a cowboy whose beast he's watching. Clyde Parker is making a catalog of all the brands in this area. See there, high on Rosebud's flank? That's your brand, a diamond canted with the wind, like on the gates."

"The Windy Diamond," she said with a smile. "I always wondered why Lucas named the ranch that."

"Well, Mr. Bennett was fond of the finer things in life," Hank pointed out. "And the wind does whistle down the canyons."

Rosebud swung majestically to the right for another clump of grass. The rest of the cows followed her.

"Why do they do that?" Nancy asked. "She's a fine cow and all, but why did they decide to follow her? And don't give me that story about her tail again."

As if Rosebud knew she was being discussed, she twitched her tail.

"They trust her," Hank explained. "She's one of the oldest and largest in the herd. Cows generally fear what they don't know. They know her, and she's seen enough that little rattles her."

Rosebud strolled past Upkins and his horse, obviously comfortable in his presence.

"And she knows and trusts you all," Nancy said. "That's why she isn't afraid."

He had never thought of it that way. Did the cow know him and Upkins and Jenks? Rosebud had certainly seen them around often enough. Did she realize they regularly scouted the best grazing, the most reliable water? That they patrolled the fence line to keep it firm so she wouldn't wander from home? That they cleared out the snakes and coyotes that might prove a danger to her and her young? Did she respect their role on the range as they respected hers?

"Well, I always had a soft spot in my heart for a pretty lady," Hank teased Nancy.

She blushed. The color reminded him of the rosy ripe peaches she'd picked from the trees behind the house. He wasn't surprised when she changed the subject.

"Has the league set the date for roundup yet?" she asked, watching as Jenks urged a straying calf back into the group.

"In three weeks," Hank told her. "With the new rail spur, we don't have to drive them as far as we used to. We'll join our herd with theirs and drive them up to holding pens outside of town, then they can take a little ride into Waco, where the buyers will look them over and make us an offer."

"Will they all go?" She sounded positively wistful at the idea of losing some of the herd.

"Only the steers big enough to bring a good price," he told her. "We'll leave the mamas like Rosebud safely behind."

She bumped her shoulder against his arm. "See? I told you she knows who to trust."

"I think she favors Upkins," Hank said with a nod toward the old-timer. Rosebud had begun heading west, and Upkins rode in front of her and reined in his horse. For a moment, the big longhorn and the cattle pony stared at each other.

"Will she charge?" Nancy asked, hand on the chest of her striped gown.

"Not unless she thinks he's threatening her calf," Hank predicted.

Sure enough, the longhorn turned and shuffled back toward the rest of the herd.

"You called them babies," Nancy said, shaking her head so that the fringe on the sombrero bounced. "But I think they mind a great deal better than some children I've met."

"Wait until you get between them and water," Hank predicted. "Or something spooks them on a dark night. Not much you can do then but hang on to your saddle and pray."

"You pray well," she said. "I admire how you say grace."

Hank reared back. "Me? I just speak my mind."

"That's just it," she insisted. "I never met anyone who spoke their mind to God. I always thought God was someone majestic, perfect. A little big and a little scary."

"Like Rosebud," he concluded.

She sucked in a breath, and he hurried to reassure her. "I wasn't trying to blaspheme. But when you ride out at night, all alone among the oaks, never knowing what's going to come running at you, you start to throw off big words and pious thoughts. You just think, *Father, help me!* Never knew the Lord to ignore a cry like that."

She bowed her head, and he wondered what was going through her mind. Was she praying right then? Or just mulling over his words? Thinking back, he realized he probably sounded preachy. What did he know about religion and praying, after all? He'd always attended church with his family, been raised on the Golden Rule. But it had taken five years of riding herd for him to make his peace with the Almighty.

"Hey!" Upkins called, waving his hand north. "We have a runner!"

One of the younger steers had bolted, hindquarters hitching as it pounded through the brush.

Nancy's head jerked up, and she stared at the steer. "What do we do?"

"Go after it," Hank said. He handed her the reins and jumped down. Untying Belle, he swung up into the saddle and urged the horse into a gallop.

He was showing off, but it felt good to fly. Belle ate up the ground, hooves churning dirt. Wind in his face, they closed in on the steer. He yanked his lariat off the saddle horn, then swung it overhead. Once, twice, let go! It sailed out to settle over one of the steer's horns. Hank pulled it tight, reining in.

The steer faltered, head twisting from side to side. It must have realized the futility, for it stopped, blowing out a breath. Knowing Belle would stay where he set her, Hank slid from the saddle and retrieved his rope.

"You head on home," he advised, backing away.

The steer turned and ambled toward the herd.

Hank shook his head as he climbed back into the saddle. A simple task, yet satisfaction rippled through him like a breeze through the trees. He could see Nancy in the distance, watching him. Why did he feel like preening?

Just then another movement caught his eye. There was something under that copse of oak. Had they lost another steer? Or had one of the other members of the herd moved closer? He peered into the shadows, trying to make out a shape.

Another rider was watching the Windy Diamond herd. And as Hank started toward him, he wheeled his mount and took off.

Chapter Ten

Nancy couldn't seem to catch her breath. Most of the men in her small Ozark town had walked or driven wagons or buggies. Certainly she'd seen Lucas and her boys on horseback many times. But there was something about the way Hank rode, lean body bent until he and his horse were almost one, swerving among the cattle like a dove skimming the grass. Watching him set her heart to racing along in time.

And the way he swung that rope. It swirled through the air like a dancer's skirts, effortless, graceful. She'd wanted to applaud when he'd turned that longhorn.

But she'd been afraid she'd startle the others.

So she remained on the wagon bench, head up and neck craned to watch his progress. She wasn't sure why he and his horse veered into a copse of trees. Had one of the other steers strayed without anyone noticing? Surely, Hank would come out the opposite side any minute, horse trotting and longhorn plodding alongside.

But though crows shot out of the tree branches,

cawing in protest at the intrusion, she caught no sign of Hank.

Where was he?

She glanced toward Mr. Upkins, who was patrolling back and forth on the north, then to Billy on the south. Neither seemed particularly concerned they'd lost sight of their leader. Should she be concerned?

From off in the distance came the bark of a gun.

Several of the steers flinched. So did Nancy. Mr. Upkins and Billy immediately circled closer to the herd, calling to the cattle, soothing. Nancy wasn't so easily settled.

Something was wrong. The surety clawed up inside her, set her hands to trembling on the reins. Surely they should act, ride out, demand answers. But aside from their calming calls, neither of her boys showed the least interest, while she could hardly sit still.

When Mr. Upkins rode close enough to hail, she called him to her.

"Mr. Snowden hasn't returned," she informed him. "Should someone go looking for him?"

Mr. Upkins tugged on his hat brim in respect. "The way I see it, ma'am, Hank can take care of himself, and this herd can't."

She glanced out over the cattle, all of which seemed to have gone back to their contented munching. A shame she couldn't forget that shot.

"Surely they'll be fine for a little while," she told him.

He pushed back his hat. "If you order me to abandon the herd, ma'am, I'll do my duty. But I don't think

Hank will be happy for my interference, and I know what Mr. Bennett would have advised me to do."

So did she, but she wasn't Lucas.

"Open a path for me to those trees," she ordered him. "I'll look for Hank, but if I shout for help, I expect you and Billy to come riding. Do I make myself clear?"

"Clear as daylight, ma'am," he assured her. Tugging his hat down on his forehead, he turned his horse and cut through the herd, calling to Billy for help. The younger cowboy immediately wheeled his mount and set about parting the cattle. Nancy gathered up the reins and turned the horses toward the widening track.

Hank says You hear a call for help, Lord. Please, protect us both.

Confidence she had nearly forgotten flowed through her. As cattle trotted off to either side of the team, she directed the horses toward the trees where Hank had disappeared. The wagon bumped over the uneven ground, rattling her bones, jarring her teeth. If Ben had kicked, she doubted she'd even notice.

Drawing closer to the trees, she guided the horses under the canopy, ducking her head as oak leaves brushed her sombrero. She pulled the team to a stop, then straightened.

The area was empty.

Nancy glanced around, trying to get any sense of what had happened. Nothing much seemed to have been disturbed, but the trampled ground and the indents from iron horseshoes told her at least one horse had recently used the space.

She knew their horses often ranged free when they

weren't being ridden or driven, but they tended to stay near the barn. It was possible her boys had used the canopy for shade, but not while she'd been with them.

So who was hiding on her land?

A breeze darted through the clearing, setting the oak leaves to clattering, but she knew the chill inside her had nothing to do with the cool air. Hank had warned her the rustling might not be over. Here was evidence he was right.

Evidence that he might be in danger.

Clucking to the team, she urged them out into the sunshine on the other side of the trees, then reined in once more. The land rippled away from her, the bright green of fresh grass bowing to the breeze. Here and there, limestone poked up, while oak stood proud. In the distance she could see the hills rising. Overhead, a hawk circled.

The chill refused to leave her.

"Hank!" she called into the clear air. "Hank Snowden! Where are you?"

The only answer was the *scree* of the hawk.

Everything in her said to go, to ride, to seek him out, to find him and bring him home safe. But she knew she couldn't go far safely, and she couldn't chance the wagon and team. The draws and canyons that cut through the land weren't exactly hospitable to conveyances. She swiveled in the seat, scanned in all directions. She felt as if she were the only person on earth.

But she knew help lay just behind her.

Hands tight on the reins, she turned the team and guided them back toward the herd. As soon as Billy was in sight, she waved him over to her.

"Ride for town," she told the youth as she pulled the team to a stop beside him. "Tell Sheriff Fuller someone's starting trouble."

Mr. Upkins had ridden over, as well. Now, he put out an arm to stop Billy from hurrying off. "Do we know there's trouble, ma'am?"

Why was he so reluctant to help? Didn't he understand that every moment counted? Hank could be hurt, shot.

"Of course we know there's trouble," she scolded him. "You heard that shot, same as me."

Mr. Upkins shrugged, but he lowered his arm. "Could have been Hank shooting a varmint or hunting meat for dinner. No call to drag the sheriff all the way out here."

The logical part of her mind, the part that wasn't fearful for Hank's life, informed her that he was right. And even if Billy rode hard, Hank could be lost to her by the time the youth returned with the sheriff.

Billy glanced between her and the older man. "So, am I going or staying?"

Mr. Upkins stared out over the hills, then smiled. "I reckon you're staying, because here comes Hank now."

Nancy clutched the reins, setting the team to shifting in the traces. Between the trees, she could just make out Hank and his horse, riding closer. Relief nearly washed her off the bench.

He didn't look hurt. She couldn't see that he favored an arm or his side. In fact, as he rode closer, she could see that his face was set, as if he'd reached some decision. She had to force herself to stay on the bench and not climb down and run to meet him.

As he came abreast of them, Mr. Upkins pointed a finger at him. "You had the lady all worried. You make peace while me and Billy round up this group."

Nancy should have been the one giving the orders, but she was too relieved to see Hank alive to argue with the older cowhand. Hank didn't argue either as Mr. Upkins and Billy returned to their duties with a tip of their hats in respect to Nancy. She could see Mr. Upkins catch Rosebud's eye and direct her away. The other cows began to shuffle past.

"Sorry about that," Hank murmured, watching them, as well.

She should accept his apology, let the matter go. But fear gnawed at her like a gopher on a fresh shoot.

"What happened?" Nancy asked. "One moment you were roping that steer, the next you'd disappeared."

"I saw someone watching the herd," he answered, bending to pat his horse on the neck. "When I rode closer, he took off, so I went after him."

"What!" Nancy stared at him, feeling as if the wagon was once more on uneven ground. "He could have been a rustler, an outlaw. You could have been shot." The very idea froze her in her seat even as her gaze darted over his body. "Were you shot?"

"No," he acknowledged, reaching out a hand as if to calm her. "I followed him to the lip of Winding Canyon, and he pulled a pistol. His shot went wide."

Thank You, Lord!

The thought was swift and heartfelt, but even as she finished her prayer, her temper flared. What was he thinking to take such chances? She'd told him how important he was to the ranch.

"I asked you to be careful," she reminded him. "Why would you take off after a gunman alone?"

He had the audacity to shrug as if he had no idea of the danger or couldn't care less. "He'd have gotten away otherwise."

"It seems as if he got away anyway," Nancy pointed out.

He grimaced. "Only because I couldn't be sure there wasn't a gang waiting for him in that canyon."

At least he had that much sense. She drew in a breath, trying to calm her nerves. For a moment, she envied her herd, soothed by no more than a call from a capable cowboy. It would take a lot more than words from Hank to relax her again.

"So I suppose you came back for reinforcements," she accused him. "I won't have you dragging Mr. Upkins and Billy into this."

"I wouldn't take them away from the herd," he said. "That wasn't the reason I came back." He met her gaze, his own solemn. "I came back because I heard you call."

Under his regard, she felt her face warming. "Then I'm doubly glad I called. You could have been killed."

"I can take care of myself."

Stubborn. She could see it in those blue eyes, the height of his head. Was it simply the nature of cattlemen? She couldn't imagine Edmund McKay or CJ Thorn being so determined to risk their lives. And if they were, she doubted Lula May or Molly would put up with such behavior.

"If you won't think of yourself, think of the other ranchers," she said. "Surely, the members of the Lone

Star Cowboy League need to know a rustler might be about."

She thought he might argue, his jaw was so tight, but he snapped a nod. "All right. I'll tell McKay and the others, just as soon as I see you safely back at the house."

Nancy gathered up the reins. "No need. You're not the only one who doesn't need help. I'll expect you and a report at dinner."

Oh, but she had her back up. Hank wasn't sure whether to apologize for his actions again or cheer her for standing her ground. She didn't give him a chance to do either. She turned the wagon and directed the team back toward the house.

He'd made a mess of things, that much was clear. Not only had he lost the fellow who'd been watching the herd, but he'd upset Nancy, as well.

Yet, what could he have done? He wasn't about to let another rustler get away with troubling the people of Little Horn.

Upkins galloped back to meet him. "Everything all right? Mrs. Snowden didn't look none too happy when she drove off."

"I'm none too happy myself." He went on to tell Upkins what he'd seen.

The older cowhand shook his head. "And here I thought things might settle down. Jenks and I will be on the lookout. Do you still want to send these west?"

"No," Hank told him. "Drive them closer to the house. The grazing's not as good there, but it will be easier for us to keep an eye on them. I'll help once I've told McKay about the trouble."

Leaving Upkins to his work, he rode to the McKay spread to talk to his friend.

Since marrying Lula May, McKay had moved his things to the Barlow ranch, but most the cattle work still took place on his spread. Hank wasn't surprised to find the tall rancher near the barn. He and his brother were watching a hand put a quarter horse through its paces. Hank was fairly sure the horse had to be one of Lula May's beauties.

Both men turned as he rode up. Like his brother, Josiah McKay was tall and powerfully built, with sandy hair and warm green eyes. The older brother, he ran the lumber mill in Little Horn.

Edmund strode to meet Hank, the planes of his face tight and hard. "What's happened?"

Did Hank look all that worried? He was careful to compose his face before swinging down from the saddle. Josiah came over as Hank started explaining what he'd seen. When he'd finished, Edmund shook his head.

"I was afraid of this. I'll send word to the others to keep watch. We'll need to talk after church services tomorrow about what else can be done."

"We're bringing the Windy Diamond herd closer to the house where we can keep an eye on them," Hank told him. "And I'll start posting a night rider again."

Josiah rubbed a hand against his trousers. "I'll finish my business and let you get to it, Edmund."

The three turned to admire the animal trotting about the corral. Hank could see it had clean lines, graceful haunches. It seemed a little dainty for a cattle pony, but then he supposed it would do for a riding mount.

"Lula May has some fine horses," Josiah said with a smile. "You were right, Edmund. She's the one for my Betsy." His smile faded. "I just don't know when she'll be up to riding her."

He looked worried. Hank knew it was none of his affair. He tried not to pry into the business of others. But Josiah seemed as if he needed a friend.

"What's the trouble?" Hank asked.

Josiah colored. "It's a woman thing. I don't really understand and neither does Doc. Betsy says some pregnancies are just harder than others."

Hank nodded. "If that's the problem, I may have an answer. Nancy's ma was a midwife, and she taught Nancy all about babies and such. I'd say she could help your wife."

Josiah brightened. "I'd be much obliged. It's not easy watching the woman you love hurting."

Hank couldn't argue with that. He didn't like seeing anyone hurting.

But the matter stayed on his mind as he rode back to the Windy Diamond. He kept remembering the look on Nancy's face as he'd returned from following the stranger. Though she'd scolded him something fierce, that sense of his told him she hadn't been angry or disappointed as his family might have been.

He'd frightened her again.

He supposed he couldn't blame her. He'd claimed he could take care of himself, and she'd seen a gun in his hand. But Lucas Bennett had been a quick draw too. Hank was quicker, and he couldn't make himself feel sorry he'd managed to stop the man before he shot his friend.

Still, he knew he had an obligation to take care of

Nancy and baby Ben. The way the bank was carrying on, Nancy needed him as her husband. And she still had a lot to learn about running a ranch. Losing help in that situation would probably scare anyone.

But he couldn't just walk away from finding Lucas's accomplice. He needed to see justice done. And he didn't want anyone else to be hurt because of his inaction.

He'd simply have to apologize again this evening. He hadn't meant to upset her. And he doubted having her upset was good for the baby.

Just thinking about the baby made him smile. He was going to be a pa, and he'd make sure little Ben understood he was loved. Oh, Hank knew some men thought too much encouragement spoiled a lad, made him soft. He thought love could be a firm foundation, the fertile ground on which a boy might grow to be a man he and his family could be proud of.

Would his pa be proud of the man Hank had become?

His fist tightened on the reins, and Belle faltered. Patting her on the neck, he released the pressure. He didn't want to fall into the pit again. Nothing he did, nothing he said, had ever been good enough for Henry Snowden senior. His father had made it clear Hank would never measure up. He shouldn't even try to think otherwise.

Yet, if Hank was going to be a father, that made his mother a grandmother again, his sisters aunts. Judith, Almira and Missy had already been married with children of their own when he'd left. Little Ben had cousins he might never meet.

Unless Hank was willing to take a chance.

Contacting his family was a risk, one he wasn't sure he was ready to take. His mother's sense of propriety could make most folks uncomfortable. His father had strong opinions, about most everything. Hank didn't want Nancy or the baby hurt by them. Yet he couldn't very well show up in Waco without his father knowing about it.

Maybe he could write, as Nancy had suggested. His family might not even answer, but at least he'd know he'd tried. Perhaps that was all that mattered.

Decision made, he urged Belle into a gallop. As soon as he returned to the ranch, he'd write to his family. He could take the letter into town when they went to church tomorrow. He'd simply have to deal with the answer, if it ever came, and hope it wasn't as bad as the letter Nancy had received from her in-laws.

Chapter Eleven

Nancy had calmed herself by the time Hank returned for dinner. She knew the source of her reaction. She was scared, pure and simple. She needed Hank, and she didn't want to lose another person in her family. But he was right to be concerned about someone watching their herd. She'd regretted being oblivious to Lucas's thefts. She could hardly look the other way now.

She had macaroni and tomatoes and a ham steak ready when he came in, but she waited until they had both been seated and served, and she'd said the blessing before questioning him.

"What did Edmund say about our stranger?" she asked as she cut the ham.

His hair was damp, a sure sign he'd stopped by the bunk room to clean up before joining her. And he hadn't been wearing that checkered shirt this morning either.

"He's going to talk to everyone tomorrow after church," Hank reported, reaching for the pitcher of lemonade between them and pouring himself a glass. "At the very least everyone will step up patrols."

She drew in a breath. "Very sensible. Surely that will detour rustlers."

He shrugged. "We had patrols before."

And Lucas had still managed to steal cattle, because he'd known precisely where those patrols were going to be. "It's different this time," she insisted. "We're more prepared. Aren't we?"

"Maybe." He picked a tomato from the layers of macaroni and cheese and studied it. "I've been thinking. Maybe we should be checking with the law in some of the other communities that have been hit. If we pool our information, we might see a pattern."

That made sense. "You should suggest that to Sheriff Fuller," she said.

"I'll talk to Jeb tomorrow at services." Still he didn't lift a bite to eat. "But I thought I might ride down to Burnet, ask around there."

Something crawled up her spine. Lucas had disappeared to Burnet on any number of occasions, claiming urgent business. Aside from the Empire Bank loan, she hadn't seen anything urgent or businesslike in the results.

But Hank wasn't Lucas. He wasn't trying to ride off and gamble. She had every proof he was conscientious about his work. She could see that the cattle were well fed and contented, and he certainly knew his way around a horse and lariat. Mr. Upkins and Billy respected him. Yet, suspicions lingered, like the sour scent of spoiled milk.

"I'd like to go with you," she said. "I came overland from Missouri and down through Fort Worth when I arrived. I've never seen Burnet."

"Not much to see," Hank said, avoiding her gaze. "And I can go faster alone."

The discussion was so like the ones she'd had with Lucas that the ham turned briny in her mouth. She'd given in before, kept to her place in the house.

Her place was no longer in this house.

"You might be able to ride faster," she said, "but I have a reason to visit Burnet too. I should talk with Mr. Cramore, assure him all is well. Shall we go Monday?"

That square jaw was tight again, and she prepared herself for an argument. But he nodded and went back to his dinner.

A shame her dinner no longer held any appeal. She hardly expected Hank to agree with her on every subject, but his determination to leave her out of this trip couldn't help but set her on edge. Was he truly trying to find the criminal who had aided Lucas in his thefts?

Or was he planning to take Lucas's example and rustle cattle?

No, she couldn't make herself believe that. Surely, she hadn't mistaken her man, not once but twice. Hank had some other reason for pursuing this vendetta when he might have handed the matter over to Jeb Fuller. If only she could understand what drove him.

He certainly looked the dedicated family man as they traveled to church services the next day. His jaw was clean-shaven; the blue of his cotton shirt made his eyes all the more noticeable. He tied up the horses before joining her in entering the new building, leading her to a bench right behind Lula May and Edmund and their family. Their smiles of welcome lit up the church.

Hank's warm voice joined with hers in the familiar hymns, his hands holding the hymnal open for her. He was so kind, so considerate. How could she doubt him?

When would she stop doubting herself?

She forced herself to focus on Pastor Stillwater's rousing sermon on the second greatest commandment. Beside her, Hank listened with a slight frown on his face, as if he too was soaking in every word. Ahead of them, she could see Lula May and Edmund exchanging glances from time to time. That's what they'd done by founding the Lone Star Cowboy League, Nancy realized. By banding together in times of trouble, they were living out the command to love thy neighbor as thyself.

Was that why Hank had offered to marry her? Was that why he was helping her learn ranching? Was he merely doing his Christian duty? Was that why he was so determined to catch the criminal who had helped Lucas?

She was so deep in thought as they left the church that she didn't hear Josiah McKay hail them until Hank caught her arm to stop her from heading to the wagon. The older McKay brother loped up to them with an apologetic smile on his rugged face.

"Mrs. Snowden, ma'am," he said, dragging his hat off his head in respect. "Your husband mentioned you were good with ladies having babies."

She glanced at Hank in surprise.

He nodded. "Mrs. McKay is having some trouble," he explained. "I told Josiah you would know what to do."

Her cheeks warmed. Lucas had always seemed embarrassed that she knew about pregnancy and childbirth. Like the people she'd left behind in Missouri, he thought a childless woman should be ignorant of such things. But how was a woman to learn if she didn't study?

"I'd be happy to help," Nancy said. "Did she come with you today?"

"Yes, ma'am," Josiah said, shoulders relaxing in his obvious relief. "But she had to return to the buggy before service even finished she was that tired." He pointed to where his black-topped buggy stood under the shade of some trees, horses placidly cropping the grass at their feet.

"Excuse me," Nancy said, and she picked up her skirts and hurried to the buggy.

The horses shifted as she approached, and she slowed her steps, calmed herself. Betsy McKay was sitting on the seat, skirts draped about her, head back and nostrils pinched as if she was having trouble breathing deeply enough. Even in the shade, her face looked white.

Molly Thorn was standing to one side, holding Betsy's hand, her own face tight with worry.

"Oh, Betsy," Nancy said, bracing herself on the other side of the wagon. "What's wrong?"

"Better to ask what isn't wrong," Betsy returned, casting her a quick glance. "Everything hurts from my head to my toes. I've weathered two other pregnancies, but none were this hard."

"My mother was a midwife," Nancy told her, "and she said every pregnancy is different just as every child is different."

"I thought maybe it wasn't entirely the baby," Molly put in, free hand fisting in her green-striped skirts. "I've had the worst trouble keeping down food the last couple months. I thought it must be the heat."

Nancy smiled at her. "Either that or you're expecting too."

Molly jerked back, then turned and dashed away from the buggy as if a coyote was on her tail.

Nancy felt as if she'd been slapped. "I'm sorry. I know some women don't like to talk about such things, but surely it's no mystery to Molly. She's been married twice."

"And never managed to conceive a child," Betsy pointed out. "I think she feels it keenly."

Nancy's heart twisted. "I didn't know. I'll apologize. But first, let's hear about you."

Betsy went on to tell her about her ailments, breath coming easier as she did so. Sometimes, Nancy had found, just having a sympathetic ear was enough to make burdens less heavy. And in listening, Nancy was able to think of a few things that might help.

Betsy smiled as Nancy finished offering her advice. "I can't wait to see Josiah's face when I tell him he has to rub my feet every night."

"Just make sure to use olive oil," Nancy told her. "That will help with some of your aches."

Betsy nodded, and Nancy excused herself to go to Molly.

She found the lady standing alone near the edge of the churchyard, where the dry lands began to stretch out into the distance. Molly stood with one hand on her belly, head bowed. Nancy hesitated to speak, afraid her friend was praying. But Molly looked up then and met her gaze, and Nancy could see tears sparkling on her cheeks.

"I'm so sorry," Nancy murmured, taking her hand and giving it a squeeze. "I didn't realize the trouble you've had. Can you forgive me?"

Molly managed a smile. "Of course. You didn't mean to hurt me. And the matter truly hasn't bothered me much since CJ and I married and adopted the twins. But hearing you say I might be pregnant brought it all back."

Nancy could hear the longing in the woman's voice. "And you're certain you can't conceive?" she pressed.

Molly nodded. "You don't know how often I've prayed about the matter. But no child ever came."

Nancy had met other couples with similar worries. Everyone always assumed it was the wife's fault, but Nancy knew that sometimes the husband was the one with trouble.

She squeezed Molly's hand again. "Well, I'm not a doctor, but I've seen quite a few pregnant women since I started helping my mother fourteen years ago. You say food has been difficult for a while?"

"Since shortly after I married CJ, yes," Molly admitted. "But the warm temperatures always make me less hungry."

"Clothes getting a little tight?" Nancy suggested. "Feeling like you just can't wake up in the morning?"

Molly stared at her. "You too?"

Nancy smiled. "Not right now, but that was certainly the case when I first discovered I was pregnant."

Molly's golden-brown eyes widened. "Oh, Nancy! I'm afraid to hope."

"One thing about pregnancies," Nancy replied, "they have a way of showing themselves. Give it another month, and you'll know for sure."

"Oh, my!" Molly pressed her fingers to her lips, tears once more starting. "Wait until I tell CJ!" She reached out to hug Nancy. "Thank you, so much!"

Nancy absorbed the warmth, the praise. *Thank You, Lord, for giving me the opportunity to show my neighbors how very much I care about them. Maybe I'll finally start feeling capable again.*

Hank stood by the church steps, following Nancy's progress around the churchyard. Everywhere she went, she left smiles behind. And he very much doubted she knew how much she was appreciated. She was always tending to someone's needs—her hands', Betsy McKay's, his. Maybe it was time someone tended to hers.

He wasn't entirely sure how to go about that, but he resolved to make their trip to Burnet as easy as possible. Her presence would make it harder to get the answers he wanted, but she was right that checking in with the banker might help prevent him from following through on his threat to foreclose.

Hank had the wagon ready for her early the next morning. The thirty-mile trip to Burnet would take much of the day, and they'd have to put up overnight before heading back the next day. They'd talked about the matter over dinner, so she was ready with a carpetbag as she came out of the house. But she eyed the back of the wagon as she handed him her case.

"Is that a bedroll?" she asked.

He shrugged before stowing her bag behind the bench. "I figured if you get tired we can lay you down right then. Plus, I can use it tonight in the livery stable."

She made a face. "We're staying in the livery stable?"

"I am," he qualified. "We'll find a nice hotel room for you."

She looked uncertain about that, but she allowed him to hand her up onto the bench. "Is this the cushion from the parlor chair?" she asked, shifting to see what was under her.

"I thought that might make the trip more comfortable," he replied. "You know the roads, full of bumps and ridges. You and the baby might need some padding. Not that you lack padding," he hastened to add. When she raised her brows, he knew he had only dug the hole deeper. "That is, Nancy, you're just fine as you are."

Her lips twitched. "Thank you, Hank."

When was he ever going to learn to open his mouth without putting his foot in it? Shaking his head, he came around to the other side of the wagon just as Upkins trotted out of the barn.

"Filled and ready," the older cowhand reported, pushing a wooden crate up into the bed of the wagon.

Nancy twisted to eye it. "What's that?"

Why did she sound so suspicious? What did she think he was packing, enough ammunition to take down the remaining buffalo on the plains?

Upkins answered easily enough. "Food and drink for the trip, ma'am," he said, stepping back to tip his hat to her. "Beef strips, biscuits, dried cherries and apple cider. Course my cooking don't come close to yours, but we figured you didn't need extra work to get ready for this trip."

Nancy eyed Hank. "Soft seat, good food and apple cider. What's next, Mr. Snowden? Flowers?"

As if on cue, Jenks darted out from behind the house. "Best I could do on short notice, Hank." He shoved a handful of carrots, dirt still sticking to their russet sides, into the bed of the wagon.

"Thank you, Billy," Nancy said kindly.

"Oh, they ain't for you, ma'am," he qualified. "They're for the horses, so they'll trot real good for you."

"It seems Mr. Snowden thought of everything," Nancy said, though he could see she was fighting a smile.

"I try," Hank said, bowing his head.

Upkins spoiled the humility by clapping him on the back. "Ain't that what I've always said? If there's one thing you need to know about Hank Snowden, it's that he's mighty trying."

Nancy's laughter played them out of the yard.

"It really was kind of you to make the journey so comfortable," she said as they crossed through the gates. "Especially after I insisted on coming with you."

"Your company is welcome," Hank assured her. "I'm just concerned for you and the baby. If you need to stop and rest anytime, you let me know."

"I will." She sat with her hands folded across her

middle. She always looked so composed. Now she wore a proper white blouse and blue skirts, her hair up under her sombrero. Except for the hat, she might have been sitting in her parlor, entertaining callers. He was glad he'd decided to wear his leather vest over his cotton shirt.

The horses plodded down the road, their hooves raising puffs of golden dust with each step. Hawks circled overhead, and off in the distance, he saw an antelope bounding between the oaks.

"Why are you so determined to catch the rustlers?" she asked. The question sounded no more than curious, but she shifted on the cushion as if the topic still made her uncomfortable.

"Because they hurt people," he told her. "CJ was knocked unconscious when they went after his horses. The Carsons lost their barn."

Her fingers tightened. "That was all Lucas's fault."

"Lucas and whoever was planning to buy those cattle," Hank insisted.

"He should be brought to justice," Nancy agreed. "But I'm more concerned about your well-being."

Was she? Her cheeks were turning that peachy color again, but he thought it had more to do with the heat of the moment than warm feelings. She needed his help. That was all.

"Thank you kindly," he said, gaze going back to the road. "But maybe we should talk about something else for a change."

She leaned back as much as she could on the stiff bench. "Very well. Tell me about Burnet. Why does everyone want to go there?"

He had a feeling everyone meant her late husband.

"It's the county seat," he allowed, "and I hear tell the politicians are already trying to see how they can pull our county into theirs to make a bigger one."

The wagon hit a bump, shaking their seats, and she clung to the sideboard. "So there are government buildings in Burnet."

"If you can call them that. Whitewashed brick and stucco, maybe two stories tall. Back in Waco, we had a courthouse shaped like a Greek temple. Burnet's not that far along just yet."

She closed her eyes. "Tell me about Waco, then."

An image of his family's ranch came to mind. Funny. He hadn't thought about it in years. He could see the road running straight and true up to the house, the two wings fanning out from the wide, shaded front porch. He could smell the sage blooming in the spring, hear the call of the cuckoo in the summer. Faces flashed past—his sisters, his mother. A longing rose up inside him.

"Waco's just a big town," he said, feeling as if the seat had hardened beneath him. "Tell me about Missouri."

She was quiet a moment, and when he glanced her way he saw a tear squeeze out from under her lashes and roll down her cheek.

Guilt struck him. "Here, now, no call to cry. We don't have to talk about Missouri. We don't have to talk at all. You just rest, and we'll be in Burnet in no time."

She nodded. In the silence, the thud of the horses' feet sounded like hammer blows.

If he was feeling heavy now, how much worse would it be when they reached Burnet and he started asking questions she shouldn't have to hear answered?

Chapter Twelve

They made it to Burnet that afternoon, after stopping several times to eat or take their comfort. Based on Hank's dismal description of the place, Nancy wasn't sure what to expect. She was pleasantly surprised to find the wide, dusty streets lined with trees and braced by neat two-story buildings, many with upper balconies. At the end of Main Street, she could see the square white block of the county courthouse, carriages and wagons crowded in front.

Hank threaded the team through the wagons and riders thronging the streets, found a nice hotel that catered to cattlemen and their wives and set her up in a room for the night.

"You're probably tired from the trip," he said as he set her carpetbag down beside the iron bedstead. "I can talk to the sheriff and come back for you later."

He was not getting away from her so easily. Nancy linked her arm with his and smiled up at him. "But Mr. Snowden, you promised to show me Burnet."

He chuckled. "I guess I did. All right. Come along."

They left the hotel together. She had to admit it

was nice strolling the stone pavement under the sweep of the balconies along Main Street. The shop windows were bright with calico and cakes, the air redolent with barber soap and cinnamon. The gentlemen all tipped their hats and smiled at her. A few ladies regarded her growing frame with arch looks, but she ignored them. Her mother had always encouraged expecting ladies to do more than recline on their beds until it was time for the birth. She didn't intend to hide from the world simply because she was increasing.

But she couldn't help pausing in front of one of the display windows. Inside was the dearest set of baby bonnets, pinks and blues and yellows with satin ties and silk flowers.

"You're not fixing to put one of those on Ben?" Hank asked, and she nearly giggled at the look on his face.

"Babies don't generally wear Stetsons," she told him.

"Why not?" he asked. "Let's see if they have one." He took her hand and pulled her inside.

The clerk was happy to direct them to an area that held a number of ready-made pieces for a baby's layette. Nancy smiled as she fingered a fine cotton gown edged in lace.

Hank lifted one of the long shirts. "Will he really be this small?"

"Very likely," Nancy told him. "At least at first. But he'll grow fast."

Hank set down the garment. "Never knew a baby would need so much stuff. I make do with a couple shirts and denim."

"Babies tend to spit and spill," Nancy explained.

"Ben will need at least a dozen gowns and twice that many diapers."

He shoved back his hat. "Well, what do you know? Why don't you pick out a few things while I go talk to the sheriff?"

There he went again, trying to leave her out. Nancy straightened, careful to keep her look and tone pleasant. "I'm making most of what Ben needs. I'll come with you."

He sighed, but he offered her his arm.

"I didn't mean to make it sound as if Burnet is such a fearsome place," he said as he held the door of the mercantile open for her. "You don't have to be scared to be alone here."

She couldn't tell him it wasn't Burnet that scared her.

Hank escorted Nancy to the sheriff's office. In truth, he would have liked to have spared her this. From the walls of the narrow room, men with angry faces glared out of wanted posters, and Hank didn't like thinking about the source of the dark stain on the plank floor near the barred cells that took up the back half of the office.

The sheriff, a burly fellow with graying hair, listened to Hank's story, then shrugged.

"Rustling's become a way of life these days," he commiserated. "My advice is to look to your herds and round up any mavericks. Branded cattle are harder to sell when it isn't your brand."

Nancy frowned at that. Likely she was remembering that the cattle Lucas had stolen had all been branded, by their neighbors. But that just meant whoever was buying the branded cattle was more conniving. Besides, Hank had another reason for talking with the lawman.

He drew out the key he'd found in Bennett's room and showed it to the sheriff. "You ever seen one of these?"

The sheriff smiled. "Seen one, but never owned one. There's a hotel on the edge of town, fancy place known for its high-stakes games and fine liquor. The lady who owns the place gives these out to her best customers. It's a promise they're welcome anytime."

Hank felt ill. He shoved it at the sheriff. "Return it. Better yet, melt it down. The man who owned it shouldn't have had it to begin with."

Turning, he took Nancy's arm and escorted her from the place.

She was pale as she walked beside him. "That was Lucas's, wasn't it?"

"I found it in his room," Hank admitted. "But he could have picked it up somewhere or won it in a game."

"Or he could have lost all our money gambling at that place," she said, voice sad. "I can see why you didn't want me to come, Hank. I don't think much of Burnet right now."

And less of her former husband.

"You wanted to see Mr. Cramore," he reminded her. "Why don't we find the Empire Bank before they close for the day?"

She nodded, and they set off in search.

But the Empire Bank wasn't located along Main Street, and when they asked at the mercantile, the clerk had no idea where to send them.

"This can't be right," Nancy protested as they returned to the pavement. "I had a letter from them. Mr. Cramore came to see us."

Hank didn't like the direction of his thoughts, but he knew he couldn't keep them to himself. For one thing, she had a right to know. For another, he was beginning to realize Nancy didn't want his protection when it came to Lucas and the rustlers.

"It may not be a bank that caters to businessmen and the like," he said. "Back in Waco, I heard tell of men who called themselves bankers but held their trade at the back of gaming establishments."

She shuddered. "Money lenders."

"For the desperate," he agreed.

"Oh, poor Lucas," she murmured. "Greed so latched into him he never shook it free. Why didn't I see it?"

She was hurting again. How could she not hurt when every bit of evidence Hank uncovered proved that her husband had been no good at the end?

"I knew a cowboy once," he said, directing her back toward the hotel. "Nicest hand on a rope you ever saw. Willing to ride all day and all night if need be. Oh, he had a habit of chewing on mint, and once in a while he'd get a little silly, but everyone thought it was just him having fun. Turned out he couldn't stop drinking—had pints stashed all over the ranch. We kept finding them for months after he rode on. We lived with him, worked beside him, and we never figured it out."

She kept her gaze on the dusty pavement. "You weren't his wife."

"And Lucas Bennett wasn't any kind of husband

to leave you like this." The words came out harsher than he intended, and she stopped and stood still for a moment.

"I'm sorry, Nancy," he said, hand on her elbow. "I told you we should speak good about the man, but when I think about the way he gambled away your future, the baby's future, I want to hit something."

"I know," she murmured. "But when I think about it all, I start to wonder why. Maybe he was pining for Alabama. Then why not sell the ranch and go home? Did he feel trapped in Little Horn for some reason, or was I such a terrible burden he could only escape through drink and gambling?"

He stared at her. "Hogwash!"

When she blinked at him, eyes swelling with tears, he seized her shoulders. "Now, you listen to me, Nancy Snowden. I was there when you arrived at the Windy Diamond. I saw what you did for your husband. You cooked, cleaned, sewed, decorated real nice, made his life more comfortable in every way. If a man can't appreciate that, it's not the lady who's lacking."

She choked back a sob and buried her head on his chest. "Oh, I want to believe that!"

People passing were looking at them oddly. Men shook their heads and hurried around. Ladies walked more slowly, scowling at Hank, and he realized the picture they must present—him a trail-dirty cowhand, her a pregnant lady sobbing in his arms.

Well, he didn't much care what they thought. He gathered Nancy close, shielded her from their judgmental looks.

"Easy, now," he murmured, rubbing her back with

one hand. "You just think on what I said. If you don't believe me, ask Upkins or Jenks or Lula May. They'll all tell you the fault of the matter lay with Lucas, never you."

She pulled back, drew an embroidered handkerchief from her sleeve and dabbed at her eyes. "Thank you. Maybe someday I'll believe it myself."

"No time like the present," he said, starting forward once more. She swept along beside him, head bowed and handkerchief still patting at her cheeks. She blew her nose with a genteel puff.

"Careful," he teased. "You'll rub off your freckles."

Her handkerchief fell even as she widened her eyes to stare at him. "I have freckles?"

He laughed. "Just one or two, right on the tip of your nose where it must have peeped out from under your hat."

She shook her head, steps quickening and hand falling to ball the hanky at her side. "No, no, no. I'll have to use milk of almonds. I think I still have some of Mother's."

Hank hastened his steps to keep up with her. "Why the fuss over a couple of freckles?"

"Ladies," she informed him, "do not have freckles."

That was news to him. He tried to remember whether his mother or sister had ever fretted over freckles. Judith and Almira sure had been determined to protect their skin from the sun, using parasols or hats whenever they went out. And he seemed to remember that creamy skin was counted a blessing.

"Well, yours are only the raisins dotting the cream

of your face," he said, rather pleased with his turn of phrase.

Her face puckered. "They're as big as raisins? Why didn't I notice?" She stopped before a window where her reflection showed like a shadow and turned her head one way and the other.

Hank crossed his arms over his chest. "You aren't going to find any flaws. Not on that face."

She straightened. "This after telling me I have spots the size of raisins."

He took her arm and drew her down the walk to the hotel. "I tell you, you don't have to worry. You're pretty as a picture, freckles and all."

She cast him a look as he held the door open for her. "And how do you define pretty?" she demanded.

"By what I've been taught," he replied. "It's not what's outside that makes a woman beautiful. It's what's in her heart. That's why you'll always be beautiful, Nancy, freckles or no."

She stopped in the hotel parlor, bit her lip, and he could see tears brimming in her eyes again.

Hank sagged. "Now, don't go looking at me like that. I meant it as a compliment."

"And it was a compliment, a lovely one," she assured him. "A reminder too. It's easy to focus on the outside, on what you can see of your circumstances. But it's important to look past all that. Thank you for helping me remember that, Hank."

Once more, she stood on tiptoe and kissed his cheek. He ought to stand there, accept the gesture, thank her kindly for it. But suddenly he wanted more than polite conversation. He turned his head and met those peach-colored lips with his own.

And the world started bucking like a wild bronco.

Emotions he'd buried for five years shot to the surface; yearning, hope, a tenderness that threatened to knock him off his feet. He cradled her close, drank her in like cool water, all while his heart beat a tattoo in his chest.

"Pardon me, sir."

The clerk's prim voice made Hank raise his head. Nancy swayed beside him, peaches ripe in her cheeks, lips dark from his kiss. He kept his arms around her.

"I do not know who let you in the door," the clerk informed Hank, hands on his aproned hips. "But this is a proper establishment. We cannot have such displays in public view."

Hank glanced around at the empty lobby, then back at the clerk standing so firmly in his fancy black-striped trousers. "You have rules against a man kissing his wife?" he demanded. "What sort of place is this?"

The clerk reddened as he stepped back, arms falling. "Terribly sorry, sir. I didn't realize, that is, I…" He straightened and snapped a nod. "We at the Palace Hotel are a staunch supporter of marriage."

"Quite right," Hank said. Nancy was biting her lip again, but this time he thought it was to keep from laughing. Taking her arm, he led her upstairs to her room.

She paused at the door. "There's plenty of space in here. You could sleep on the settee instead of at the livery stable."

He'd seen the settee when he'd brought in her bag. After an hour on the hard-backed little seat, he'd be bent tighter than a branding iron. Besides, after that kiss, he needed to walk a pace.

"I'll be fine," he told her. "You're not scared, are you?"

"No," she allowed. "I'll be fine too, thanks to you." She ducked her head and slipped through the doorway.

He couldn't help smiling as he descended the stairs. Maybe there was hope for them. Maybe he could regain the life he'd once dreamed of having—fine ranch, sweet wife, children to love and teach. All he had to do was open his heart.

And there lay the danger. He remembered the pain when his father had criticized his least move. He still felt the sting of Mary Ellen's defection. He'd never been good enough, smart enough, strong enough for any of them. What made him think Nancy would find him good enough to love? The only reason she'd married him was because she'd been desperate.

And the main reason he'd offered to marry her was because he needed to atone. That need hadn't gone away. But he wasn't sure what to do next. He didn't think Nancy would appreciate him finding that fancy hotel, taking up with determined gamblers, just to see if any might remember Lucas Bennett. And likely the gambling den had little to do with buying the stolen cattle. Gambling had merely been the goad that had driven Lucas Bennett to steal. Someone else had abetted those thefts, made it possible for him to gain money from them.

That someone might reside in this very town, but Hank had no way of finding him.

What else can I do, Lord? I just want to see justice done.

He stepped out of the hotel into twilight. The streets were emptying of wagons, and a few horses were carrying their riders away, as well. Best he head for bed.

He started for the livery stable, and a man fell in beside him. Something about him seemed familiar, but Hank was certain they'd never worked together.

"Heard you rode for the Windy Diamond up near Little Horn," the stranger drawled.

Who had been telling tales? He glanced at the man, taking note of the trail-darkened skin, the narrowed green eyes, the pearl-handled pistol sticking out of his holster.

A pistol that looked a lot like the one Lucas Bennett had lost gambling.

Hank stopped, washing cold. "I'm not looking for trouble."

"But you are looking for something," the man insisted, pausing beside him.

Hank nodded, careful to keep his hand not too close but not too far from his own six-gun. "The owner of the Windy Diamond was caught moving cattle. You happen to know where he sold them?"

"Heard tell there's quite a few head of cattle up that way looking for a new home," the stranger countered. He cocked his head, putting his face into shadow, but something about the way he moved pricked a memory.

Was this the fellow who had been watching their herd?

"Cattle have been known to go astray," Hank said, keeping his tone neutral.

"And men like us have the job of rounding them

up," the man agreed. "I might know someone interested in buying, no questions asked. You interested in selling?"

"Maybe," Hank said. "If I knew the buyer could keep his mouth shut. Any chance of meeting?"

"A little eager, cowboy." The stranger widened his stance, and Hank's heart jerked into a faster clip. "First you have to prove yourself. I hear Edmund McKay's herd is too big. Think you could thin it out?"

"McKay's not the fellow to cross," Hank said, mind whirling. How could he get the fellow to tell him the whole story? "But I might know some others in the area with mavericks to pick off. Where would I take the cattle to get paid? It's not easy moving a herd this time of year with roundup close. Too many men on the ground."

"Which is why one more won't be noticed." He leaned closer, gaze drilling into Hank's. "And why do you care what McKay thinks? I heard before you worked for Bennett you used to ride from spread to spread, didn't make ties."

How did they know that? "I'm married now," Hank said.

He laughed, an ugly sound. "The widow Bennett? She's none too picky who she weds from what I can see. She'll find another fellow to fill your place. Those kind always do."

"You're wrong." His hand was shaking, and he forced it to still. "About Nancy and about me. I aim to find the man who was waiting to pay Lucas Bennett for the cattle. You either tell me his name now, or I reckon things are going to get unfriendly."

Things got unfriendly.

Chapter Thirteen

It was a long while before Nancy could sleep that night. She kept reliving the moment Hank's lips had met hers. She'd been kissed before, by a young man at a church picnic back in Missouri, by Lucas any number of times. She wasn't the type of woman to deny she'd enjoyed being kissed. But Hank's kiss had been different: richer, fuller, like fresh milk after water. It satisfied something deep inside her, made her feel beautiful, loved.

Was it possible she and Hank might make a true marriage?

Ben wiggled inside her, and she pressed a hand against her lawn nightgown at the spot.

"You like that idea, do you?" she murmured in the night, head resting against the soft pillow as she pictured a dark-haired little boy listening to her. "Mama's learned love doesn't come as easily as dreaming, present company excepted. What if he doesn't love me back? What if I'm wrong about him?"

What was she doing talking to someone who couldn't answer?

Of course, she couldn't answer the questions either. But she knew someone who could.

She'd always uttered formal prayers, until she'd heard Hank pray that night over dinner. Now she closed her eyes, focused her tumultuous thoughts.

Lord, I remember a passage in the Bible that says You give wisdom to any who ask. Well, I'm asking. I don't know whether to trust what I see, what I feel. I don't know whether You put Hank in my life to help me or to be the helpmate You intended me to love. Won't You please show me what to do?

She fell asleep with a prayer still fading from her mind.

The morning dawned bright and clear, and she drew in a breath before rising to change. The long drive back would give her and Hank ample opportunities to talk, to share. Maybe that's why she felt so unburdened.

She thought Hank was planning to leave early, so she was downstairs with her bag by seven. Cattlemen and their wives passed her spot on the upholstered chair in the lobby on their way to the hotel dining room beyond. Even where she sat she could catch the scent of bacon cooking. Other guests stopped to settle their bills before leaving. Any number glanced her way, and she made sure to sit with her hands folded so that her wedding band was visible.

Twice the clerk came out from behind his post to see if she needed anything. The second time she agreed to his suggestion to have tea and biscuits brought from the kitchen for her while she waited.

She was pouring herself a cup when a gentleman came in from the street. Portly and balding, black coat and trousers oddly formal in the frontier town, he made his stately way toward the dining room, starting to pass her as if she were no more than a familiar painting on the wall.

Nancy set down her cup and rose to put herself in his path. "Mr. Cramore."

He stopped, blinked for a moment, then offered her a tight smile. "Mrs. Bennett. I had no idea you were in town."

"It's Mrs. Snowden now," she informed him. "I won't detain you. I just wanted you to know that we are making a go of the ranch and should be able to pay you what we owe in the next few months."

Something flickered behind his pale eyes. "Excellent news. You will, of course, remember that there will be additional fees on the principle."

Nancy frowned. "Fees? I don't recall you mentioning fees."

He tutted as if he thought she should have known without him saying so. "Filing, administration, interest. The usual things associated with business matters."

He made it sound as if she could not possibly understand. "May I see these fees itemized," she asked, "so I know exactly what I owe?"

"I do not carry paper and pencil around with me, my dear," he answered with a chuckle. "And the amount of interest will change in any event, depending on when you actually arrange a payment. Perhaps next time you come to Burnet, you can make an appointment at my place of business, and I can review everything with you then."

"Delighted," Nancy said, feeling as if she'd had

honey poured over her head. "If you would be so good as to tell me the èxact address. Mr. Snowden and I looked all over Burnet yesterday and even asked your direction. No one could tell us the location of the Empire Bank."

He raised his head, making his double chins quiver. "You must have asked the wrong people, Mrs. Snowden. Our location is no secret." He glanced at the tall case clock against the far wall. "Ah, I fear I must leave you or I shall be late for my appointment." He leaned closer, the scent of his flowery cologne washing over her. "A word of advice, if I may, my dear? As you are learning, many people are ignorant of the ways of the world. Be careful who you trust."

With a fatherly smile, he turned and strolled past her into the dining room.

Nancy plopped down on her seat, fuming. It was one thing when she questioned her own judgment. It was another to have her intelligence questioned. No, not questioned, assumed! Did he really think she would blindly hand over money at whatever amount he decreed? That she'd accept anything he said to her, simply because he was a man and a banker?

Her hand was shaking so hard she could scarcely lift her cup. She'd relied on Lucas, and he'd failed her. She'd believed Mr. Cramore's papers that said Lucas owed him money, and now she was beginning to think the man's story held more holes than a sieve. Why did she keep putting her trust in people? Was she as dim as Mr. Cramore seemed to think?

Just then, the door to the hotel opened to admit Hank. His clothes were rumpled and stained, and his mouth was swollen on one corner. She was up and moving even as he stumbled.

"What happened?" she cried, putting her shoulder under his arm and leading him to the chair she had vacated.

"I might have run into a feller who thought I'd steal McKay's cattle and sell them to him on the sly," he answered, sinking onto the chair. "It seems it took my face hitting his fist to dissuade him."

"Oh, Hank." She pulled a handkerchief from her case, wet it with the tea and handed it to him. "Press that against the spot. It will help the swelling go down."

"Much obliged." He did as she'd suggested and grimaced as the tea must have stung. "Doesn't look nearly as bad as it feels," he assured her.

She shook her head at his jest. "Did you at least learn something about the rustlers? Did this man know Lucas?"

"He certainly gave me that impression," Hank said, words coming out thicker around the handkerchief. "The discussion attracted the sheriff, who put the other feller in jail and promised to look into the matter. So I may have made some progress."

"Mr. and Mrs. Snowden." The clerk nodded a greeting as he approached, wringing his hands. "Really, we are a proper hotel. We simply cannot have such displays in our lobby."

Hank frowned at him over the lace-edged handkerchief. "I didn't even reach for her hand."

Nancy smiled. "It's all right. If you'll provide the bill, Mr. Snowden will settle up, and we'll be on our way."

And she could not wait to shake the dust of Burnet off her feet.

* * *

"If I ever leave Little Horn again, it will be too soon," Nancy said as Hank directed the horses out of town. He was having a hard time keeping his eyes open. The sheriff had locked him in jail all night for disturbing the peace. What peace? He'd heard gun shots, whooping and hollering on the street until nearly dawn. His only consolation was that the rustler was confined to the other cell, and being questioned mercilessly by the sheriff.

"You have what you need to make an arrest?" Hank had asked as the lawman let him out that morning.

"Close," the sheriff advised. "But I'll probably have to let him out while I check into his story. You willing to testify against this fellow, tell the truth about your boss?"

Nancy didn't deserve to have her husband's secrets trotted out for public consumption. But it was the only way to see the rustlers brought to justice.

"I'm willing," Hank had told him. "Send word to the Windy Diamond whenever you need me."

Now the jostling of the wagon on the rutted road north made him aware of every ache and injury earned in his fight with the rustler and on that hard cot in the jail cell. As the wheel hit a rock, pain shot through his jaw.

He must have made a face, because Nancy stuck out her lower lip in sympathy. Then she bent to rummage through her bag again. She'd placed it at her feet this time, as if expecting she might need it.

"Here," she said, handing him a gnarled stick. "Try chewing on this. It can ease the pain."

He recognized the little root as ginger. He stuck

it in his mouth and clamped down on it. The sharp warm taste poked his tongue.

She glanced down at her belly. "What are we going to do with your pa, Ben? He can't go picking fights with men twice his size. We need him."

Hank pulled the ginger from his mouth. "He wasn't twice my size. And you didn't see *his* face this morning."

She regarded him with raised brows.

Hank shook his head, sending a fresh spasm through his cheek. "All right. My face looks worse than his, at least at the moment. But I didn't start the fight. All I was doing was looking for answers."

"So you endangered your life again," she accused him.

Did she want the villain to go free? "You have to kill a steer to get steak," he countered.

She rounded on him, eyes blazing. "I don't need steak! I have acres filled with cattle! What I need is a husband."

He turned his gaze toward the front, afraid of what she might see in his eyes. "You had one. I'm just trying to figure out why he left the way he did."

"Oh, chew on your ginger," she snapped.

He did. And she was right, as she always was in matters of medicine. The pain in his jaw slowly subsided.

The pain in his heart grew heavier.

He pulled the root out of his mouth again. "I didn't go looking for trouble, Nancy. The feller sidled up to me on the street, said he knew I rode for the Windy Diamond, offered to introduce me to someone who would take cattle, no questions asked."

Nancy frowned, gaze on the oaks clustered to one side of the road. "He knew you were from the Windy Diamond?"

"Named it specifically," Hank assured her.

"Then he knew Lucas." Her voice had a finality about it he couldn't like.

"Could be," he allowed, "or he might have learned the names of all the ranches between Burnet and Little Horn and guessed the brand. Pays to know who you're stealing from, I guess."

"He must have been involved in the thefts," she said. "Can we prove it?"

He sure hoped so. "The sheriff said he'd look into the matter."

She cast a quick glance his way. "You don't sound convinced."

"After our first meeting with the sheriff, I wasn't," he admitted. "But it's possible he's coming around. He questioned the feller most of the night."

"You heard him?" She swiveled to face him fully. "What did he say? Are there other rustlers near Little Horn?"

"I don't think so," Hank told her, easing the horses into a canyon that cradled the road. One thing about driving in the hill country, you never knew who or what might be waiting in the draws and around the bend. He was just glad the way ahead looked empty, with nothing more dangerous than a jackrabbit bounding into cover under the low-hanging branches of a scrub oak.

"All he'd say was that he was just trying to help out hands like him who weren't riding for the brand at the moment."

"Riding for the brand," she repeated. "What does that mean?"

"It means a cowboy is attached to a spread, like Upkins and Jenks and I are part of the Windy Diamond. A cowboy without work tends to find ways to get himself in trouble."

"So we still don't know how Lucas was planning to sell those cattle," she surmised.

"Not yet," he said. "But we do know it was someone around Burnet."

She cast him another glance. "So I suppose that means you'll be going back to Burnet."

Somehow she made it sound as if he planned to ride to California and never return. "I'd like to hear how the sheriff's investigation goes," he admitted.

Her fingers were knitting together over baby Ben, as if she was determined to hold him close. "I need you on the ranch."

There was that. Particularly with roundup starting in only a week or two, she needed all the help she could get. Transferring the reins to one hand, he reached out and patted her arm with his other hand.

"Don't fret. I won't go until the cattle are to market. We'll need to head into town then in any event to pay off the Empire Bank."

He felt her hands tense and pulled away.

She offered him an apologetic smile. "Maybe, or maybe not. I meant to tell you. I saw Mr. Cramore."

Hank stiffened, and the horses picked up their pace in response to the pressure on the reins.

"When? Where?" he demanded. "Don't tell me you went looking for him."

She brushed off her skirts as if she hadn't a care in the world. "You sound concerned."

"Of course I'm concerned," Hank told her. "As far as we knew, Cramore worked out of the back of some gambling establishment. I don't want you anywhere near one of those."

She turned her head to watch him. "Worried about my safety?"

"Well, sure," Hank said, wondering how she could be so calm. "You should have heard the goings-on in the streets last night. And there are unsavory types who frequent those places. No telling how they'd react to a pretty gal sashaying in. I don't want anything to happen to you."

The words seemed to echo from the canyon walls, hover in the air between them. That feeling was coming over him, and he knew he'd been wrong.

"Oh," Hank said.

She cocked her head at his obvious realization. "Yes?" she said, batting her honey-colored lashes. "You were saying?"

"You're right," Hank said, tucking the remains of the ginger in his pocket. "I don't like the idea of you in danger any better than you seem to like the thought of me in danger." He wasn't willing to confess to more than that. "Where did you run into Cramore?"

She relaxed back against the seat, as much as she could on the hard wood. "He came into the hotel to meet someone," she said. "I practically had to accost him to get him to stop and talk. And I didn't much like what he said."

Hank gripped the reins, wishing the pushy little banker was in front of him right then. "Did he threaten you?"

"In a way," she admitted. "He refused to give me the location of his bank, and he warned me to be careful who I trusted. As if the most untrustworthy person I've ever met wasn't the one speaking to me!"

Her righteous indignation rolled off her like steam from a hot springs.

"We'll pay him off," Hank promised. "And you won't have to deal with him again."

"That's just it," she said, pushing back a tendril of hair that had come loose in the breeze. "I'm not sure he wants us to pay him off. He gave me some vague excuse about fees and claimed we owe more than we thought."

From the first, the so-called banker had tried to put himself forward—dismissing Nancy's plan to learn enough to run the ranch, trying to install his own man to manage things for her. Had Lucas Bennett really signed away such rights, or was Cramore taking advantage of the situation?

"We'll pin him down," Hank told her. "That new lawyer in Little Horn might be able to help prove the truth of the matter. All I know is that nobody owns one acre of the Windy Diamond but you."

"And you," Nancy reminded him, hand once more covering Ben.

They discussed their options on the ride back. Nancy was for approaching Jeb Fuller about the matter or going all the way to Austin to talk to the federal marshal at the state capital. Hank wasn't sure the law would step in on what some might see as a closed case. Besides, the more questions a lawman asked, the more likely Nancy would hear about Hank's role in Lucas's death. Given her concerns, now didn't seem the best time to confess.

He was just glad to find everything at the ranch in good shape when they pulled the wagon into the yard later that afternoon. Hank unloaded while Upkins sat with Nancy on the porch and gave her a detailed report on the ranch. Jenks came to help Hank unhitch the horses. They let the pair out into the corral and started back for the house.

The young cowhand dug into his pocket before they reached the porch. "Letter came for you," he said, handing Hank the battered missive. "Hope it ain't bad news."

Hank recognized the elegant hand immediately. He stopped in the yard and stared at it. His own hand shook as he broke open the letter and read the words from his mother.

"Hank?"

Nancy's voice seemed to come from a long ways off. He looked up to find her and his friends all gazing at him with obvious concern.

"What's wrong?" Nancy asked, rising from her seat on the porch.

He cleared his throat of the lump building there. "My pa's dying. Ma says he wants me to come back to Waco to say goodbye."

Chapter Fourteen

Nancy knew the pain of loss—her father, her mother, Lucas. She remembered the dark days when it had seemed as if the world would never be the same, when she might not be able to go on. But she'd never seen such pain and confusion that blazed from Hank's face a moment before he blanked the emotions out.

"Well, then," she said, "it seems we're going to Waco."

"Nancy," he started, but she turned to her other two boys.

"The trip will take quite a few days, I imagine. Mr. Upkins, will you and Billy need another hand to see to the cattle while Mr. Snowden and I are away?"

"Nancy," Hank pressed.

Mr. Upkins and Billy exchanged glances, ignoring him, as well.

"Reckon we could use some of those youngsters Mr. Thorn and Mr. McKay have been teaching in their young rancher's program," the older hand mused. "They can ride herd with me during the day while Jenks does the night riding."

The younger cowboy nodded his agreement.

Hank took a step forward as if to make sure they couldn't overlook him this time. "I can't ask that of you two. And Nancy, I can't take you to Waco. It's too far by wagon."

She was not about to let him face his family alone. "You didn't ask anyone a favor, Hank. I did. Mr. Upkins and Billy have given you their answers. And as far as going by wagon, if that is impractical, we'll go by train."

Hank shook his head. "Train tickets cost money we can't spare."

Billy cleared his throat. "I've a little money put aside. You're welcome to it if it helps."

Hank stared at him, but warmth bubbled up inside Nancy, and she put a hand on the cowboy's thin shoulder. "That is very kind of you, Billy."

"But you don't need to do this," Hank insisted.

Billy ducked his head, but Nancy could still see that his skin was turning as red as his hair.

"My ma died when I was born," he murmured. "My pa, when I was ten. I've been riding from spread to spread ever since. I reckon you three are the closest thing I got to family. That's what families do—help each other."

Hank sagged as if he couldn't protest against that. Nancy squeezed Billy's shoulder. "That's exactly right. But I'll only take that money as a loan. I'll pay you back once the cattle are sold."

"*I'll* pay you back," Hank replied, looking from Billy to Mr. Upkins. "For everything. Thank you."

The veteran nodded, stepping back. "Well, those steers won't watch themselves. I best be riding."

"And I best get some shut-eye so I can ride to-night," Billy agreed.

Nancy released him. "Very well, but I expect you both at the house at six. I'm cooking dinner, and I won't take no for an answer."

Now even Mr. Upkins was reddening, but she thought it was from pleasure. They both tipped their hats to her before heading out.

"Are you sure you're up to this?" Hank asked as she turned for the house.

"I'll keep it simple," she promised. "There is some ham left in the larder, and I can easily add mashed potatoes, biscuits and peach preserves."

Hank caught her arm. "I wasn't talking about dinner. Are you certain you want to come to Waco? I told you a little about how it was between my father and me. With him ailing, it's not likely to be a pleasant reunion. I can't be sure what I'll walk into."

"Which is precisely why you will not walk into it alone," she informed him. "I agree with Billy. We are a family. We stick together, through thick and thin."

"For richer, for poorer, in sickness and in health," he murmured, releasing her.

She'd said those vows twice now, but never had she felt them more surely. "That's right. I mean to honor those commitments."

His smile inched into view. "Even the obey part?"

"Don't be absurd."

He laughed as she climbed the stairs for the house.

With Hank off to see to the horses, Nancy set to work inside. Bless Billy for keeping the wood box full. It was easy for her to stoke up the fire in the black iron stove. One of her boys must have been hunting earlier, for she found a brace of pigeons in the larder. She smiled thinking how they had to be from Mr. Upkins. Billy still couldn't bear to kill a helpless critter.

Her boys. Her family.

Her husband?

Hank had resisted her coming to Waco, but she felt the bonds knitting them together—concern for the ranch, preparations for the baby. Yet how could they become a true family if Hank couldn't overcome the wound his family had caused? Like her, most of the time he went on with life as if the past was forgotten, then something brought it to front of mind with sharp clarity. But people changed, learned, grew. Maybe Waco wouldn't be as bad as he thought. Either way, she intended to stand beside him.

Her boys started arriving a little before six. Billy came first, damp hair slicked back from his freckled face, plaster sticking to one cheek, where he must have cut himself shaving. He handed her a bunch of daisies, stems cracked here and there from his grip.

"To pretty up the table," he said. "Though I reckon it will be pretty enough with you sitting at it."

Nancy thanked him with a smile and pointed him to a chair. But he stood awkwardly beside it, shifting from foot to foot on his pointy-toed boots.

"It's all right, Billy," she assured him, going to put his flowers in a vase. "You can sit until the others arrive."

"Mr. Upkins says it ain't right to sit while a lady stands," he protested, hands gripping the back of the chair as if he defied anyone to force him into it.

"If the lady tells you to sit," Nancy countered with a look his way, "you sit."

He yanked out the chair and plunked himself down onto it.

Mr. Upkins was next. Once more he had donned the black coat and trousers he'd worn when he'd walked her down the aisle.

"Mrs. Snowden," he greeted her, taking her hand and bowing over it like a courtier of old. "Right honored to be invited to your table." He frowned at Billy as he straightened, and the youth popped to his feet once more, standing at attention as if he'd been conscripted into the army.

"Please," Nancy said, "sit down, both of you. I'll just bring out the rest of the food. I'm sure Mr. Snowden will be here shortly."

She turned for the stove to find Mr. Upkins there ahead of her. "Now, you just set down and rest a spell," he insisted. "I know my way around a stove. I'll have everything on the table quick as a wink."

Faced with his determination, Nancy could only thank him and go to sit, while Billy went back to shifting from foot to foot.

Mr. Upkins had the pigeon pie, ham, biscuits and potatoes on the table and had taken a seat across from the trembling Billy when boots thudded up the back steps. Hank paused in the doorway as if to take in the tableau. He too had a clean-shaven jaw and damp hair, but the black locks were curling around his face as they dried. He kicked the dirt off his boots before entering, then nodded a greeting to his friends.

Taking his seat beside Nancy, he clasped his hands

and bowed his head. Nancy saw Mr. Upkins and Billy follow suit before doing so herself.

"Dear Lord," Hank prayed. "You sure are generous. Around this table, You've given us good friends, good food. I want You to know we're thankful, and I for one won't be taking it for granted. The Good Book says You own the cattle on a thousand hills. Thanks for sharing some with us. Amen."

"Amen," Nancy murmured along with Mr. Upkins. She raised her head to find Billy staring at Hank.

"God owns cattle?" he asked, wide-eyed.

Hank tucked his napkin under his chin. "That's what it says in the Bible. Pastor Stillwater read it to us a few weeks back."

Billy grinned as he glanced around at them all. "Why, then, that means Jesus must be a cowboy!"

Nancy pressed her lips together to keep from laughing.

Mr. Upkins went so far as to point his fork at the youth. "Now, then, don't you go putting on airs."

Billy shook his head. "No, sir. But it does set a body to thinking."

Yes, it did, though at the moment Nancy's thoughts were more focused on the man who sat next to her and what he would find once they reached Waco.

They left three days later, after Hank had had time to tell Edmund and CJ about what he'd learned in Burnet. The other ranchers agreed to help Upkins and Jenks while Hank and Nancy were gone.

"And tell Nancy she was right about Molly," CJ said to Hank as he was getting ready to ride back to the Windy Diamond. The rancher's lean face broke into a grin. "Looks like the twins are going to have a baby brother or sister in a few months."

"Congratulations," Hank said, clapping him on the back. "I can see our Ben and your young'uns growing up together."

"More recruits for the Young Ranchers," Edmund agreed with a smile.

Hank was smiling too as he set off for the ranch. The next generation of Little Horn was rising up all around. He'd never seen CJ so happy. He knew the feeling. He could hardly wait to be a pa.

But just the idea of fatherhood sobered him. He and his father had never managed to come to terms. He'd meant what he'd said to Nancy—he didn't know what he'd face in Waco.

Still, he knew what he wanted here in Little Horn—a home, a family, friends and neighbors who looked out for one another. More, he wanted a chance with Nancy to make a real marriage.

And that meant he had to tell her the truth about his role in Lucas's death, even though telling her could cost him everything.

It was that thought, more than the reunion with his father, that set his stomach to churning as he waited with Nancy on the platform for the train to arrive. She was dressed in blue skirts with white piping running down the panels like icing, a white bodice gathered high at her throat and a darker blue cape over the top. He could feel her bouncing on the toes of her boots as she glanced down the track.

"Nervous?" he asked.

She shot him a grin. "More like excited."

He willed her attitude to flow over him. Better

excitement than dread. "My first time on a train," he acknowledged. "You too?"

She shook her head. "I rode on one on the way from Missouri, but my father introduced me to them when I was a child. He worked for a time as a dispatcher for the Frisco Line out of Springfield. Steam engines fascinated him. He said riding in them was the closest we'd ever get to flying."

Hank wasn't so sure. He could see the smoke belching out of the stack as the massive black engine rumbled into view. The platform at his feet trembled. He clapped his hands over his ears as the train roared to a stop. The whole thing looked mighty earthbound to him.

The conductor, a tall fellow with a neat brown cap and bushy white mustache, made them wait while passengers filed off and collected luggage, townsfolk came to unload freight and Nancy and Hank's bags were stowed. Every moment that passed he felt his nerves tightening. He was jumpy as a herd of cattle on a stormy night, ready for the least sound to set them stampeding. Only he had nowhere to run.

"All aboard!" the conductor called, deep voice cutting through the hiss of steam. "All aboard for Waco and points north!"

Nancy seized Hank's hand and dragged him onto the train.

He had to own the inside was impressive, with walls paneled in fine wood and high-backed benches covered in green velvet upholstery. Nancy chose two seats opposite each other. His seat even gave a bit as he dropped onto it, and he bounced experimentally.

"Isn't it grand?" Nancy asked, eyes shining.

It was grand, until the train's horn blared. He nearly jumped out of his seat. Then, he had to grab hold of the armrest to keep from falling over as the car jerked into motion.

Nancy was looking out the window, waving at some of the folks on the platform. "Here we go!"

He realized his fingers were digging into the seat and forced his hands to relax. "Bit unsteady," he remarked.

"You wait until we get up to full steam," she promised, turning to face him and settling back in her seat. "It will go as fast as a galloping horse, for hours."

Hank drew in a breath and nodded. He knew the feel of his horse beneath him—warm, sure, alive. He trusted her to respond as he ordered, to any situation. She'd carried him through rainstorms and stampedes alike. The train rocked and clanked and spewed out black smoke, and he had no faith he could command it or tell it where to go.

The conductor came around, even though Hank could not understand how the man remained upright much less looked so calm and cool as he inspected and punched Nancy's ticket.

"How long until we reach Waco?" she asked him as he returned it.

"About three hours, ma'am," he replied with a nod. He took Hank's ticket and peered down at it a moment with a scowl before punching it and handing it back. Hank wasn't sure if the conductor thought there was something wrong with the ticket or with him.

Nancy settled her skirts about her. "There you are. Only three hours to travel more than a hundred miles. Isn't that amazing?"

Hank closed his eyes. Three hours? Already he wanted out of the confining car. "Sounds good," he said for her sake.

"Hank?"

He opened his eyes to find her regarding him with a frown. Meeting his gaze, her look softened.

"It will be all right," she promised. "Your father asked for you to come. He wants to see you."

She'd mistaken his concerns, but he couldn't help a laugh at her assumption about his father. The laugh sounded hollow even to him.

"He likely asked me to come to tell me one last time what a disappointment I am," he replied.

"He's dying," Nancy protested. "Surely he wants to make peace."

Hank shook his head. "Pa's not the peaceful type. His parents died when he was young. He started riding when he was about nine."

"So young?" She glanced down at the baby as if she couldn't imagine that for her own child.

"I'm not sure Pa was ever really a boy. He was more determined than any man I ever met. He had a dream of owning his own spread, of being beholden to no one. He never stopped until he had achieved that dream. And, then, all he could think about was having everything be the best—his cattle, his horses, his hands and his family."

"Surely your mother had something to say about the family," Nancy said.

"My mother has a way of making her opinions known," Hank answered, remembering. "But make no mistake, Nancy. I may be going home after a long time far away, but I'm not expecting anyone to kill the fatted calf."

She reached out and touched his hand. "Whatever happens, we'll weather it together."

Her kindness only made it harder for him to make his confession. He pulled back, swallowed, determined to get it over with. "Nancy, there's something I have to tell you."

She nodded, encouraging. "I'm listening."

He felt as if each word was being yanked from his heart. "It's about the day Lucas was shot."

Her lips tightened, and she folded her hands over the baby. "Must we talk about that again?"

He didn't like it any more than she did. "Sorry. I know it's not a pleasant subject. But yes, it's important we talk about it again. Did Sheriff Fuller explain that Lucas drew on us?"

She nodded, face puckering. "Yes. I don't know what he was thinking. Why would he threaten his friends?"

Hank had wondered the same thing. "Likely he was scared, not thinking straight. I wasn't thinking straight myself. Here was my boss, the man who had made me part of Little Horn, who had given me a place in the league, pointing a gun at me."

"It must have been dreadful," she commiserated.

"What came next was worse," Hank told her, feeling sweat starting on his brow. "I'd already figured it was my fault the cattle had been stolen. I'd told Lucas all about the patrols. He knew just how to avoid them. Now here he was threatening to shoot my friend McKay. I couldn't let that happen."

He swallowed and met Nancy's gaze, which was

growing darker with each word. "I drew and shot him, Nancy."

She shook her head. "No, the sheriff shot him."

"Jeb Fuller shot at the same time," Hank told her. "Not one of us was even sure which bullet had hit Lucas. But I had to know. I rode down into the canyon later and checked. I pulled a rifle bullet out of a fence post. My bullet went into Lucas."

Her face was twisting, and he hurried on before she could protest further. "I only meant to wound him, make him drop the gun, but he must have moved at the last moment and stepped straight into the path of the bullet."

The peaches in her cheeks were fading away. "That can't be right. You wouldn't hurt anyone."

"I didn't want to," Hank assured her. "But I'm afraid it's my fault you're a widow, Nancy. I killed your husband."

Chapter Fifteen

Nancy felt as if all the air had left the train car in a whoosh. With it went sound and sensation. She couldn't move, couldn't think beyond one simple, horrible fact.

Hank had killed Lucas.

"No," she said. "No. Not you. I won't believe it."

His blue eyes were dark and heavy, his face sagging. Pain radiated out of him like heat from a stove. "I'm telling the truth, Nancy. I should have confessed weeks ago, but I couldn't find the right time or place."

There was no right time or place to tell her what made no sense. How could Hank—loyal, steady, helpful Hank—have killed anyone, let alone Lucas?

"But he befriended you," she protested. "His hospitality was one of the good things you said we should remember. You told me you were honored by his trust."

His hands were fisting so tightly on his knees she thought his rough nails might be gouging into his palms.

"It was an honor to be entrusted with membership

in the league," he said. "I finally started feeling like a man again, working beside Thorn and McKay to make Little Horn a better place."

"And it is a better place," she reminded him. "We have a church for worship. The Carsons have a barn. I just don't understand why Lucas had to die."

His sigh sounded as if it had been ripped from his heart. "I don't know that he had to die. I couldn't believe at first that he was the one causing all the trouble. He had everything! A ranch of his own, friends, you. How could he possibly be the rustler stealing everyone's cattle?"

She felt as if his bewilderment had reached across the space and grabbed her by the hand. "I've asked myself that so many times. But now we know. He wanted the money because he was gambling. And he started gambling because he was disappointed about not being invited home to Alabama."

He rubbed a hand down his face as if he could wipe away his emotions. "Now we know. Then, all I saw was a gun pointing at a good man. I couldn't let him be shot, especially not when it was my fault McKay and the sheriff were there to begin with."

She struggled to see a killer sitting across from her, but all she saw was a penitent, someone trying desperately to make amends, to atone.

Nancy gasped, and his head snapped up.

"That's why you're working so hard to find his accomplice," she accused him. "You're trying to make up for the fact that you shot Lucas."

He winced as if he didn't like anyone else saying the truth aloud. "I can never make up for taking a man's life. I'm just trying to do right by all those affected."

All those affected—CJ, Edmund, the Carsons. Her.

Her breath hurt in her lungs. "So, you married me to atone? You don't care anything about me or baby Ben."

He stiffened. "That's not true. I married you because I care about you and the baby."

At the moment, she didn't know what to think.

"Next stop, Temple," the conductor called, moving through the car. "Connection to the Waco and Northwestern Railway, transfer for Houston, Galveston and points east."

Nancy struggled to her feet. Hank reached out a hand to help her, and she shook it off. "I need some air."

He did not move to stop her as she turned and hurried down the car.

The other passengers must have assumed she intended to get off at Temple, for only a few looked at her askance as she passed. Many were preparing to disembark themselves. As the train slowed, clanked to a halt, let off a blast of steam, she followed them out onto the platform. The air felt cold on her cheeks, and she reached up a hand to find that tears were tracking down her face.

I've cried enough for Lucas, Father. Now am I crying for Hank?

People jostled her as they passed, murmuring apologies. Wives were waiting for husbands who had traveled to points west. Children greeted mothers who had returned. She felt as if there was a bubble insulating her from them and them from her.

She was alone.

Hank had killed Lucas.

Father, I don't understand. Is he not the man I thought him? Have I been blind again?

Memories drifted into her mind, each a clear picture from the last few weeks. Hank riding down the longhorn to keep it safe in the herd. Mr. Upkins deferring to his judgment above anyone else's. Billy gazing up at him, trusting him to guide. CJ and Edmund standing in conversation with him, listening to his advice. The smile of pride on Hank's face when he'd offered her as someone who could help Betsy McKay.

This man she'd married was no murderer.

"All aboard!" the conductor called. "All aboard for Waco!"

She glanced back. Hank was gazing out the window at her, face haunted. He wasn't sure of her, doubted he'd done the right thing in telling her. He could have kept the matter to himself, rationalized that he was protecting her. She would never have known the truth.

Now the truth was looking her in the eye. Hank had ever put her needs before his own. He had walked each step beside her. He was a man she could trust, a man she could believe in.

She was sure of that even if she was sure of nothing else at the moment.

"Ma'am?" the conductor asked, stopping beside her with a frown. "Your ticket said Waco. Are you stopping at Temple instead?"

Nancy shook her head. "No, thank you. Forgive me for keeping you waiting." She hurried to board the train.

Hank watched her come up the aisle and take her seat across from him.

"I wasn't sure you were coming back," he said.

"I wasn't sure either," she told him. "But I needed to come back. And you needed me to come back."

He blew out a breath. "That's true enough. Nancy, tell me what to do. I don't know how to make this right."

And that was so very important to him. She could not deny him.

"That day, you were faced with an impossible choice," she murmured, fingers tightening in the soft blue fabric of her skirts as the train started out of the station. "I don't know what I would have done if I had been in your place. Probably stood and stared in disbelief."

"I just drew and fired." He squeezed shut his eyes a moment as if to block out the memory. "I've lived through the moment over and over. What if I'd aimed lower? Higher? What if I'd let Sheriff Fuller talk to him, calm him down? Would he be alive today? I don't know, Nancy. I don't know."

In that one act, she'd lost a husband and little Ben had lost a father. She ought to be angry with Hank for keeping the truth from her, denounce him for a killer. But she didn't feel angry, and her confusion, for the first time in months, was fading in the face of certainty.

Because in that moment, she realized, Hank had lost something almost as precious to him—his sense of honor.

She reached out and took his hand, feeling his fingers cold against hers, as if all the blood had drained from him along with his hope.

"Lucas made his choices," she said. "He decided to steal from people who had only ever shown him kindness and friendship. He risked the ranch he'd worked so hard to build, the future of his wife and child. He threatened the lives of those who came seeking the truth."

Hank's gaze was on her fingers entwined with his. "That doesn't change the fact that he's dead, and I killed him."

She edged out on the seat, putting herself closer to him, wanting to feel his heart beating, willing the warmth back into him.

"After doing so much damage, to himself and those who cared for him," she said, "what do you think he would have done if you hadn't stopped him?"

"I wonder," he murmured.

She knew. "He would have shot. Edmund or Sheriff Fuller or you could be dead. Their families would be grieving now. Lula May could still be a widow, with no hope of marrying the man she was coming to love. Stella Fuller would be struggling to raise her little brother alone."

"It might have been better if he shot me," Hank said. "You'd still have a husband."

"I have a husband," Nancy told him. "And I couldn't ask for a better one."

His head jerked up, and he searched her face as if afraid of what he might see there.

"Lucas made his choices," she repeated, holding that brilliant blue gaze as she held his hand. "You chose to stop him. I choose to live for the future."

He cocked his head, dark hair spilling over his brow. "You still willing to live that future with me, after what I told you?"

Never had she felt so sure of herself. Nancy reached up and brushed back the silky locks. "You are the future, Hank. Thank you for telling me the truth. It proves to me that this time I married the right man."

He pulled her the rest of the way onto his seat, held her close, murmured her name like a prayer. And she knew from that moment that things would be different.

She murmured a prayer of her own that this time, things would be better.

He finally appreciated what her father had said about trains and flying. He felt as if he'd been lifted right up through the roof of the train car and into the sky. The world looked brighter, smelled cleaner. This was grace—forgiveness where none was warranted.

"I'll never let you down," he promised. "Every day I'll work to be the best for you." He pulled back to look into her dear face. Those peaches he loved had returned to her cheeks. Those hazel eyes held his gaze with a tenderness that rocked him harder than the train.

She shook her head. "Please don't say such things. You told me how you felt when you were bound by your father's expectations. I don't want you to feel that way about me."

"This is different," he started, but she pressed a finger to his lips.

"Perhaps. But it seems Lucas had a similar problem. His father sent him West to mature, and he convinced his father he was his own man so thoroughly his father insisted he stay where he'd grown. That's not what he wanted. That's why he started gambling."

Another reason Hank would never understand his former boss. Lucas had seen the Windy Diamond as a prison rather than an opportunity to blaze his own path.

Hank pulled back from Nancy's touch. "I don't know why his father's orders made Lucas decide to throw away everything he should have protected. Maybe he never lived up to his own expectations. Maybe he woke up one morning and didn't like the feller he saw in the mirror."

He took both her hands, held them in his. "All I know is, ever since I started working with you on the Windy Diamond, I like the feller looking back at me from my mirror. The only shadow on the image has been the secret of how Lucas died."

Her smile was soft, as welcome as a breeze on a hot day. "Just don't keep things from me again, Hank. I can't bear secrets and lies. They tear at your heart, your beliefs." She dropped her gaze. "They make you start to question yourself."

And she'd done that, he realized. Discovering her husband's hidden life had made her question everything she knew. He was only glad she had decided to trust him.

He drew in a breath. "Never again. I promise." He managed a chuckle. "Until recently, my life wasn't nearly exciting enough to have something worth keeping secret."

He could see her smile deepening. "Mine either."

He touched her cheek, savoring the warmth, the softness. She raised her gaze to his, eyes wide.

"I don't deserve your forgiveness," he murmured. "But I cannot thank you enough for offering it. You've given me back my life."

She dropped her gaze again, gave his hands a little swing. "We both have an opportunity for a new life. You and me and Ben."

He pulled her close again, rested his chin against the satin of her hair. Like his tangled fears, the land outside straightened out, the plains flat in all directions. The sky above seemed to go on forever. So did his hopes. Even the rocking ride of the train seemed gentler, smoother.

"How much farther to Waco?" she murmured against his chest.

He chuckled again. "You suddenly in a hurry to get there? I thought you liked trains."

She started to yawn, then quickly covered her mouth with her hand. "I do like trains. But I'm ready for us to climb the next mountain."

She sure was brave. Most people would think twice before going up against Henry Snowden senior. Yet he knew how she felt. He wanted to ride across those plains, dive into a creek, build a barn, knowing he was finally free.

"Put your head on my shoulder," he said, "and rest awhile. I'll wake you when we get closer."

With a grateful smile, she leaned against him.

All he could do was gaze down at her. With her nestled against him, he could see only the shine of her brown hair, the freckles that had made her so aghast. He felt her sigh as she drifted off.

A wave of tenderness rolled over him.

You've given me a chance, Lord. I won't let You or her down.

He waited for the familiar feeling of frustration for a burden he was afraid he couldn't carry. It didn't come. He'd worked his whole life to fend off expectations that choked and bound. He'd told her this time was different, and he knew why. He had tried to meet his father's expectations out of duty. He would meet Nancy's out of love.

Love. He wanted to gather her even closer, protect her from all harm, help her reach her dream of running a successful ranch. He hadn't asked for love, hadn't thought it possible, yet now he felt it growing inside him, binding her to his heart.

Maybe it was their shared work. Maybe he just felt so good that nothing lay between them anymore with the confession about Lucas's death. But he felt as if hope was pushing the train across the ground for Waco. He could only pray it would follow them out to the family ranch and through the next few days.

They reached Waco an hour later. The church bells were tolling noon as Hank escorted Nancy off the train onto the packed dirt that surrounded the station. She gazed about, neck craning to look up at the tower that was the center of the Waco train station. What would she do when she saw the multistoried buildings in town? The famous Waco Suspension Bridge the townsfolk had built to span the Brazos River?

He'd planned to hire a wagon at the livery stable and drive out to the ranch, but they had barely collected their bags and turned from the train before a big man in a Stetson pushed his way forward through the crowd.

"Well, I'll be. Hank Snowden." He seized Hank's hand and pumped it up and down. "You are a sight for sore eyes."

Hank stared at him. Matching him in height, the burly man had russet hair peeking out from under that dun-colored hat and an impressive mustache a shade darker than his hair. But it was those green eyes, always twinkling, as if he knew something the rest of the world had missed, that Hank remembered most. "Red?"

"Sure enough," he said, smile so wide it stretched the curl of his mustache. "I can understand why you didn't recognize me straightaway. Your sister's cooking has made a new man of me, or should I say two men?"

Laughing at his own joke, he released Hank's hand and whipped the hat from his head to beam at Nancy. "And this must be Mrs. Snowden. I'm your brother-in-law, Rufus Winslow. They call me Red. Welcome to Waco."

Nancy nodded her thanks, then cast Hank a look of pure confusion around the man. Hank knew how she felt.

"You in town for supplies?" Hank asked, taking Nancy's arm and directing her around the building for the street that pointed toward the town square across the river.

"No, sir," Red declared, pacing them. "I came to meet you at the train. Got a buggy waiting with room for you and your luggage."

Hank frowned. "I don't understand. I didn't have time to write and tell you we were coming."

Red grinned at him. "You didn't have to write. We knew you'd come. One of us has been meeting the northbound train every day since your mama mailed that letter."

Nancy's smile popped into view as she cast Hank a glance. "See? Your family knows you care."

"Yes, ma'am," Red assured her. "Besides, few folks ever say no to a Snowden. Henry and his wife are famous in these parts. But Hank probably told you all about that."

Nancy raised her brows at Hank. He'd told her a little about his family, and he'd hoped to go into more detail on the ride out to the ranch. As usual, his family had had other plans, and it was up to him to make sure Nancy wasn't hurt by them.

Chapter Sixteen

❧

Nancy stayed close to Hank as Red led them to a waiting buggy. The open carriage had two sets of seats and a black leather top, and it was painted a jaunty green. A young man with hair the color of Red's sat behind the reins, dividing his attention between the fretting team and the ladies who were passing. When he looked toward the station, he immediately straightened.

"Scoot over, Tom," Red ordered. "And say hello to your aunt and uncle."

Hank grinned up at the lad. "You're probably tired of hearing this, but you sure have grown."

"I'm as tall as Pa now," Tom bragged, sliding over on the seat to make room for his father.

"But not nearly as wide," Red joked. "Sometimes I think that boy has a hollow leg. All the food he eats has to be going somewhere." He held out his hand to Nancy. "I'll take your bag, ma'am."

Nancy smiled her thanks as she offered him her carpet bag. He went to stow it and Hank's bag at the rear of the buggy.

Hank took her elbow and helped her up onto the back seat, then went around to jump up beside her.

Tom twisted to look at them, hands gripping the padded leather of the seat back. "I'm sure glad you're here, Uncle Hank. I've been wanting to talk to you on account of you being famous."

Nancy eyed Hank, and he grinned, leaning back in the seat and crossing his hands behind his head. "Sure, I'm famous. I reckon I hold the record for the Texan cowhand who can sleep in latest most often."

Nancy pressed her lips together to keep from laughing.

Tom frowned. "But Grandpa says you're a gunslinger and an outlaw. Don't you have any notches on your belt?"

Nancy felt Hank stiffen, but he merely shook his head as he lowered his arms. "Sorry to disappoint you, Tommy, but I'm just a cowboy. Mostly, I use my six-guns to scare off rattlers."

The boy's face fell.

"But he's more than a hand," Nancy felt compelled to put in. "He runs our ranch, the Windy Diamond. We have nearly two hundred head of cattle."

"Nancy," Hank murmured gently, but she heard the warning in his voice.

"Must be nice having a little place like that," Tom said wistfully. "Pa won't even let me ride to the other side of our ranch."

"That's because it would put you in another county," Red teased. He climbed up into the driver's seat, and the whole buggy tilted with his weight. Nancy slid against Hank, who put an arm around her to steady her.

"Gee-up!" Red called to his team, and the horses

obligingly headed away from the station. Hank bent closer. Over the rattle of tack, Nancy could hear his murmur.

"Cattlemen don't talk about the size of their herd," he said. "It's like bragging about the amount of money you have in the bank. And, as you can probably tell, someone in my family always has more."

She could almost believe that as the buggy rolled toward Waco proper. The train station was actually across the Brazos from the town, and Nancy couldn't help gawking at the graceful suspension bridge that spanned the muddy waters.

"The whole town banded together and built the thing a few years back," Red told them as the wheels rumbled over the wooden slats. He directed the horses up the street to the town square, where a majestic county courthouse, looking like a Grecian temple as Hank had said, stood surrounded by trees. They passed any number of shops, and hotels as tall as three stories with clock towers on one end.

And everywhere she looked, she saw the name of Snowden.

There was the Snowden civic auditorium, the Snowden Conservatory for the Performing Arts and Harriett Snowden Park. Even Hank's mother, it seemed, had something named after her.

"Your family must have invested in the community," she commented as the horses pulled the buggy to the north and east of town.

Red barked a laugh. "That's a nice way of putting it. Henry Snowden likes to control things. You pay for something that needs building, and folks tend to listen to how you want it done."

She glanced at Hank, who shrugged. "I'd be the first to admit Pa likes things just so." He leaned forward to speak to his brother-in-law. "How's he doing, Red? Ma said he might not have much time left."

Red shook his head, gaze on the fields of cotton on either side of the road. White tufts bobbed in the breeze over dusky green plants, and she could see workers bent over, picking.

"He has good days and bad," Red admitted. "But you know your Pa. He's not likely to let the Lord take him until he's good and ready."

Nancy found that hard to believe. Certainly her father and mother had had no choice as to when they left this earth. Even Hank's powerful father had to bow his will to the Master's.

But as they left the cotton fields behind, she began to appreciate what Hank's father had built. It took them nearly an hour to reach the ranch house, the last half hour after passing through the iron gates of the Double H. The land was flatter here. Nancy saw none of the draws or limestone lifts common around Little Horn. Instead, the land was either cultivated with corn and hay or left to tall grasses where cattle grazed. The air smelled crisp, clean. Everything seemed organized, peaceful. She had a hard time imagining Hank here.

As they drew closer to the center of the ranch, she saw that the layout was as well planned. The storage buildings were massive—barns with haylofts, two on either side of the road and open-air sheds that held plows and wagons. The house was just as grand. A single story, the center block was of stone, red marbled with white, while a wing in planks painted red led in either direction off a wide front porch. Red drew the buggy up in front, then climbed down along with Tom, who ran to hold the horses.

Hank got out of the buggy more slowly. Nancy could see him eyeing the house a moment before he came around to help her.

"Has it changed much since you left?" she asked.

He glanced at the house again. "It hasn't changed at all that I can see. Same flower boxes under the windows, red and white geraniums. Same blue rug on the porch. I'm just hoping not all the changes were in me."

Nancy hoped so too, for his sake as well as his family's.

The sound of the buggy must have alerted the house, for people began spilling out onto the porch. First came three boys, between six and eight, she guessed, their eyes wide and spirits high, black hair tumbling onto their foreheads. Next came a tall lady dressed in purple, hair piled up behind her and face serene. Tom wasn't too grown-up to wave at her, so Nancy assumed she must be his mother. Behind her was a blonde beauty who had one hand gripping that of a toddler who walked with halting steps. She put her free hand to her back as if struggling with her advanced stage of pregnancy.

Finally, a woman whose black hair was turning a shining silver came out onto the porch. At the sight of Hank, she steepled her fingers and pressed them to her lips as if whispering a prayer of thanks.

"Came on the noon train, just like you predicted, Mother Snowden," Red said, pulling Nancy's bag from the back of the buggy. "And with his blushing bride beside him." His expansive wave took in Nancy and Hank.

"Henry," his mother said. Were those tears glistening in the blue eyes the exact shade of her son's? "I've been praying for this day ever since you left."

Still Hank didn't move from beside Nancy. She thought he might be holding his breath.

"Go on," she whispered. "Greet your mother."

He drew in a breath and nodded, then squeezed Nancy's hand. "Thank you." Raising his head and his voice, he spoke to the group. "It's good to be here. I want you all to meet the lady who made Little Horn feel like home—my wife, Nancy."

That took the focus off him. His nephews bounded down the steps to surround him and Nancy, peppering her with questions. Judith came more slowly. She was the only one in the family, Hank thought, who had ever earned Pa's approval. Pretty and proper, she'd married the fellow Pa had picked out for her, the irrepressible Red, who owned a spread to the south. Even though the two had had a rough start, they seemed to be devoted now. Hank could see that in the way the big man approached his regal wife, slipping an arm around her slim waist and murmuring something in her ear. Judith glowed.

"Boys! Boys!" Missy called from the porch. "You'll scare the poor thing out of her wits before she even has a chance to learn your names."

Her sons ignored her, as usual. Though she'd married young and to a former hand to their parents' dismay, Missy had done the one thing guaranteed to please his father—given him a passel of grandsons. It looked as if another was on the way. The closest sister to him in age, she grinned at him as if completely unapologetic for her unruly brood.

"This is Clovis," Hank told Nancy, trying to match the talkative boys to the shy toddlers he'd left behind. "This is Daniel. And this must be Buford."

One of the smaller boys shoved himself forward. "No, I'm Buford, and that's Clovis."

Clovis must have been eating his greens, for he was already a head taller than his older brother. He offered Hank a gap-toothed grin as if he knew it.

"Very pleased to make your acquaintances," Nancy said with a smile.

"Who's that gonna be?" Buford demanded, pointing at Nancy's belly.

"Boys!" Missy handed her toddler to Judith and navigated the stairs surprisingly fast. "Go fetch your pa and tell him Uncle Hank is here."

The three boys obligingly ran off toward the closest barn.

"Sorry about that," Missy said, rubbing her side. "They've grown used to seeing me like this, so they know what's going to happen."

"Nancy," Hank said, hiding his grin at his sister's honesty, "this is my sister Matilda."

Immediately his sister elbowed him. "Missy, you scoundrel. You know I hate Matilda."

"We all change as we mature," Hank said, careful to sound appropriately pious.

She laughed. "Oh, I doubt you've changed all that much. You still came running when Mother called."

He glanced up at the porch, where his mother waited in the shadows of the overhang. Now in her sixties, Harriett Snowden stood with hair perfectly arranged, lavender-colored dress with its lace at the throat looking as if she was ready to take tea rather than run a ranch.

Judith looked nearly as composed as she glided up to them, Missy's youngest in her arms. "Henry, welcome home."

"Nancy, this is my oldest sister, Judith," Hank offered.

Missy chortled. "*Oldest* sister. I like that."

Something flickered behind Judith's blue eyes, a shade lighter than his. Was she vain about her age? He very much doubted anyone looking at her lovely face and willowy frame would suspect she was ten years his senior or the mother of a fourteen-year-old boy.

"I'm very glad to meet you," she told Nancy, ignoring her sister. "Congratulations on your marriage to my brother. I only wish I'd known sooner so I could send you a card and gift."

She glanced at Hank again, and he knew he was supposed to beg her pardon, call himself lazy or ignorant. But he was not about to slip back into old habits and apologize for every little thing just because he was back at the Double H.

"No gift necessary," he assured his sister. "I'm the one who was given the greatest gift when Nancy agreed to be my bride."

Nancy blushed, but Missy sighed. "That's so romantic."

Judith's smile was more contained. "Indeed it is. Don't let me keep you. We'll have time to talk later. You should go to Mother."

Again, Hank glanced to the porch in time to see his mother extend her hand.

"Henry," she called. "Introduce me to my new daughter-in-law."

A command from the queen was never to be disobeyed. Both his mother's demeanor and his father's strict discipline had drummed that into them all. Still, he hesitated. What was he going to say to her?

Missy arched a brow. "Well, go on. You know she isn't going to holler. That's simply not ladylike."

And his mother never did anything that wasn't completely appropriate and proper.

Nancy slipped her hand into his and gave it a squeeze. Certainty flowed from her touch into his heart. Raising his head, he escorted her to the steps and up to his mother.

The two women eyed one another a moment. He'd seen similar looks between steers, sizing each other up, wondering who'd give way first. Under different circumstances, he could imagine them pawing the ground and snorting, ready to defend all they held dear.

After all, this was his mother's castle. She'd never ceded her place to any of her three daughters. She wasn't about to bow down to a newcomer.

But if he'd had to stake his life on someone, it would have been Nancy.

She was the first to smile. "Mrs. Snowden. It's a pleasure to meet you."

"Mrs. Snowden," his mother returned, then she raised her feathery brows. "My, how odd that sounds. May I call you Nancy?"

"Please," Nancy insisted. "And what shall I call you?"

His mother's precise smile appeared, the one she reserved for moments of command. "Why, Mother Snowden, dear. I've always been rather proud of my last name, unlike some."

It hadn't taken long for the claws to come out. "I never lost pride in the Snowden name, Mother," Hank told her. "I just lost faith in my ability to live up to it."

His mother softened. "I never had any doubts."

A shame he didn't believe that.

She glanced to where Missy was moving back up the steps, Judith patiently behind her. "Girls, why don't you get your boys cleaned up for dinner? Take Nancy with you. I'd like a moment alone with Henry." She smiled at Nancy. "I'm sure you don't mind, dear."

Nancy glanced at Hank, and he could see the uncertainty in her gaze. She was concerned about him, but he was not about to leave her to his sisters' not-so-tender mercies until he knew she felt comfortable. He threaded her fingers with his.

"Nancy and I tend to stick together," he told his mother. "I'm sure you understand."

His mother's mouth quirked, but she was too polite to put up a fuss in front of his sisters. "Certainly. This way."

"Good luck," Missy called before heading down the porch with Judith.

Hank led Nancy into the house. It too looked exactly as he remembered it. From the beginning, his father had planned for a large family. The wide hallways opened onto a central parlor, where a stone fireplace big enough to roast an ox took up one of the walls. From the polished wood floor to the open beams in the ceiling, the room spoke of space to live, to grow. He'd simply grown beyond it.

His mother went to perch on the settee his father had brought from back East for her. The camelback piece with its rose-colored brocade still looked out of place in a Texas ranch house, though the six dun leather-covered chairs surrounding it seemed more at home. She gazed pointedly at the space beside her, but Hank escorted Nancy to the chair opposite before sitting on the one next to his wife's.

"I wasn't sure you'd come," his mother said.

"Oh, I think you were," Hank replied. "Red was waiting at the station. Missy and her family are here to greet us."

"Missy and her family are always here," his mother said, and she didn't sound all that pleased about the fact. "She and Ernesto moved in when your father fell ill."

If his father had accepted that much help, something was seriously wrong. Hank leaned forward. "How is he?"

His mother spread her hands, dropping her gaze to the lavender of her lap. "Doing as well as might be expected."

The answer was as vague as Red's, and his frustration inched upward.

"What does the doctor think is wrong?" he pressed. "You didn't say in your letter."

"That's because she doesn't like to think about it."

The gruff voice behind him set Hank's hair rising on the back of his neck. Climbing to his feet and turning, he saw his father leaning in the doorway to the east wing.

Here the changes he'd been seeking were at last evident. His father had always been a big man, powerful shoulders, strong legs. Now his blue shirt and denim trousers hung on him, and his shoulders sagged in the black leather vest. A face made rugged by forty years of riding looked gray, lined. Hank could see his father's chest heave with each labored breath. Their gazes locked.

"If you're expecting your inheritance soon," his father said, gray eyes hard as steel, "get used to disappointment. I intend to outlive you all, and I don't need your pity. So you can take that woman with another man's child in her belly and get out now."

Chapter Seventeen

Nancy's hands were shaking at the insult Hank's father had just uttered. She'd always been taught to be respectful to her elders, to speak when spoken to. Those rules had held her bound in the past. But Hank wasn't the only one who'd grown through adversity.

She surged to her feet and faced his father. "Don't talk to Hank that way! He married me precisely because he knew I was pregnant and alone, my first husband dead. He was there when I needed him, and he came here because he thought you needed him. He never asked for your money, and he certainly doesn't deserve your contempt."

As if in agreement, Ben squirmed inside her.

The others were staring at her, but she refused to quail. All they saw was the past. She saw the man Hank had become, and she was proud of him.

"Well," his father drawled, "at least she has spunk."

Hank took a step closer, his smile all for her. "That's just one of the things I admire about her."

Nancy blushed under his regard, but his father

limped into the room and sank onto the settee beside his wife.

"Sit down," he ordered Hank and Nancy. "No need for me to crick my neck having this conversation."

She wasn't sure she even wanted to talk to him. The gray tones to his skin, the sag of his mouth told her he was indeed gravely ill, but she didn't think his illness was the only reason he didn't resemble Hank. Hank had a buoyant spirit about him, rebounding from any trouble. His father seemed to have welcomed trouble more than he welcomed his son.

Still, Hank had come here for his father. So long as that discussion was civil, she should encourage it. She returned to her chair, and, after a moment, so did Hank.

"So you came to help, did you?" his father asked, gray eyes watchful. "I have plenty of hands, and your sister's husband is doing his best to confound and confuse them. What can you do?"

"I didn't come here looking for work," Hank answered. "Nancy and I have a spread outside Little Horn. Nothing as big as this, but it keeps us plenty busy. I came because Mother said you were sick."

His father shook his head. "Vultures always gather around carrion."

Nancy felt her temper rising again, but Hank's mother intervened this time.

"I asked Henry to come," she told her husband, laying her hand over his. "He was kind enough to accept my invitation. Please leave it at that."

As if certain her husband would comply, she turned to Hank. "You'll stay here, of course. I have a room made up for you. Find Missy and ask her to

show you the way. I'm sure you'll want to change before dinner. Shall we meet in the dining room at six?"

Nancy was beginning to realize that when Mother
Snowden phrased things as questions, they were just
as much orders as her husband's commands. Indeed,
even Hank didn't argue.

"Thank you, Mother." He rose and held out his
hand to Nancy, who took it to rise. For a moment,
their gazes locked, and she thought she saw thanks
written in the expanse of blue.

Unfortunately, she had another concern.

"One room?" she whispered as they left the parlor and headed out onto the porch to locate Missy.
"Shouldn't we ask for two?"

"I wouldn't worry," Hank said, giving her hand a
squeeze. "I can sleep in the parlor. We can tell them
it's best for you and the baby."

He always knew what to say to allow her to breathe
easier. His sister, however, was another matter.

"Don't you go upsetting Pa, Hank," Missy said
as she led them down one of the wings of the house
past plastered walls braced by timbers and side tables
holding tall vases of dried flowers. "The doctor says
we shouldn't rile him. It's bad for his heart."

"You assume he has a heart," Hank muttered.

"Be nice, I said." She stopped and held open a
door. Nancy peered inside. The neat room was paneled in oak, with a warm red-and-blue rug on the
floor and an elaborate lace doily on the mirrored bureau. The oak-framed bed in the center was edged
with wrought iron and covered with a colorful quilt.
Nancy couldn't help moving closer to admire the care-

fully stitched pattern of red-white-and-blue-striped triangles around a center square.

"I won't rile him if he doesn't rile me," Hank was saying to his sister as they stood by the door. "Best offer I can make. I suggest you take it."

Missy laughed. "It's going to be an interesting dinner." She turned to go, then pressed a hand to her back and groaned.

Nancy glanced up with a frown, but Hank stepped toward his sister. "Are you all right?"

Missy shook her head as she lowered her hand, then looked to him with a rueful smile. "I'm getting too old to be pregnant. My skin feels tighter than a rattler's who's ready to shed."

"You might try olive oil," Nancy suggested. "My mother relied on it."

"Nancy's mother was a midwife," Hank explained.

Missy's eyes widened. "Oh, sister, where were you on the last five pregnancies? We have a lot to talk about."

Nancy smiled. "I'm happy to help in any way."

"What do you advise eating?" Missy asked eagerly. "I've craved odd foods before. Ernesto was sure Clovis would be born with a fiery temper I ate so many chili peppers while I carried him. But now peppers and cucumbers and the like don't sit well. And don't tell Pa, but beef makes me green."

Hank was examining the doorframe as if trying not to listen.

"Try fruits," Nancy suggested. "Apples, plums, bananas if you can get them. They should be easier on your constitution and good for the baby."

Missy nodded. "Thank you. I'm sure I'll think of

other questions." She lowered her voice. "Only don't talk about babies in front of Judith. It's a sore point in the family that all she ever managed was her Tommy."

Nancy couldn't help thinking of Molly Thorn and how happy she'd been to learn she was going to have a baby. Tommy seemed an honest young man willing to help. A shame the rest of the family didn't realize that could be blessing enough.

Missy rubbed her hands together as she straightened. "Oh, this is going to be fun. See you at dinner." She swayed back down the hallway.

"Fun, she says." Hank shook his head as he closed the door behind his sister. "I'm sorry, Nancy. I knew you and my sisters would get along. But Pa reacted the way I feared he might."

"I reacted worse," Nancy said, running her fingers along the pattern of the quilt. "I didn't mean to upset him, Hank, or to push myself forward, but I just couldn't bear to hear him talk to you that way."

"You'd better get used to it," Hank said, moving farther into the room. "I have a feeling there's more to come." He went to his bag, which someone had placed on a chest at the foot of the bed. "Mother will expect us in our finest for dinner. I'm just going to change my coat, but I'll leave you to dress."

Nancy glanced up at him. "Won't your family find it odd you have to leave the room to change? Did you tell your mother about our agreement?"

Hank shook his head. "As far as my family knows, we're a happily married couple. But I doubt Mother will find our arrangement all that odd. Even after four babies of her own, she doesn't consider it proper for her and Pa to share a room."

Nancy had known a few women in Missouri who had felt the same way. They were the ones who had insisted she couldn't be the local midwife. Certainly Lucas had kept his own room at the Windy Diamond, but she no longer considered him any sort of example of what a husband should be.

"Your mother is different than I expected," Nancy said, sitting on the bed. "You said your father had high expectations. It seems your mother does too."

Hank pulled out the coat he'd worn to their wedding. "Sometimes, I think she raised her expectations to counter his. I told you that she and Pa met in Dallas. Pa had big dreams, and her family had the money to back them."

"So, they married for convenience, as well," Nancy mused.

"They might not have been in love to start," Hank allowed, "but I think Pa came to respect her. He may boss around the hands, us kids and pretty much anyone in Waco who would let him, but all of us always knew Mother was the power behind the throne. Still, when Pa sets his mind to something, even she has to step aside. Like my sister said, this could be an interesting dinner."

Hank did his best to appear calm as he escorted Nancy to the dining room just before six. They had taken turns in the room changing into their Sunday best, him in the brown coat he'd worn to their wedding and her in the green dress the ladies had sewn for her, the one that made her eyes look as bright as a field of clover. Her color was high, her steps firm, as they entered.

The dining room at the Double H was built for company. The heavy oak table with its scroll-backed wooden chairs could easily seat thirty. Judith and Missy were already in the long room with their husbands, stationed near the door as if ready to intercept Hank and Nancy. Tommy had been allowed to join the group for dinner, but Missy's boys were absent, likely dining in the kitchen under the watchful eye of the staff. If his father intended to be difficult, Hank was just as glad most of his nephews would be spared.

"And who is this fair flower brightening our gathering?" Ernesto Rodrigues said. Missy's husband took Nancy's hand and bowed over it. The vaquero had joined the Double H as a horse wrangler when Hank was fifteen. The wavy jet-black hair and intense nearly black eyes had not changed since the day Ernesto had charmed Hank's sister. Lean and wiry, he exuded confidence.

Hank introduced him to Nancy, who smiled at his attentions while Missy gazed fondly at her flamboyant husband.

Voices behind them signaled the arrival of his middle sister. Like their mother and Judith, Almira moved with stately dignity in her silk skirts as blue as a robin's egg. The most thoughtful of his sisters, she paused to regard him and Nancy before greeting him. She and Missy were the only ones to inherit Pa's blond hair, though hers was clean and shiny and carefully braided behind her head.

"Henry," she said, smile hovering as Judith, Red, Missy and Ernesto went to take their seats. "It's good to see you again. And this must be your Nancy." She held out her long-fingered hand. "Please call me Mira. And welcome to Waco. I know you'll love it here."

She made it sound as if he and Nancy had come to stay. "This is only a visit," Hank assured her as her husband and two daughters joined them.

Like his nephews, his nieces had grown. The oldest wore her blond hair up and blue skirts down. The youngest still wore the wider skirts of youth, and her hair was a curly chestnut like her father's. After curtseying to Hank and Nancy, they hurried around the couples to join their cousin Tommy on the other side of the table.

"Whether you stay or not may depend on your father," John Fulton, Mira's husband informed him. A slender man, shorter than any of the Snowdens, he had nonetheless impressed the family with his sharp intellect and warm wit. Pa had been persuaded that it might come in handy having a lawyer in the family, so Mira had been allowed to marry him, and the two lived in Waco and came out to the ranch on business and for family occasions.

"Is Mr. Snowden truly that ill?" Nancy asked.

John winked at her. "No, ma'am. He's truly that stubborn."

Mira tsked. "Now, John, don't scare her before she's even had a chance to meet him. He may not feel well enough to join us for dinner."

"We met him this afternoon," Hank explained. "He's already told us how he feels about this visit. And he's planning to be here tonight."

Mira raised her delicate brows. "Oh, this could be interesting. Come along, John."

With a supportive smile to Hank, John followed her into the room.

"I have a feeling your family and I use the term *interesting* differently," Nancy murmured to Hank.

He linked arms with her. "Sorry you came?"

"No." As always, her smile warmed him. "I like meeting your family, seeing where you came from. You're fortunate to have had siblings. When my mother died, it was just me."

"It was just me when I left here," Hank reminded her. "It actually felt good, for a while. Then I met a lady who changed my mind."

Ah, there were those peaches. A shame he couldn't lean in and kiss them. Now, wouldn't that shock his oh-so-proper mother?

Of course, the feelings that rose when he looked at Nancy surprised him enough.

"What are you two doing over there?" Missy demanded, saving him from having to explain to Nancy why his own cheeks were blazing. "You know you can't escape that easily. Ernesto and I have been trying for years."

Ernesto laughed, but Judith offered her a prim look.

"Now, Missy," she started with a tone so much like their mother's that Hank could only exchange glances with Nancy and smile.

Perhaps that was the biggest difference in this dinner, he realized as he escorted Nancy to the table. By the time he'd been allowed to sit on these scroll-backed chairs, Judith and Mira had already moved on to homes of their own, and Missy had followed shortly thereafter. He'd never had anyone to stand up for him with his father.

Until Nancy.

She couldn't know how rare it was for anyone to put Henry Snowden in his place. Hank hadn't been sure whether to cheer her or hide her from the coming wrath. It must be a sign of his father's illness that he'd taken her scold so well.

Now Hank just had to protect Nancy through this dinner.

He chose spots farther down from his sisters and their families, pulled out the chair for her, scooted it in just a little so she could sit without the edge of the table discomforting her or baby Ben. When she smiled her thanks up at him, he had to wonder whether he might pop the buttons right off his waistcoat he was so proud to be her husband. He still couldn't believe how forgiving she'd been of his confession.

If only he could find similar forgiveness in his heart for his father.

He had just taken his seat beside Nancy when his mother led in the cook and his helper. Hank didn't recognize either, but that was no surprise. Except for the maid who helped the ladies of the house dress, his mother had never been able to keep staff for long. His father claimed she always chose men and women with ambition, who wanted to advance themselves beyond playing servant. Hank thought it had more to do with an unwillingness to meet his mother's demands for perfection.

Now the savory scents of garlic and onions lingered in the air as the men set the dishes on the table. There was a platter of roast beef surrounded by vegetables, a bowl of fluffy mashed potatoes and a boat of rich gravy, plus fresh-baked bread and apricot preserves. With a nod, his mother dismissed the staff, then took her seat to the right of the head chair. Everyone seemed to be staring at the empty spot.

From down the hallway came a series of thumps, and his father moved into the room, leaning heavily on a brass-headed oak cane. As when he'd first seen his father that afternoon, Hank could not help noticing the changes. His father's back was hunched as if he were in pain, and his breath came in shallow gulps. Still, he walked to the head of the table and stood for a moment, gazing out at his gathered family. Hank didn't think it was his imagination that his father's look rested longest on him.

"Nice to see everyone here," his father commented before lowering himself onto the chair. "Rufus, say the blessing."

"An honor." Red bowed his head with clasped hands, and everyone else followed his lead.

"Dear Lord," he said, deep voice resonating against the hard wood, "we thank You for the friends and family You've brought together today. May this food bless our bodies and our conversation bless Your ears. Amen."

Amens echoed around the table, and Hank's mother began passing the dishes.

While Hank served Nancy and filled his plate, he couldn't help glancing down the table at his father. The man took little and ate less, even with his wife's encouragement. Hank recognized the dishes; they were some of his father's favorites. Was it the illness or Hank's presence that was keeping his father from enjoying them?

"You tamed that bronc yet, boy?" his father asked Tom, who was seated near him on the left.

Tom hurriedly swallowed his mouthful of potatoes. "Almost, sir. I'd be farther along if you were there to help me, I know."

His father had been a genius with breaking cow ponies. Now he shook his head. "Time you did it on your own. And what about you, Lizzie? That a new dress?"

Mira's oldest preened. "Mama had it made for me in Waco."

"Humph." His father's hand came down on the table. "You'd better learn how to use the needle yourself. Can't always count on having money to pay a seamstress."

"Yes, Grandfather," she said, lowering her gaze. The shoulders of the blue dress sagged.

"Both of my girls know how to sew," Mira informed her father. "They made that lap quilt for you last Christmas, if you recall."

"I recall," their father said, glint in his gray eyes. "And I recall it came apart in the first washing."

Mira glowered at him.

"I expect you're having to do a great deal of sewing for the baby, Nancy," his mother put in smoothly. "This being your first and all."

"It has kept me busy," Nancy acknowledged with a smile. "I'm sure you've had to go through that."

All the ladies smiled and nodded.

Mira perked up. "Of course we have. And I know we all have diapers and nightgowns folded away. We should give them to Hank and Nancy."

Judith's face tightened, and Missy went so far as

to shake a finger at her sister. "Speak for yourself! I still need those diapers."

"I have quite a store put by," Nancy assured them. "But thank you for the thought."

"And what about you, Junior?" his father asked, and Hank had to fight to keep from cringing at the hated nickname. "Are you ready to be a father now? You didn't think much of marriage before you left."

And there came the next shot fired. He wasn't the only one to notice. His mother and Mira were gazing across the table at nothing. Judith's face saddened, and Missy's gaze darted between him and their father as if she was eager to see the flames erupt. His brothers-in-law and Tommy offered commiserating looks, but he thought they were just as glad the sharp questions were directed at him now.

Yet the only look around the table that mattered to him was Nancy's, and she was smiling encouragement.

"Guess it just took me a while to find the right bride," he said, returning her smile.

"True love," Missy said, squeezing her hands together with a sigh. "It's so romantic."

"You didn't think so when you and Ernesto were living in that hovel," her father reminded her.

Missy dropped her hands, pouting, but her husband took her fingers and pressed a kiss against them. "I would never subject my wife to a hovel, though she would make it a castle by her very presence." As Missy melted, he turned to Hank's father. "I returned to the Double H at your request, Señor Snowden, not because of need."

"Same story I heard from Hank," his father complained, but his usual gruff voice sounded more petulant than commanding. "You all think you can go on without me."

His sisters squirmed.

"Isn't that what we want for our children?" Nancy's soft voice spoke into the silence. "That they will learn and grow and go on to greater things?"

Ernesto lifted his glass to her. "Well said, senora."

"Hear, hear," Red agreed, raising his glass, as well.

Most of the others murmured their ascent, took a sip in toast. But Hank watched his father and mother, neither of whom had touched their glasses.

It was going to be a long few days.

Chapter Eighteen

"That went better than I expected," Nancy said as they returned to the bedroom later that night. She and Hank had spent the evening with his family around the dinner table, trading stories and catching up on each other's lives. His father had been, for the most part, quiet, though she'd noticed he'd turned more gray as the evening wore on, as if he was staying upright through sheer force of will.

"That went better than I'd ever dreamed," Hank replied as they reached the door. He paused to smile down at her. "Having you beside me made all the difference, Nancy. Thank you."

Why was it even the littlest praise from him warmed her whole heart? She returned his smile, watched as he leaned closer, then shut her eyes, waiting for his kiss.

Instead, she heard the sound of footsteps in the corridor. Opening her eyes, she saw Hank's sisters sweeping toward them with the energy of a Texas twister.

"We're having a hen party," Missy announced as

they drew abreast of Hank and Nancy. She flapped her fingers at Hank. "Go on, now. Find a rooster or two to visit while we get to know your bride better."

"Red and Tommy are out by the main corral," Judith offered. "I'm sure they'd love your company, Henry."

Hank glanced Nancy's way as if doubting she wanted his sisters' company as much. She nodded to him. "It's all right. I'd like to talk to your sisters."

He held her gaze a moment longer as if he couldn't quite believe her.

Missy tugged on his sleeve. "Move along, cowboy. We'll send word when it's safe to come back."

With a commiserating look to Nancy, he went.

Nancy led his sisters into the room she and Hank had been given. She was glad she'd tidied up a little before going to dinner so that his sisters at least had a place to sit.

"You don't mind the intrusion, do you?" Judith asked as she arranged her skirts around her on the bed.

"After all, you are still newlyweds," Mira agreed, perching on the chest.

"Though you don't act like any newlyweds I know," Missy said, flopping down on the other side of the bed and lifting her legs to stretch them out on the red-white-and-blue quilt. "I heard Hank tell Mother he intended to sleep in the parlor."

While her older sisters exchanged glances and Nancy's face heated, Missy frowned at her. "Did he do something boneheaded or are you still pining for your first husband?"

"Missy," Judith scolded before Nancy could answer. "It's really none of our affair."

"Why not?" Missy asked with a puzzled frown. "We're family."

"Only recently," Mira reminded her. Then she turned to Nancy. "I'm sorry we assumed, dear."

Though Nancy went to sit next to Judith on the bed, she felt as if a gulf had opened between her and Hank's sisters. They were right; they were family. She'd told Hank she wanted no more secrets. Surely, she should follow her own advice.

"No apology necessary," she told them. "You see, Hank and I married to save the ranch. My first husband had mortgaged it without my knowledge, and the bank didn't have faith that I could manage it on my own. Hank offered to marry me. He would run the ranch while teaching me more about ranching, and he'd be father to my baby."

Missy sighed, blue eyes softening as she lay her head back on the pillow. "Such a romantic, our Hank."

"That was well done of him," Mira agreed.

"But I don't see any reason why the two of you can't be husband and wife," Judith protested, glancing between her sisters as if for support. Both Missy and Mira nodded.

"Well," Nancy said, finding it hard to meet their concerned gazes, "he doesn't love me."

Judith waved a hand. "That's hardly an insurmountable problem."

"Certainly not," Mira said. "It only took me a month to convince John he couldn't live without me."

Missy snorted. "A month? Please! I had Ernesto eating out of my hand in a week."

"Some of us take our time," Judith replied with an arched look to her sister.

"Some of us are too high in the instep, you mean," Missy shot back.

"I don't understand," Nancy interrupted. "You can't make someone fall in love with you, can you?"

"Not if they don't care to begin with," Judith acknowledged.

"But Hank cares," Mira assured Nancy. "We can see it in his eyes."

"And in the way he treats you," Judith added. "We know our brother, Nancy. He's already halfway in love with you. We just need to convince him to let go and give love a chance."

Missy made a face. "I wouldn't be so sure. You know why he's so gun-shy."

"Missy," Judith warned.

Missy rolled her eyes. "Honestly, Judith, you have no idea what a woman needs to know about her husband." She sat up and turned to Nancy. "Hank was in love once, with a girl here. She broke his heart. It never mended."

"Now, Missy," Mira said, "we don't know it never mended. He's been away for five years."

Missy pointed a finger at her sister. "Well, he never came home until now. That ought to tell you something."

It certainly told Nancy something. He hadn't wanted to talk much about the girl he'd nearly married. At times, he seemed to be guarding his heart from further hurt. Nancy could understand that; she'd done the same thing. But was he any more willing to let go of his first love now?

"The fact that he came home with Nancy ought to tell us all something," Judith countered beside her. "I do believe he has feelings for you, Nancy. You just have to encourage them."

Could she? Should she? Was she ready to open her heart again?

She must have taken too long to respond, for she caught the three sisters exchanging glances once more.

"Oh, dear," Mira said. "It seems we've assumed yet again."

Missy glowered at Nancy. "Don't you want Hank to fall in love with you? He's a fine fellow."

"Missy," Judith said, exasperation in each syllable.

Missy turned her frown on her sister. "Well, he is! Any gal would be proud to have him beside her."

"Hank is beside her," Mira reminded her. "They're married."

Missy shook her head. "Marriage, real marriage, means more than working side by side. It's loving and striving and hurting and healing and laughing and praying. Otherwise, you're just two people playing house."

"Never mind her," Judith said. "You must do as you see fit, Nancy."

As she saw fit. She had doubted her ability to understand people, to recognize their true nature. She had realized she needed to learn enough to run a ranch. She had wondered how she might contribute to the Little Horn community.

When it came to what she wanted from her marriage, she knew.

"Missy's right," she told Hank's sisters.

"Of course, I am," Missy said with a lift of her nose.

Nancy hid a smile. "Marriage is about sharing everything, the good and the bad, the triumphs and disappointments. I want that for Hank and me. I love him."

Missy applauded while Judith and Mira beamed.

"And I'm certain he just needs a little help to return that love," Judith said.

Nancy's certainty, flying as high as a hawk, suddenly dipped. "What sort of help?"

Missy nudged her with her foot. "You know. Use your woman's wiles."

Nancy stiffened. "I won't trick him. That's not right."

Mira rose, grace and determination personified. "No one will trick anyone. That's no way to build a marriage."

"And there's no need," Judith agreed, rising, as well. "In fact, all we need do is gild the lily."

Missy pushed herself off the bed. "Lilies are for funerals. Besides, I think Hank should be the one to pick the posies."

Judith stared at her. "Were we even raised in the same house?"

"Ladies." Mira's stern look silenced both her sisters. She turned to Nancy. "Consider us your advisors, dear. We can tell you everything about our brother."

"His favorite foods," Judith suggested.

"His favorite colors," Mira offered.

"His favorite horse," Missy put in. She rubbed her hands. "Oh, this will be fun."

Baby Ben did a little dance of excitement as if he couldn't wait either.

Nancy stood as well, meeting each of their eager

gazes in turn. "Very well, ladies. I'll do it. Tell me how to encourage Hank to fall in love with me."

Hank found all three of his brothers-in-law in deep discussion out by the corral closest to the house. Inside the wood rail fence, he could see a solid quarter horse trotting about under Tommy's watchful eye. The moon had risen, full and fat, casting a silver glow over the space. The cool breeze bathed Hank's face.

"Kicked you out, did they?" Red commented as Hank walked up to where the men stood by the fence, looking over the boy and horse inside.

"My sisters said they wanted to get to know Nancy better," Hank answered.

John shook his head. "They're plotting against us. You wait and see."

Red nodded. "Tomorrow we'll be roped into some family hoo-haw."

"Or set to watch the little ones while they go to town," Ernesto added with a shudder.

His complaint didn't fool Hank. Missy had always been the most determined of his sisters, willful, but the day she'd met Ernesto Rodrigues, she had met her match. And his sister's love had softened the brash vaquero into a true family man. The fact of the matter was that all his sisters had married men of character. He thought the pairs evenly yoked.

"I wouldn't mind spending more time with your pack," Hank told Ernesto.

"You say that now," Ernesto warned.

Red clapped Hank on the shoulder. "Don't let him tease you. Being a father is the best thing that can happen to a man." He nodded to his Tommy, who had walked up to the horse and was stroking its nose. "Tom is my pride and joy. I know that baby will steal your heart too."

"He already has," Hank said with a smile.

"*He,*" John scoffed. "I thought it was going to be a boy too, both times, and then I got my beauties."

Ernesto propped a tooled-leather boot up on the lowest rung of the fence. "I knew my boys were coming. Just as I know this one will be a señorita."

Red snorted. "I can't tell whether a calf is going to be a heifer or a steer. I doubt anyone knows for sure about human babies."

"Nancy thinks it's going to be a boy," Hank explained. "Her mother was a midwife and taught her about such things." He leaned his elbows on the rough rail. "But I don't care. Boy or girl, I aim to love the little one."

"And maybe his mama?" Red joked.

Hank wasn't ready to discuss his feelings for Nancy with anyone, particularly not his brothers-in-law. He pushed off the fence. "So, what's all this about Pa? No one seems able to answer my questions. What's wrong with him, and how bad is it?"

They sobered.

"Tommy!" Red called. "Take her inside."

Tommy obediently picked up the bridle and headed for the barn. Only when he was safely out of hearing did the big man turn to the others and nod permission to speak. The fact that he didn't want his son to listen to this part of their conversation sent a chill through Hank.

"Henry is sicker than he wants us to believe," John volunteered. "And he won't tell anyone the truth. Mira offered to go with him to see the doctor in Waco, and he refused."

"That sounds like Pa on the best of days," Hank protested.

"But he doesn't eat enough to keep a bird alive," Red complained. "He stays in his room most days, from what I hear."

"And he gave me much of the responsibility for the ranch," Ernesto added. "I do not like it. I learned long ago that I work better when someone else does the planning."

"Plans are easy," Hank told him. "I've had them for years, but Pa didn't want to hear about them. He'd already arranged my life, down to where I'd live and who I'd marry."

"Mary Ellen Wannacre," Red remembered with a smile. "Now, there was a fine filly."

"A most beautiful señora," Ernesto allowed. "Then and now with three children."

Three babies? Good for Mary Ellen and Adam. "I hope they're happy," Hank said, surprised to find the words easier to say.

"You'll have a chance to see for yourself," Red predicted. "Tomorrow's Sunday. I expect you'll be joining us for services in Waco."

His stomach gave a decided lurch. He'd left Waco five years ago because he couldn't face his father's disdain. Truth be told, he'd felt nearly as uncomfortable facing Adam and his bride. He wasn't sure what he felt now.

"You still go all the way into Waco for church?" Hank asked, nudging them away from the topic of his lost love. "I'd have thought Pa would have convinced a preacher to relocate out this way by now."

"Your Pa is a big supporter of the pastor in Waco," John said, tone appropriately pious.

"Particularly after Mira threw him over for John," Red added with a laugh. "Guess keeping the Snowden family in the congregation was the consolation prize."

Hank glanced between Red and John. He could see Ernesto watching them with similar interest.

"Is that how it happened?" Hank asked.

Red cocked his head while John gazed at the moon, all innocence.

"You don't remember?" Red asked Hank.

"I suppose I wasn't paying that much attention," Hank admitted. "I was too young to understand when Judith and you were courting. I was fourteen when Mira met John, and I was too busy trying to figure out the attraction between boys and girls to pay attention to my sister's courtship."

John winked at him. "I'll tell you all about it, once you've had a daughter or two of your own and can appreciate your father's point of view."

They all chuckled at that.

Tommy stuck his head out of the barn. "Can I come out now, Pa? I'm old enough to hear about the attraction between boys and girls."

"We're done talking," Red said, more to his brothers-in-law than his son, and even in the moonlight Hank could see that he was turning as dark a red as his hair.

Hank spoke awhile longer with his nephew, praising him for skill and patience in training the horse, then headed back to the house. He couldn't remember ever talking with his brothers-in-law like that, but then things had been more strained when he'd lived on the Double H. Now these men treated him like an equal for all they'd watched him grow up. Why was it his father couldn't see him as a man? He was certainly older than Tommy! And he knew exactly why boys were attracted to girls.

He didn't hear any voices or giggles as he approached the closed door of the bedroom. Had his sisters gone? Had Nancy changed for bed? He should have found a way to explain to his mother that his and Nancy's marriage was unconventional. As it was, she'd accepted his excuse about sleeping in the parlor to give Nancy more room in the bed. At least his mother's settee was longer than the one in the hotel in Burnet. He might still be able to stand without groaning come morning. Now he just had to collect his shaving kit before he headed for the parlor.

The door opened just then, and Missy swayed out into the hallway. With her came the scent of roses, bringing back memories of the garden his mother had so lovingly tended behind the house. His sister grinned when she saw Hank.

"Everything's ready for you, little brother," she said. "Sweet dreams."

Bemused, he passed her to enter the room.

His sisters had evidently settled Nancy for bed, because she was sitting against the headboard with the covers pulled up to her chin, as prim and proper as his mother could hope. But it was her hair that caught his attention. Unbound, it draped about her like a satin cape, shining in the lamplight.

"Did you have a nice visit with your brothers-in-law?" she asked.

Hank forced his gaze away and went to his bag. "We talked some. How did things go with my sisters?"

"They have some interesting ideas," she said as he shucked off his coat. He glanced up to find her sitting up higher in the bed and gazing at him wide-eyed.

"Do you want me to leave for a moment so you can change?" she asked.

Hank grinned at her. "No need. I sleep in my clothes often enough on the trail. I figured I'd just take off my coat, boots and belt, and I'd be fine."

"Oh." She settled back against the headboard. The covers slid a little, giving him a glimpse of a high-collared flannel nightgown. It was the color of bluebonnets, his favorite flower. He ought to buy her a dress that color, maybe a hat with the flower on it.

What was he thinking?

He wadded up his coat and shoved it into the bag, determined only to quit the room and shake off these feelings.

"Would you put out the lamp before you go?" she asked.

He glanced her way. Her gaze was wistful, as if all she wanted was for him to step closer. His feet seemed to think that a fine idea, because they were moving before his brain registered the fact. He walked to the table near the bed and bent over the flame. The movement put his gaze on a level with hers. She bit her lip watching him. Such pretty lips, warm, sweet.

Hank straightened. "Maybe you should put out

the lamp after I leave. I'll need to see my way to the door."

"Yes, of course. You're right." Her voice was soft and sweet as she lowered her gaze.

But something was wrong. That feeling was coming over him. He'd disappointed her for some reason. He hated disappointing people.

"What's wrong, Nancy?" he asked. "Did my sisters say something to concern you?"

She sighed. "No. It's me. I'm not very good at this."

"At what?" he asked with a frown.

Still, she kept her gaze on the quilt, fingers picking at the striped patterns. "Your sisters gave me all kinds of advice on how to make myself more attractive to you, but I just can't do it."

"Whoa, there." Hank sat on the edge of the bed. "You don't have to do anything to make yourself more attractive. I reckon you're one of the prettiest girls in Texas."

Her smile trembled on her lips as she shot a glance his way. "That's so sweet of you to say. But you told me Mary Ellen Wannacre was beautiful."

"She was," Hank agreed, puzzled by her attitude. "So's the river when the sun is rising. So's the sound of a mother singing her baby to sleep. What's that got to do with anything?"

"Well, I…" She drew in a breath as if making a decision, then glanced up at him again. "I wish you thought I was that beautiful too."

He could see what it had cost her to admit that. Her cheeks were flaming, and her head immediately ducked. He put a finger under her chin and returned her gaze to his.

"I reckon if I thought you were any more beautiful, they'd have to lasso me to keep me back," he said. Then he bent his head and kissed her.

Chapter Nineteen

At the sweet pressure of Hank's lips against hers, joy, delight and hope burst inside Nancy like poppies opening to the sun. She slipped her arms about him, feeling the strength of him, the surety. This closeness was what she'd yearned for, what she needed. She never wanted to let go.

But Hank pulled back, his smile soft. "You are beautiful, Nancy, and if it takes me telling you that every day for the rest of our lives for you to believe that, I'll do it."

The emotions crowding inside her sealed her lips.

He rose and pressed a kiss to her forehead. "See you in the morning."

The air felt colder as he moved toward the door. Was it her imagination, or were his steps a bit unsteady? Had the kiss affected him as much as it had her?

"Hank?" she asked as he reached for the door handle. "Is there something more I should be doing to be a good wife to you?"

"No, ma'am," he said, so quick and hard she

couldn't doubt him. "You're nigh close to perfect. I reckon most men have to fight to keep from falling in love with you. I certainly did."

He yanked open the door and bolted out of the room as if afraid she'd ask him to explain that statement. As it was, his words hung in the air. She wanted to jump from the bed, race after him, demand that he elaborate. Was that his declaration of love? Was letting down her hair, using her sweetest tone and sharing a kiss all it took to win a heart as sheltered as his?

She couldn't believe it, so she stayed put. She'd dressed well, cooked well, cleaned and sewed and tended the garden, catered to Lucas's least need, and he hadn't fallen in love with her.

She lay on the bed, listening to the sizzle of the lamp. One evening of tenderness wasn't enough to build love in her experience. Of course, Hank seemed more spontaneous. Look at the way he'd ridden after that rustler who'd been watching the herd, the way he'd sawed the legs off her sewing chair in a burst of inspiration. If he was going to fall in love with her, wouldn't he have done so by now?

What more could she do? What more should she do to earn his love?

The statement hit her as hard as his words. Was that what she'd been doing, trying to earn first Lucas's love and now Hank's? She knew better than that. Love wasn't something you earned through hard work but something that grew naturally, like the bluebonnets that blanketed the fields every spring.

Oh, she thought a marriage required nurturing and tending, like any garden, but maybe it wasn't her efforts that made the seed sprout any more than it was the farmer who made his crops begin growing.

That part was up to God.

She closed her eyes, shut out all sound. *Lord, I'm learning that You're part of my life in ways I never imagined. You must have given me Hank for a reason. Was it love? Can we forge a marriage that's strong enough to last?*

The door opened, and so did her eyes. Hank offered her a sheepish grin. There was something soft, vulnerable about his face, as if humility had wiped away all the bravado.

"Forgot my shaving kit," he said before going to fetch it.

Kind, considerate, gentle.

Loyal, sweet, hardworking.

This was a man she could love.

The feeling was so strong, so right, she knew it for the truth. Once more joy trembled through her.

He paused at the door. "Good night, Nancy. Sweet dreams."

She nodded, unsure how to express the feelings singing through her. All she knew was that they had a chance. He closed the door behind him.

"Good night, husband," she whispered.

Hank's sisters had told Nancy about Sunday arrangements, so the next morning she donned the blue dress she'd worn on the train. She was just finishing buttoning up her boots, a process that was becoming more challenging as the baby grew, when Missy flounced in wearing a white organza gown that floated about her own widening figure.

"Well?" she demanded, blue eyes merry. "How did it go?"

"Fine," Nancy said, standing to check her hair in the mirror on the bureau. She turned to find Missy frowning at her.

"Fine?" Hank's sister tapped her pink kid leather shoe against the floorboards. "Details, dear. Details."

Nancy put out a hand to her. "I truly appreciate your help, Missy, but the details must remain between me and Hank."

"Oh." Missy wiggled her blond brows. "I understand. Really. And I'm so glad things went well. Maybe he can give up sleeping on the settee soon."

Nancy knew she was blushing as she followed Hank's irrepressible sister out of the room.

With all the family in residence for once, Mother Snowden had arranged a big breakfast, but Nancy found it hard to do justice to the poached eggs covered in melted cheese, the crisp fried potatoes mixed with peppers, the generous slabs of steak and ham and the fresh-baked bread dripping with butter and preserves. Missy had no such trouble, but she slowed down when she met Nancy's gaze.

"Here, Ernesto," she said, sliding her plate toward her handsome husband. "You finish the steak. I'll have some more of Mother's apple preserves."

The children joined them in the parlor afterward, and there was much scurrying as mothers attempted to put hats on their children without losing their own.

A boy of about five with Missy's golden hair stepped in front of Nancy where she and Hank were waiting by the door. "You're new," he accused.

Hank squatted to put his face on a level with the lad's. "I'm older than you."

His nephew paused to consider that. "Who's she?" he asked, pointing at Nancy.

Hank glanced up at her and smiled. "That's the most beautiful gal in Texas."

Delight rippled through her, but the boy regarded her, head cocked.

"I think you're right," he said. And then he turned and scampered off.

Hank took her hand in his. "See? Even my nephew agrees with me."

"He's still young," Nancy pointed out, feeling her cheeks heating under Hank's regard.

"Doesn't make his opinion any less valid," Hank insisted. "Now, let's see what we can do to get this herd a-moving."

"They aren't cattle," Nancy said with a smile.

His eyes sparkled, reminding her of his sister. "Same principles apply. I'll ride flank. You take rear."

She laughed, but he peeled off from her to stalk around the edges of his milling family. Like Mr. Upkins urging the herd, Hank nudged here, spoke a word of encouragement there. Nancy dropped to the back and tried to mimic his actions. With protests punctuated by laughter, his family began moving toward the door. Nancy kept any from escaping back into the house.

"That was some roundup," she teased as she met Hank on the porch, watching as his family climbed into various buggies and wagons for the trip to Waco.

He tipped his hat. "Just doing my job, ma'am."

"Do it without blocking the steps," his father ordered, coming out onto the porch, wife on his arm. Mother Snowden was dressed in a fine black velvet gown with a cream-colored lace front. A hat crusted with black lace and pearls sat above her carefully confined silver-and-black hair. Henry Snowden likewise wore a black suit and crisp white shirt with a black bow tie at his throat. Nancy didn't think it was the contrast of the colors that made his skin look sallow.

At the sight of his father, Hank stood straighter. "Sorry, sir. I wasn't sure if you would be joining us today."

"What have I always told you about services?" his father returned, pausing at the top of the steps and leaning heavily on his cane.

"If you're too sick to make it to church, you're too sick to do anything else," Hank replied. "Glad to see you're not so sick, Pa."

His father humphed as he eased himself down the steps, but Hank's mother cast them both a grateful look.

"This could be interesting," Hank said.

"If you say that word one more time, I will personally show you what interesting is," Nancy threatened.

Laughing, Hank led her to the waiting buggy.

Hank expected to feel some trepidation at the possibility of meeting Adam and Mary Ellen again, but he found himself more entranced with Nancy. She sat between him and Tom in Judith and Red's buggy, taking in the sights and answering Judith's questions about Little Horn. Though Nancy's hair was now bound up at the top of her head, he couldn't help remembering how it had looked last night, soft and sleek around her face. Her gaze had been nearly as soft when he'd kissed her.

"Why are you staring at me?" she murmured when he helped her down from the buggy near the church. "Have I sprouted more freckles?"

"No, ma'am," he assured her. "And that's a real pity as they look so fine on you."

She dropped her gaze, and he could see a smile tugging at her mouth.

But her head came up as they approached the church. The brick building with its sweeping arches and five-story tower could be seen from miles around.

"It always reminded me of a castle," Hank confided as they followed his family toward the massive front doors. "All those stones on top look like fortifications."

His mother must have heard him, for she glanced back at the pair. "Nonsense, Henry. I should hope we have more originality. Why, those stained glass windows came all the way from Paris."

Nancy's eyes widened.

He supposed the Waco church was a far distant style from the chapel in Little Horn, much less the tent they had been meeting in until recently. Growing up, he'd taken the polished wood pews, the twining arches overhead as typical of any church. Now as he and Nancy walked down the center aisle, he felt the weight of the place slip over him. With the flickering lamps along the paneled walls and the jewellike tones of the stained glass windows, this was a church for reflection, for awe of one's Maker.

The preacher seemed to know this, for his sermon was thoughtful, encouraging. The only thing that kept

Hank from full appreciation was the knowledge that this was the man his father had intended for Mira. He could not see the tall, thin, determined fellow with his sister.

It seemed as if his father hadn't really known his children, based on the spouses he'd tried to choose for them. At times, Hank thought his father never saw his children as individuals but as a reflection of him. And just as a man worked to control his reflection in a mirror—combing his hair, adjusting his bandanna, forcing a smile on lips curved by sorrow—so his father had worked to control his children. Was he happy with the results?

Nancy's hand slipped into Hank's, and his troubled thoughts were replaced by a wave of thanksgiving. She'd said on the train here that Lucas Bennett had made choices, and so had she. It struck him now that his father had made choices as well, but it was Hank and his sisters who had to decide what to do about them. All of his sisters seemed sincerely in love with their husbands, contented for the most part in their families. Maybe he had a chance for the same.

He stood with Nancy to sing the final hymn to the thunder of the big pipe organ, hopes swelling along with the grand music. His family had filled the first three pews to the right of the aisle. Now Judith, Red and Tommy as well as Mira, John and their girls all joined their voices together, and even Missy and Ernesto managed to coerce their brood into tune.

Still, Hank knew the eyes of the congregation were on them all. Henry and Harriett Snowden were too well-known to have their activities go unnoticed. Maybe that was why, when Hank's father stumbled coming out of the pew, Hank managed to prop him up without anyone being the wiser.

"Thanks," his father murmured before turning to answer a question from Hank's mother. As everyone else filed out, Hank paused to look back at the golden cross above the altar.

"Thanks," he murmured before following Nancy and his family down the aisle.

In the churchyard, old friends and acquaintances stopped him to welcome him back, and he introduced them to Nancy and learned about their lives over the past five years. He wasn't surprised to find most had married, and quite a few had babies of their own.

"We all grew up," he told Nancy with a grin.

"People generally do," she allowed.

"Well, you might not have been so sure if you'd seen us a few years ago," Hank told her.

Just then he heard his name being called. Turning, he saw Adam striding toward him. His friend looked much the same as Hank remembered him, brown hair curling around a boyish face, muscular body ready for action. But the green eyes that had once held mischief were now wary.

"Welcome back," he said, stopping a little ways away from Hank and Nancy. "Sorry I didn't come up right after service, but I wasn't sure you wanted to see me again."

Hank held out his hand to the man who had once been as close as a brother. "Adam. Of course I want to see you, and Mary Ellen too. I heard you had children. Congratulations."

Adam nodded. "Three so far. I've been blessed.

That is…" his voice trailed away, and he dropped his gaze.

Hank felt for him. Even a year ago, he might have been the one to stutter in front of Adam, trying to find a way around a topic that could not be ignored.

"I'm glad for you both," Hank told him now. "Mary Ellen knew what she was doing when she chose the best man."

Adam's head came up, and he stared at Hank. "You mean that?"

"I do." And even though Adam's face broke into the smile Hank remembered, he was sure no one was more pleased than him to feel the truth of those words.

Nancy had stepped back at Adam's approach. Now Hank reached out and drew her forward. "I want you to meet my wife, Nancy. Marrying her changed my life."

Nancy raised her brows at that, but she smiled at Adam and accepted his hand in greeting.

"So are you back to stay?" Adam asked.

Hank exchanged glances with Nancy. "No, we have a nice spread out by Little Horn. I just came to see my pa."

Adam looked to where Hank's father was talking to the minister. By the frown on the pastor's face, it was not a pleasant conversation.

"I heard he was feeling poorly," Adam said. "Nothing serious, I hope."

"I hope," Hank echoed.

Adam turned to Nancy. "Even if it's just a visit, I'm glad you came. I'd like you to meet my wife." He turned and waved.

And there she was. Mary Ellen Turner glided across the grass, hair still as golden and wavy, eyes still the color of bluebonnets in the spring. Her smile was gentle as she came to a stop beside her husband and linked her arm with his.

But no birds sang, and no rainbows sprang from her smile. She was just a pretty gal who had married his friend.

"Henry, so nice to see you again," she said, and Hank couldn't like the name on her lips any more than he could on anyone else's.

Nancy was at his elbow, and he could feel her tension. She had to wonder how she compared to the acknowledged beauty.

In his mind, there was no comparison. He had the perfect gal for him.

"This is Hank's wife, Nancy," Adam said into the silence.

Mary Ellen extended a hand. "Pleasure."

Nancy shook the hand. "Very nice to meet you, Mrs. Turner. I've heard a great deal about you."

Mary Ellen dimpled, taking the compliment as her due. "How sweet. Adam and I talk often about the days we were all friends."

"We're still friends," Adam protested. He glanced at Hank. "Aren't we?"

"Of course we are," Hank assured him. "But people change. We even learn a few things along the way." He smiled at Nancy. "We might even learn who we ought to be."

Her eyes brightened.

"So, you'll be moving back to the ranch," Mary Ellen surmised.

Hank shook his head, sparing her a glance. "No plans in that direction. God had something else in mind for this cowpoke."

Across the churchyard, he could see his family starting to fill their buggies and wagons.

"We should go," Nancy said as if she'd noticed, as well.

"It was very nice seeing you again," Mary Ellen told Hank.

He nodded and shook Adam's hand, then took Nancy's elbow and led her away. And he wasn't surprised to feel a spring in his step.

"Was that difficult?" Nancy asked as they approached the buggies, where Missy and Ernesto were trying to corral their herd and Mira was attempting to pull her girls away from a group of eager young men.

Hank shook his head. "Not at all."

She beamed at him. "I am so glad, Hank. Truly."

There was something in her tone, as if his meeting with Mary Ellen and Adam had set her mind at rest, as well. But why would she care, unless...

"Let's round everyone up and head for home," she said, giving his arm a squeeze. "I'll take flank. You take rear."

He couldn't fault her logic. Still, it was a long ride back. His two oldest sisters and their families peeled off for their own homes partway along the road. He and Nancy rode with his parents, and his father was quiet, coughing from time to time into a handkerchief. Nancy nudged Hank at one point and nodded to where the white cloth was stained with red. Hank's heart sank. When his father stood to get out of the buggy, it was all Hank could do to keep him upright.

"Walk me back to my room," he ordered his son. "The rest of you can amuse yourselves."

His mother looked less than pleased by this pronouncement, and Nancy glanced at Hank askance. He nodded her toward Missy, who was calling to her boys again. Knowing Nancy could hold her own with his sister, he escorted his father up the steps.

"Mrs. Turner is a fine figure of a woman," his father commented, cane loud against the floor.

"She and Adam seem very happy," Hank acknowledged.

His father scowled at him. "Your Nancy isn't that pretty."

"I could argue that," Hank countered, opening the door to his father's room. The massive center bed was flanked by the heads of buffalo and antelope his father had shot in his youth.

"You've changed," his father said.

Hank wasn't sure whether his father thought that was a good thing or a bad thing. He was just glad the changes were evident.

"I'm the man I want to be, Pa. Nothing more."

His father levered himself down onto a chest at the foot of his bed. "I want you to come home."

Hank stepped back. "I have a home. It's with Nancy in Little Horn."

His father whacked his cane against the floor with all of his former energy, but Hank could see his knees shaking from the morning's exertions. "Your place is here. Always has been. I can see the time away matured you, and I'm glad for that. But there's a ranch to run."

"Ernesto runs it," Hank pointed out. He went to the bed and drew off one of the brightly-colored blankets.

"Ernesto's running it into the ground, you mean," his father complained, but he didn't protest when Hank draped the blanket over his trembling legs. "He's a hard worker, I'll give him that. But he has no head for business."

"So, hire someone else," Hank said.

His father glowered. "I didn't build this ranch to hand it over to a stranger. I built it for you."

Hank leaned back. "I was under the impression you built it for you and Mother. The two of you had a place to uphold in the community, you always said, a reputation to maintain. I can't be one more medal on your chest, Pa. That's why I left the first time."

His father looked up to meet his gaze. "I'm dying. The doctor figures I have six months."

Hank felt as if the beams overhead had caved in on him. "He must be wrong."

"I aim to prove him wrong," his father declared. "But to do that, I need to concentrate, and I can't do that worrying about the ranch." He drew in a breath, and his voice softened. "I need you, Hank. More than that, I want you here beside me. I didn't do well getting to know you as a boy. Maybe I pushed you too hard."

"Maybe," Hank allowed.

His father nodded as if accepting the criticism. "I want a chance to do better. I want to get to know the man you've become, to meet my newest grandson."

"Nancy could be wrong," Hank warned. "It could be a girl."

"Then I'll love her all the same," his father insisted. "It would mean the world to me to have you run this ranch, to make it your own. What do you say, son?"

Chapter Twenty

Nancy could see the change in Hank when he came out to rejoin the family in the parlor. He looked a little unsteady on his feet again, but there was a new light about him, as if he was finally at peace with the things that had kept him from home. She met his gaze with raised brow, but he mouthed, "Later," and she had to be content with that.

They didn't have a chance to talk privately until they retired that night. Judith and Mira had returned with their families for Sunday dinner, an expansive affair that involved dozens of dishes that set the long table to groaning under the combined weight of good food and fine china. Hank's sisters seemed to think their stratagems had worked because they kept grinning at Nancy and giggling at things Hank said. All the children were welcome at the table, and Nancy could only smile at the happy chatter.

Hank's father joined them for a short time. Having all his family around him seemed to have done Henry Snowden good, for he encouraged all his grandchildren in one way or another. Though it seemed as if he had been a demanding father, he had a word for each of his grandchildren, for the most part kind, particularly to the littlest ones. Nancy could only hope he might have time to get to know Ben, as well.

Between the ladies' coy glances and the children's antics, it had been a delightful evening, but Nancy was glad to retire to the quiet of the little room. Once more, Hank walked her to the door.

"You and your father seemed to be getting on better," she murmured as they paused in the hallway.

"We settled a few things," he admitted. "He seems willing to accept who and what I am."

Nancy smiled. "I'm so glad. Did you get a better sense of what's really wrong with him?"

He was quiet a moment, and she felt her smile fading as she waited to hear the news.

"The doctor's given him six months to live," he said.

"Oh, Hank! I'm so sorry." She wanted to enfold him in her arms, but she wasn't sure that would bring him comfort.

"He asked me to stay," he continued, and the amazement in his voice was mirrored on his face, "to take over the ranch from Ernesto. And I think Ernesto would be glad to see that happen. But I can't run this ranch and the Windy Diamond too."

"No, of course not." She should have known this was coming. How could she and the baby compare to a whole family, a history of friends and past loves? He'd grown into a man in Little Horn, but a part of him would always belong to Waco. Much as she loved him, she couldn't put herself between him and his family. She wanted what was best for him.

Even if that broke her heart.

"I'll understand if you want to stay," she made herself say. "I can go back on the train alone."

"Nancy." Her name sounded soft, murmured in the quiet. His face looked soft as well as he reached out to caress her cheek. "I'd never leave you. You and me and baby Ben are a family. We stick together."

Emotions welled up inside her, and she nearly cried with the sweetness of his touch. But she had to be strong. She couldn't let him sacrifice himself for her and the baby.

"But your family here needs you," she insisted.

He pressed a finger to her lips, stilling them. "My family in Little Horn needs me too. Or am I mistaken in that?"

She pulled back enough to free her lips. "No. We need you, Hank. I need you. But I can't be so selfish as to deprive you of your last moments with your father. I know I wouldn't have wanted to miss one moment with my mother."

She could see the smile on his face. "I reckon it's more important to be there when Ben breathes his first than when Pa breathes his last. We'll stay a couple more days, if you're willing. Then we'll head back to Little Horn."

"I'm willing," she said. "If that's what you want."

"It's what's best," he said. He pressed a kiss to her forehead as if in pledge, then turned to go. And Nancy could only hope his decision was for the best, for all of them.

The next two days flew by. Hank's sisters and their families came by when they could, sharing meals and taking rides about the ranch. Unlike the Windy Diamond, the Double H lay on good, flat grazing lands. When Hank took Nancy up in the wagon, she thought she could see forever.

"Does the sky ever end?" asked Daniel, who had insisted on driving with them. Missy's five-year-old son had taken a liking to Hank and refused to let him go anywhere without his company.

Nancy smiled at him. "Not on your ranch, apparently."

"We have a few more trees and rocks and a lot of draws and canyons on the Windy Diamond," Hank agreed.

"Why?" Daniel asked as Hank guided the horses back toward the ranch house.

Hank grinned at Nancy. "You know, I ask myself that question every time I have to chase down a steer."

Daniel wasn't the only one who liked being around Hank. He and Ernesto spent several hours discussing plans for the ranch. Missy tried to get Nancy to come out with the children, but Nancy demurred. Because of what she'd learned at the Windy Diamond, she was able to contribute to the discussions and delighted when the more experienced gentlemen listened to her suggestions.

"But we do not dare drive the cattle to the south pasture," Ernesto protested one day as they stood overlooking the herd. "The water there does not last in the summer heat."

"That's why we need to put in a windmill," Hank told him. "What rain we get may evaporate, but the grass tends to stay nice and green because of groundwater."

"We just need to tap that water and bring it up for the cattle to drink," Nancy promised.

"Señor Snowden will not like the expense, I think," Ernesto said.

"Not at first," Hank agreed. "But once he sees how fat the cattle grow with the extra food, he'll come around."

Nancy wasn't sure whether any member of the family besides Hank knew that his father's time might be short, but she liked the fact that Hank acted as if his father would be around for some time to come.

The biggest surprise for Nancy was the change in Hank's mother. From the moment she and Nancy had met, it had seemed to Nancy that Mother Snowden had found her lacking. Hank's mother wanted the best for her son, and a pregnant widow likely didn't qualify. But one afternoon, she called Nancy aside.

"I am not the most demonstrative person," she admitted, head high and back straight as she perched on her settee. "I see no reason to shout or cry when circumstances vary from what I'd hoped. But Henry, Hank, was always one to share his heart, with his sisters, with his friends, with me. It was one of his most endearing traits. I thought Mary Ellen Wannacre stole that from him. You gave it back, and for that I will always be grateful."

She opened her arms and hugged Nancy close, and when they separated, Nancy could see tears sparkling in the matron's eyes despite her brave words.

They also discovered they shared a love of quilting and spent several hours looking over Mother Snowden's pattern books and fabric to choose a quilt she could make for Ben.

"I've made a birth quilt for each of my grandchildren," she told Nancy. "I don't intend to make an excuse for this one."

But even with all that activity, it seemed only a few hours before Nancy and Hank were standing near the train in Waco, waiting to board.

John and Mira had driven them back from the ranch. As John took the baggage to be loaded, Hank's sister kissed them both on the cheek. Then she braced her hands on Hank's shoulders.

"You will write," she said, sounding more like her father than her mother. "We don't want to lose you again."

"You won't lose us," Hank promised. "I'll have to write to tell you when Ben is born."

"Oh, no," she said, dropping her hands and sharing a smile with Nancy. "Nancy told me when the baby is due. You'll be meeting me at the train two weeks earlier. I may not be a midwife and I may not have Judith's cooking skills, but I know how to take care of family."

"We'll be glad to see you," Nancy assured her.

Just then the conductor called for everyone to board. Hank and Nancy said their goodbyes and hurried to find seats. She waved to John and Mira as the train pulled away from the station.

"I think my family likes you better than they like me," Hank teased as she turned to face him.

Nancy laughed. "I think they love us both. I'm so glad that's how it turned out, Hank."

He reached over and took her hand. "It wouldn't have turned out that way if you hadn't insisted that we come together. I've never felt so blessed. Thank you."

"Thank you for sharing them with me," Nancy said. "I always wanted a big family."

He released her to lean back with a grin. "Then we have a lot of work ahead of us, Mrs. Snowden."

She blushed, afraid to believe his teasing. "We do, indeed. We have roundup coming."

He groaned. "You had to remind me. We'll need to staff up. Upkins and Jenks and I can't do it alone, even if we team with the others."

They spent the next little while talking through options and costs. Hank didn't want to try looking for cowboys in Burnet after their reception there, but Nancy thought it might be the best spot for recruiting. Hank had launched into an impassioned argument, when he paused and cocked his head. "Why are you grinning like that?" he asked.

"Because of this," she said, feeling as if she might burst with the joy of it. "Look at me. Trying to find the best way to get my cattle to market, just like a real rancher."

"And look at me," he countered, "a down-on-his-luck cowpoke who married the prettiest gal in Texas, trying to figure out how to convince you to see things my way."

"Guess we both have things to grin about," she said.

Hank's smile faded as he glanced past her, toward the back of the train car. Turning, she saw a man standing near the door, six-gun in each hand.

"This is a robbery, folks," he called. "Reach your hands up nice and easy, and no one gets hurt."

Hank couldn't help stiffening, one hand dipping toward the gun at his hip. Nancy jerked around to face him. Those wide hazel eyes all but begged him not to start something. He didn't want to cause trouble, but he wasn't about to let her get hurt.

Besides, he knew that man. It was the same rider from Burnet who'd tried to convince him to steal cattle. The sheriff must not have been able to make a case against him. The man had already lit into Hank once. Would he take it out on him now? Would he take it out on Nancy?

A chill went through Hank. He carefully relaxed his arm and tugged his hat down over his forehead, slumping in his seat to shadow his face.

"You there," the robber ordered the nearest man, who was wearing a bowler. "Take off your hat and pass it around. I expect you all to donate handsomely."

The passenger removed his hat and held it out to the people closest to him, who dropped in coins and jewelry. Hank waited for the robber to demand more, but he didn't even seem to be watching as the hat progressed down the aisle.

Instead, he was watching Hank.

Hank turned his head away, but the robber started down the car. "You looking for trouble, mister?" he demanded.

Hank shook his head. "No."

"No, eh?" The robber stalked closer, people cringing away from him as he passed. One man in a black Stetson caught Hank's gaze and shook his head as if to warn him not to react.

"You getting smart with me again?" the thief asked, stopping between Hank's and Nancy's seats.

"Never claimed to be any kind of smart," Hank said, trying to think of a way to convince the fellow to move on. A lady offered Hank the hat, and he reached in his pocket for a coin.

The robber stiffened, leveling his guns at Hank. "Now you think you can draw on me?"

Hank held up the coin, then made a show of dropping it in the hat. "Just donating, like you asked."

The robber lowered his guns, even as he nodded. "Good. Glad to see you learned something after our time together in Burnet." He looked to Nancy. "What about you, pretty lady? You have anything I might want?"

Hank tensed, but Nancy shook her head. "No. I'm sorry."

"Well, now, aren't you a peach?" He raised his voice. "See there, people? That's how you answer a man, sweet and proper as you please." He bent closer to Nancy, though his gaze darted to Hank's for a moment. "How about a kiss for my trouble, sweetheart?"

Nancy blanched.

"Leave her alone," Hank said.

The robber straightened. "Oh, so you do want trouble. Come on, then. Draw. Let's see who's faster."

Another place, another time, he might have obliged the fellow. He'd drawn on Lucas Bennett without thinking through the consequences. Now all he could think about was Nancy.

What if the bullet went astray and hit her? What if he lost the draw, leaving her alone again with a ranch facing roundup and a baby to raise? Much as he would have liked to put this fellow in his place and stop the robbery, his pride wasn't worth her pain.

"I'm not going to draw on you," Hank told him.

"I will," said another voice.

Hank hadn't seen him coming, but now the man in the black Stetson reared up behind the robber, putting his gun against the thief's head. "Drop your weapons. Now."

The robber hesitated a moment, and Hank's hand went to his gun, ready to protect Nancy at all costs. But the thief released the triggers of his pistols and let his arms fall. Hank took one of the guns while the man in the black hat took the other.

"I noticed a cage in the baggage car," the man said. "It was designed to hold hunting dogs, but I figure it will do for a cur like you. Move."

The other passengers broke into applause as the man turned the robber back the way he had come.

"Don't go anywhere," their rescuer warned Hank and Nancy over his shoulder. "We need to talk."

Hank felt as if he'd ridden the trail all day. He reached out and gathered Nancy against him on his seat, feeling her tremble.

"Easy, now," he murmured. "It's all right. You're safe."

She pulled back to meet his gaze. "You nearly weren't. I thought he was going to shoot you."

"I thought he might at that." He rubbed a hand against her shoulder, relieved to have her close. "That was the man I met in Burnet, Nancy, the one who tried to convince me to become a rustler."

"I don't understand," she said. "What was he doing here?"

Hank didn't know either, but he couldn't like it. Still, he didn't want to worry her. "I don't know, but at least that man stopped him before he could hurt anyone." He tried for a smile. "Just think, this will be a story we can tell baby Ben."

Nancy shuddered. "I'd rather not relive it, thank you very much."

Another passenger came up then with the hat, and Hank rose to help him redistribute the belongings. Several of the others thanked him for his bravery. By the time he had returned to his seat, the man in the black Stetson was back.

He sank onto the bench beside Hank with Nancy returned to her seat across from them. "That was some smooth talking back there, Mr. Snowden."

Hank frowned at him. "How do you know my name?"

"Sheriff Fuller told me to keep an eye out for you and your lady," he explained. He pulled off his hat to reveal hair the color of a well-used saddle. "Mrs. Snowden, ma'am," he said with a nod of respect to Nancy. "I'm Justin Blacock. The folks outside Burnet asked me to look into cattle thefts in their area."

"Are you a deputy?" Nancy asked.

"No, ma'am," he said. "Former Texas Ranger with too much time on my hands and a willingness to help my neighbors."

He turned to Hank. "Sheriff Fuller said you were looking into rustling, as well. I thought maybe we could share information."

Hank leaned back in the seat. "I told Sheriff Fuller and the sheriff in Burnet all I know. It didn't seem to help."

Blacock grimaced. "Too few hands, too much work. But that's neither here nor there." He turned his hat as if his thoughts were moving as quickly.

"Here's what I know," he said, glancing between Hank and Nancy. "Folks around Burnet noticed cattle missing—a few head here, a few there, mostly from big spreads that could afford to absorb the loss. We figured someone was trying to build a herd at the expense of others."

Hank exchanged glances with Nancy. "We thought the same thing when cattle started disappearing near Little Horn."

Blacock nodded. "Then some of the smaller spreads were hit, larger numbers stolen, to the point that those ranchers needed to take out loans to keep their spreads afloat. Banks down our way refused them, all except one. And the terms were none too friendly."

Nancy eyed him. "Did the bank demand payment sooner than expected? Threaten to take over the ranch?"

He shrugged. "I guess bankers are the same all over."

"Maybe," Hank allowed, but he felt as if the sun was finally rising and shedding light after a long winter's night. "Maybe not. These small spreads, did they take out their loans from the Empire Bank in Burnet, by any chance?"

"From a banker named Winston Cramore?" Nancy added.

Blacock stared at them. "Yes. Every one."

Hank shook his head. "All this time, we were looking at it wrong. We thought it was a rustling ring. It's not about the cattle. Cramore is trying to get his hands on land."

"Good land too," Blacock said. "Places with water

rights, along cattle trails. He couldn't afford to buy them out, so he found a way to force them out."

"We must stop him," Nancy said, glancing between Hank and the former Ranger.

"That shouldn't be a problem, ma'am," Blacock assured her. "I reckon he's already running scared, sure he's about to be discovered. Someone took a shot at me the other day, and I tracked him to Waco before losing sight of him. I wouldn't be surprised if the fellow I locked up in the dog kennel hadn't been sent to stop you, Snowden."

Hank raised his brows, but Nancy paled. "Is that why he kept needling Hank?"

Blacock nodded. "He wanted an excuse to shoot him. Cramore must know the two of us are on his trail. He's afraid we'll put the pieces together, shut him down before he can make good on his threats."

"Then why not just shoot me?" Hank asked.

Blacock shrugged. "Gun down a man for no reason, and people talk about plots. Kill a man in a robbery, and people say what a shame."

He slapped his hands on his knees. "But the trouble stops here, folks. As soon as we reach Little Horn, I'm turning our robber over to Sheriff Fuller for questioning and I'm riding for Burnet to catch Cramore and bring him to justice. You in, Snowden?"

Hank stared at him. Something inside him urged him to go, to capture Cramore and see him stand trial for all the trouble he'd caused.

Yet that meant leaving Nancy behind. Focusing on the past when the future was looking at him with hopeful eyes.

After all he'd been through, from fleeing his father's impossible expectations to shooting Lucas Bennett, he knew what mattered now. And that told him exactly how he should respond.

Chapter Twenty-One

Nancy bit her lip, waiting for Hank's answer. Those sapphire eyes were bright with interest. His lean body was tensed, hands firm on the denim of his Levi's. From before they had married, he'd been striving and struggling to learn the truth behind why Lucas had chosen to steal those cattle.

At first, she hadn't understood his determination. Now she knew why finding Lucas's buyer was so important to Hank. When Lucas had moved into the path of that bullet, Lucas had lost the ability to atone for his crimes. By bringing those responsible for the thefts to justice, Hank was atoning not only for Lucas but for the shot Hank had fired.

But much as she wanted him to put that fateful day behind him, she knew capturing Cramore could be dangerous. The banker had already sent a killer after them, if Mr. Blacock was right. Surely, he'd protect the scheme he'd worked so hard to perpetuate. What if Cramore killed Hank?

How would she go on? Losing Lucas, who she'd

come to care for, had been hard. Losing Hank would break her. She loved Hank.

Maybe it was time he knew it.

Across from her, Hank smiled at the former Ranger. "Much obliged for the offer, Blacock, but I'll leave this one to you. Just send word once you've captured the crook so everyone in Little Horn can rest easy."

"Will do," Blacock promised. "But you'll miss all the fun."

Hank turned his smile on Nancy. "I have everything I need, right here."

Relief was so strong she nearly sagged against the seat. But more than relief that he would be safe was the knowledge that he'd chosen to stay, with her.

Thank You, Lord. Give me the words to tell him how much he's come to mean to me.

Blacock's laugh made her glance his way in time to see him shake his head. "I envy you. Now, I think I'll go dangle Cramore's name in front of our robber and see if he bites." He rose and nodded to Nancy. "Ma'am."

"Mr. Blacock." Nancy watched him leave, then turned to Hank, wanting to seize hold of him and keep him next to her. "Thank you for not going to Burnet to capture Mr. Cramore."

Hank shrugged, leaning back in the seat. "All I ever needed was to know I'd done the right thing. You've helped me see that, Nancy. Someone else can have the satisfaction of bringing Cramore in."

Nancy drew in a breath, feeling as if the train car had brightened. "So, it's over. We can go home."

He took her hand and entwined his fingers with hers. "Home is wherever you are."

If he truly meant that, then she had a chance. She tugged on his hand, and he slipped across the space to share her seat.

"I have a confession to make," she said. Her heart started pounding harder, and she could only think that poor baby Ben was probably wondering at the noise.

"You taught Missy how to cook," he guessed.

"No," she said with a smile.

"Ah. You and Tommy came to agreement on that bronco, and you expect me to break her for you."

"No," she said. "You leave Tommy's horse alone. I saw how you looked at her."

He chuckled, and she felt the movement against her side. "Never took you for the jealous type."

Nancy sobered. "Oh, but you're wrong. I am jealous. That's part of my confession. I offered to let you stay in Waco without me, and I would have let you go off with Mr. Blacock to capture Winston Cramore, if that's what you wanted. But I didn't want you to go, Hank. I want you here beside me, for the rest of our lives. I love you."

She emboldened herself to meet his gaze, and the tenderness in it drove any last doubts away. He reached up and tucked a strand of hair behind her ear.

"I have a confession too," he murmured, gaze holding hers even as his arms cradled her close. "Managing the Double H and riding after Cramore would have been a whole lot of fun. But neither of those things nor anything else will ever compare to being with you. I love you too, Nancy."

Trembling from the joy of it, she leaned closer, and he met her lips with his own. In that kiss, she felt the love between them, stronger, warmer and brighter than she could have dreamed. With such a love, there was nothing they couldn't do.

Ben seemed to approve, for he was dancing once more as Nancy finally pulled back.

"So," Hank said, arm about her shoulders, "does this mean we'll be husband and wife?"

Nancy nodded, then dipped her gaze, feeling suddenly shy. "I'll clear out Lucas's things, and you can have his room."

"I am not my mother," he declared. "You clear out Lucas's room for the two of us, and little Ben can have the other room. I'll put in a door so we can reach him quickly."

"Perfect," she agreed with a contented sigh, snuggling into his arms. "Just perfect."

The trip to Little Horn seemed faster than the ride to Waco, but maybe that was because Nancy was so eager to get home. As it was, the sun was heading toward the horizon when they reached the station. Hank had sent a telegram to Little Horn to alert Mr. Upkins to meet them, but Nancy didn't see the wagon waiting.

Instead, Josiah and Betsy McKay were standing on the platform.

"I called at the ranch and your man told me when you were arriving," Josiah explained, shaking Hank's hand in welcome. "Betsy and I were hoping to treat you to dinner at the café before we take you home."

"I'm feeling much better," Betsy confided to Nancy. "Your suggestions worked wonders. Please, let us pay you back."

Nancy and Hank both tried to demur, but the couple would hear none of it. It seemed they had already arranged for Edmund and Lula May to watch their children. So, Hank and Nancy found themselves around a table at Mercy Green's café. The roast beef and gravy on special that night wasn't nearly as good as the food Nancy had eaten at Mother Snowden's table.

Hank told Josiah about the confrontation on the train and the former Ranger's plans to apprehend Cramore. Josiah's smile blossomed.

"That's great news! Truth be told, I was almost afraid to invite my brother here given the troubles recently."

"Your brother?" Nancy asked. "I thought Edmund was your only brother."

"There were three of us," Josiah explained. "When our folks died, the rest of the family parceled us out, fairly far away from each other. It's taken me years to find Edmund and David."

"But now David, his daughter and the woman who raised him want to come settle here," Betsy put in, slicing into the apple pie Mercy had brought them for dessert. She glanced at her husband. "If we can just find somewhere to put them."

"We'll need a hand or two for the roundup," Nancy offered. "That might tide him over until he finds something more permanent."

Josiah shook his head. "Thanks, but David's looking to run his own spread. He has the money to buy into one and improve it to his liking. I just don't know anyone looking to sell hereabouts."

Nancy felt Ben wiggle inside her, and her hand went to her belly. Was this an answer to a prayer she hadn't known she'd prayed?

All along, she'd fought to save the Windy Diamond for her baby. But a few thousand acres was nothing compared to the love of family. Was this encounter with the McKays God's way of telling her it was time to move on?

Were they meant to go to Waco after all?

Hank felt a jolt at Josiah's comment. He'd pledged himself to Nancy and the Windy Diamond, but he couldn't shake the feeling that his family in Waco needed him as much. Was it possible he could help both his families?

Mind whirling, he managed to keep the conversation casual as Josiah and Betsy drove them out to the ranch, then sent the couple off with their thanks. Jenks crawled out of the barn just long enough to check on the ruckus and welcome Hank and Nancy home.

"Upkins is riding herd tonight," he reported, "but I'm clean tuckered. Can we talk at first light?"

Hank promised him they could, then escorted Nancy to the house. Everything was exactly as they'd left it, from the hook hanging by the mirror next to the door waiting for Nancy's hat to the armchairs sitting at precise angles in the parlor. Suddenly, Hank wanted to shove them around, throw up the rug, make a mess that was his own.

"I've been thinking," he said as Nancy removed her hat and set it on the hook.

"Me too," she said. "Go on."

Something was troubling her. He could see it in the way her teeth tugged at her lip. He decided to plunge ahead anyway.

"You've been working hard to save this ranch," he told her. "You always said the Windy Diamond was baby Ben's inheritance. But I can give him a better one, Nancy—a spread more than twice as big and a family with cousins to spare. Only I don't want to do that if it means taking away your dream."

"I've had the same thoughts." She trailed her finger along the back of one chair, then grimaced at the dust that marred her skin. "The Windy Diamond has been all I can think about for the last few months. Preserving the ranch for Ben kept me from focusing on what I lost." She glanced up at him. "But I'm tired of living in the past. Everywhere I look here, I see Lucas."

"We could redecorate," he offered, still unwilling to give up on something that had meant so much to her.

She shook her head. "It's more than the decorations. It's bone deep. You told your family you had grown. I've grown too, and so have my dreams. I want to start fresh—you and me and Ben. I'm ready to let go. We can tell the bank we agreed to sell the ranch and keep the money in trust for Ben."

Hank blew out a breath, then moved closer and took her in his arms. "You're a strong woman, Nancy Snowden. I'm honored you chose me to stand beside you."

"And I can't wait to make us a real family," she murmured. Then she pulled back, eyes widening. "Oh, Hank. What about Mr. Upkins and Billy? They're family too!"

Hank nodded. "We'll talk to them in the morning. From what Ernesto told me, there's enough work at the Double H that I can offer them both a job. Taking them with us to Waco will leave Josiah's brother shorthanded with the herd, but the league should be able to help him until he can hire more workers."

Nancy gripped his hands. "Oh, Hank, I just know this is the right decision."

So did he. And it wasn't just that feeling coming over him this time. Now it was his love for Nancy that told him the truth of it.

Nancy cooked a big breakfast the next morning. Hank could see she was happy to have all her boys around her table again. She complimented Jenks on his new haircut, which cropped his rusty-colored hair away from his lean face, and made sure Upkins had an extra slice of apple bread. She caught Hank's gaze on her and blushed. He hoped she always would.

"We have a proposal for you," Hank told them after the two cowhands had tucked into the food. He explained about the reconciliation with his father, Josiah and Edmund's brother coming to the area looking for a ranch, and his and Nancy's plans to relocate to Waco.

"There's room for two more cowboys at the Double H," he concluded. "I'd be proud to have you with us."

Jenks hastily swallowed his eggs. "Yeah, sure," he declared, head bobbing. "I heard you have sisters."

Hank chuckled. "Three pretty ones, all older than you and all happily married."

Jenks's face fell.

"But he has at least two nieces a little younger than you," Nancy put in with a smile. "And I'm sure there are more young ladies in the area."

Jenks grinned.

Upkins cleared his throat. "I think I'll stay put."

Nancy sagged. "Oh, Mr. Upkins, are you sure?"

He nodded, though he avoided her gaze. "I'm getting too old to pull up stakes again. And Mr. McKay will need someone who knows the spread." He glanced over at Hank. "But I'll come up to Waco for a visit after roundup."

"You'll be welcome at the Double H any time," Hank promised. "There will always be room in my bunkhouse for you."

Upkins nodded again and returned to his food. "So long as Mrs. Snowden keeps cooking like this, you couldn't keep me away."

"I guess it's settled, then," Nancy said with a look to Hank. He could see the excitement in her eyes. "We're going to Waco."

"Reckon you better tell them other folks on the league," Upkins put in.

"And my family," Hank agreed. "I'll write to my father today, and we can tell our friends at church on Sunday." He raised his coffee cup in toast. "To the future!"

"To the future," they all chorused, raising their cups, as well.

And he knew, wherever he went, with Nancy beside him, that future would be blessed.

Chapter Twenty-Two

❧

Of course, the members of the Lone Star Cowboy League threw Hank and Nancy a going-away party. The cooler air of October made the grass of the field next to the church especially inviting. Bright gingham bunting draped the tables, Mercy Green and the ladies of Little Horn donated apple and pumpkin pies, and the band was tuning up their instruments for dancing.

Near the church, Molly and CJ stood listening to Lula May while the twins chased the youngest Barlow boy around the fiddler's chair. The scrappy horsewoman was badgering Bo Stillwater, who was considering running for mayor, about the need for a bigger school. Beside her, Edmund put in his support for the idea. Nancy knew from Edmund's conversation with Hank that the cattleman and his wife had big plans for the community.

But the smile on Molly's face as she held CJ's hand brought a smile to Nancy's face, as well. She could see the gentle swell under her friend's skirts and knew the couple would welcome the new life growing there.

"I can't wait to bring my daughter here," David

McKay told Hank as the three sat at a table under a cottonwood tree. Edmund and Josiah's brother had come out ahead of his daughter and the woman who had adopted him to get things settled. "I'm just glad you and I could reach an agreement on the ranch."

"I know your brothers are glad to have you near them," Nancy put in.

David looked toward Edmund and Lula May and smiled. "I thought I'd never see them again. There's nothing like having family close." He excused himself to go join Josiah and Betsy, who were restocking the cinnamon sticks in the spiced apple cider.

Hank put his arm about Nancy. "He's right, you know. I'd forgotten how good family can feel, until I married you."

Nancy rested her head against his shoulder. "And you were what I needed to be part of a family again."

"No second thoughts about Waco?" he asked, chin rubbing against her hair.

"None," she assured him. "Oh, I'll miss everyone here, but I know I'm going to love having your sisters nearby."

"You and my sisters." Hank whistled. "I think Red, John, Ernesto and I are in trouble."

So was someone else. With a yell, Charlie Donovan and Adam Carson dragged a wagon to one side to reveal Daisy Carson and Calvin Barlow, arms around each other and sharing a kiss. The two hastily broke apart, though Calvin stepped in front of Daisy as if determined to protect her.

"Looks like we're leaving the future of Little Horn in good hands," Hank said with a laugh as their parents moved in. "Everyone can rest easy knowing Cramore and his crew are behind bars awaiting trial."

Mr. Blacock had honored his promise and sent word to Sheriff Fuller, who had alerted the members of the league about the end of the banker's scheme.

"What do you think it will be like here in the future, say a hundred and twenty years from now?" Nancy mused.

"I reckon there will be doctors and shopkeepers," Hank promised her. "Maybe a Texas Ranger and a soldier or two."

"And still ranchers," Nancy insisted.

"Oh, this area was made for ranching," Hank agreed. "I reckon the Lone Star Cowboy League will be making sure they have all they need to thrive."

Nancy tapped her chin. "Hmm. Maybe Waco needs the Lone Star Cowboy League too."

"Mrs. Snowden," Hank said, kissing the freckles on the tip of her nose, "I like how you think."

"You weren't so sure when I made my proposal," Nancy reminded him as he pulled back. "I had to do a lot of talking to convince you to teach me how to run a ranch."

"And I recall you were equally unsure about my marriage proposal," Hank countered. "You didn't much like being a rancher of convenience."

"That was before I knew the truth," Nancy said. "The most important factor in running a ranch, being married, or raising children is love."

His arms tightened. "Why then, Nancy, we're sure to be a success."

* * * * *

Dear Reader,

Thank you for joining me for Nancy and Hank's story, finishing up the Lone Star Cowboy League: The Founding Years. If you missed the first two books, be sure to look for *Stand-In Rancher Daddy* by Renee Ryan and *A Family for the Rancher* by Louise M. Gouge.

1895 Texas is a new time period and location for me, so it was a real thrill to dig into the research. Having set most of my books much earlier in the nineteenth century, I had fun incorporating things I never could have before—train travel, Levi's and new words like *hen party*. If you'd like more information about the setting, visit my website at www.reginascott.com, where you can also sign up to receive a free email message to alert you when my next book is out.

Blessings!
Regina Scott

MONTANA COWBOY DADDY
Big Sky Country • by Linda Ford

With a little girl to raise, widowed single father Dawson Marshall could sure use some help—he just didn't expect it to come from city girl Isabelle Redfield. The secret heiress who volunteers to watch Dawson's daughter wants to be valued for more than her money, but will hiding the truth ruin her chance of earning Dawson's love?

THE SHERIFF'S CHRISTMAS TWINS
Smoky Mountain Matches • by Karen Kirst

After confirmed bachelor Sheriff Shane Timmons and his childhood friend Allison Ashworth discover orphaned twin babies, Shane offers to help Allison care for them—temporarily. But as Shane falls for Allison and the twins, can he become the permanent husband and father they need?

A FAMILY FOR THE HOLIDAYS
Prairie Courtships • by Sherri Shackelford

Hoping to earn money to buy a boardinghouse, Lily Winter accompanies two orphaned siblings to Nebraska. But when she discovers their grandfather is missing and the kids are in danger, she hires Jake Elder, a local gun-for-hire, for protection—and marries him for convenience.

THE RIGHTFUL HEIR
by Angel Moore

Mary Lou Ellison believes she inherited the local newspaper from her guardian...until Jared Ivy arrives with a will that says his grandfather left it to *him*. The sheriff's solution? They must work together until a judge comes to town and rules in favor of the rightful heir.

REQUEST YOUR FREE BOOKS!

2 FREE INSPIRATIONAL NOVELS
PLUS 2 *FREE* MYSTERY GIFTS

Love Inspired HISTORICAL

YES! Please send me 2 FREE Love Inspired® Historical novels and my 2 FREE mystery gifts (gifts are worth about $10). After receiving them, if I don't wish to receive any more books, I can return the shipping statement marked "cancel." If I don't cancel, I will receive 4 brand-new novels every month and be billed just $4.99 per book in the U.S. or $5.49 per book in Canada. That's a saving of at least 17% off the cover price. It's quite a bargain! Shipping and handling is just 50¢ per book in the U.S. and 75¢ per book in Canada.* I understand that accepting the 2 free books and gifts places me under no obligation to buy anything. I can always return a shipment and cancel at any time. Even if I never buy another book, the two free books and gifts are mine to keep forever.

102/302 IDN GH6Z

Name	(PLEASE PRINT)	
Address		Apt. #
City	State/Prov.	Zip/Postal Code

Signature (if under 18, a parent or guardian must sign)

Mail to the **Reader Service:**
IN U.S.A.: P.O. Box 1867, Buffalo, NY 14240-1867
IN CANADA: P.O. Box 609, Fort Erie, Ontario L2A 5X3

Want to try two free books from another series?
Call 1-800-873-8635 or visit www.ReaderService.com.

* Terms and prices subject to change without notice. Prices do not include applicable taxes. Sales tax applicable in N.Y. Canadian residents will be charged applicable taxes. Offer not valid in Quebec. This offer is limited to one order per household. Not valid for current subscribers to Love Inspired Historical books. All orders subject to credit approval. Credit or debit balances in a customer's account(s) may be offset by any other outstanding balance owed by or to the customer. Please allow 4 to 6 weeks for delivery. Offer available while quantities last.

Your Privacy—The Reader Service is committed to protecting your privacy. Our Privacy Policy is available online at www.ReaderService.com or upon request from the Reader Service.

We make a portion of our mailing list available to reputable third parties that offer products we believe may interest you. If you prefer that we not exchange your name with third parties, or if you wish to clarify or modify your communication preferences, please visit us at www.ReaderService.com/consumerchoice or write to us at Reader Service Preference Service, P.O. Box 9062, Buffalo, NY 14240-9062. Include your complete name and address.

LIH15

*Sheriff Shane Timmons just wants to be left alone,
but this Christmas he'll find that family is what he's
always been looking for.*

Read on for an excerpt from
THE SHERIFF'S CHRISTMAS TWINS,
the next heartwarming book in the
SMOKY MOUNTAIN MATCHES series.

"We have a situation at the mercantile, Sheriff."

Shane Timmons reached for his gun belt.

The banker held up his hand. "You won't be needing
that. This matter requires finesse, not force."

"What's happened?"

"I suggest you come see for yourself."

Shane's curiosity grew as he followed Claude outside
into the crisp December day and continued on to the
mercantile. Half a dozen trunks were piled beside the
entrance. Unease pulled his shoulder blades together.
His visitors weren't due for three more days. He did a
quick scan of the street, relieved there was no sign of the
stagecoach.

Claude held the door and waited for him to enter first.
The pungent stench of paint punched him in the chest.
His gaze landed on a knot of men and women in the far
corner.

"Why didn't you watch where you were going? Where
are your parents?"

"I—I'm terribly sorry, ma'am" came the subdued reply. "My ma's at the café."

"This is what happens when children are allowed to roam through the town unsupervised."

Shane rounded the aisle and wove his way through the customers, stopping short at the sight of statuesque, matronly Gertrude Messinger, a longtime Gatlinburg resident and wife of one of the gristmill owners, doused in green liquid. While her upper half remained untouched, her full skirts and boots were streaked and splotched with paint. Beside her, ashen and bug-eyed, stood thirteen-year-old Eliza Smith.

"Quinn Darling." Gertrude's voice boomed with outrage. "I expect you to assign the cost of a new dress to the Smiths' account."

At that, Eliza's freckles stood out in stark contrast to her skin.

"One moment, if you will, Mr. Darling," a third person chimed in. "The fault is mine, not Eliza's."

The voice put him in mind of snow angels and piano recitals and cookies swiped from silver platters. But it couldn't belong to Allison Ashworth. She and her brother, George, wouldn't arrive until Friday. Seventy-two more hours until his past collided with his present.

He wasn't ready.

Don't miss
THE SHERIFF'S CHRISTMAS TWINS by Karen Kirst,
available wherever
Love Inspired® Historical books and ebooks are sold.

www.LoveInspired.com

Love the Love Inspired book you just read?

Your opinion matters.

Review this book on your favorite book site, review site, blog or your own social media properties and share your opinion with other readers!

Be sure to connect with us at:
Harlequin.com/Newsletters
Twitter.com/LoveInspiredBks
Facebook.com/LoveInspiredBooks